Edward softly brushed his mouth over Bianca's. It was no more than the merest touch, but it was enough to send a jolt of searing heat through his body.

With a groan, he feathered kisses upon her mouth.

"I have wanted to do this for days," he muttered.

"Then why haven't you?" she whispered.

He shivered. She might be too innocent to realize the danger of the heat that smoldered between them, but he wasn't. With every kiss it became more and more difficult to restrain the need to ease his aching passion in the sweet heat of her body.

"If you knew what I was feeling, you would not encourage me," he whispered as he moved to explore her cheeks and the line of her jaw. She tasted of paradise. Sweet heaven. And he was quite certain he would never have enough of her.

She gave a small sigh of pleasure. "Is that what I'm doing?"

"God, I hope so."

Sweeping his tongue along the curve of her ear, he returned to claim her lips in a demanding kiss . . .

Books by Deborah Raleigh

SOME LIKE IT WICKED

SOME LIKE IT SINFUL

SOME LIKE IT BRAZEN

Published by Zebra Books

DEBORAH RALEIGH

Some Like It Brazen

ZEBRA BOOKS
Kensington Publishing Corp.
www.kensingtonbooks.com

ZEBRA BOOKS are published by

Kensington Publishing Corp.
850 Third Avenue
New York, NY 10022

All Kensington titles, imprints, and distributed lines are available at special quantity discounts for bulk purchases for sales
promotion, premiums, fund-raising, educational, or institu-
tional use.

Special book excerpts or customized printings can also be created to fit specific needs. For details, write or phone the office
of the Kensington Special Sales Manager: Attn. Special Sales
Department. Kensington Publishing Corp., 850 Third Avenue,
New York, NY 10022. Phone: 1-800-221-2647.

Zebra and the Z logo Reg. U.S. Pat. & TM Off.

ISBN-13: 978-0-8217-7857-9
ISBN-10: 0-8217-7857-9

First Printing: March 2007
10 9 8 7 6 5 4 3 2 1

Printed in the United States of America

To Mom—

Thanks for giving me the world.

CHAPTER ONE

"For God's sake, Edward, halt your fidgeting before I have you tied to the bedpost," Lord Bidwell groused.

Edward Sinclair, fifth Earl of Harrington, smiled with rueful amusement. He was a large gentleman with the thick muscles of a person accustomed to hard labor and chestnut curls that were brushed toward a countenance too bronzed for fashion and features too forceful for beauty. He was, however, blessed with warm hazel eyes and an unexpected pair of charming dimples.

Thankfully, he was also blessed with rare good humor and a patient nature. A stroke of fortune considering most would have bolted after a fortnight of enduring Biddles's wretched notions of how to mold a proper gentleman.

"I defy any gentleman not to do a measure of fidgeting after three tedious hours of being brutally bathed, brushed, and bedeviled. I can assure you that I have been more kindly handled during taproom brawls."

"Halt your complaining. You are fortunate your form is such that I had no need to order a corset. They are damnably uncomfortable, according to most," Biddles retorted with a supreme lack of sympathy. "Of course they are all the rage since the Prince has taken to wearing them. Perhaps we may yet consider one."

Edward lifted one warning brow. "You would not dare."

The slender, flamboyantly attired dandy with a narrow countenance and piercing eyes smiled with a bland superiority.

"Not only would I dare, my dear Edward, but I would twist, tuck, and squeeze you into it myself if I thought it necessary." With a flourish the gentleman produced a lacy fan to wave before his pointed nose. "I have warned you that all of society will be anxious to cast their judgment upon the new Earl of Harrington. Especially since they are already titillated by your elevation from farmer to earl in one fell stroke. Do not doubt every eye will be searching for some exposure of your rustic manners and lack of worldly experience."

"Meaning that they will expect me to arrive at their soirees complete with mud on my boots and a cow in tow?"

"That is precisely what they will expect."

Edward smiled wryly. "It is not that I doubt your judgment, Biddles, which is always quite beyond question," he murmured. "But I must admit that I have yet to comprehend how being scrubbed until I am raw, and then strangled by my valet—who by the way is taking inordinate pleasure in my torture—is to assure the *ton* that I do not reek of the country."

The ebony fan was abruptly snapped shut as Biddles advanced across the hideous paisley carpet. During his rigorous training in manners, deportment, and dancing since arriving in London, Edward had not yet had the opportunity to do more than make a cursory inspection of the enormous townhouse. Certainly there had been no time to renovate the opulent grandeur to a more simple style suitable to a bachelor of modest taste.

"Dear God, Edward, how often must I remind you? A gentleman can always be distinguished by his attire, and most importantly by the tie of his cravat. It is what sets apart a true nobleman from those of lesser quality."

Edward could not help but chuckle at the absurdity of his friend's words. It was precisely the sort of logic he would never comprehend. Regardless of the number of titles that were dumped upon his unwilling shoulders.

"Do you mean to tell me, my dear Biddles, that among a nation with the greatest minds and the most progressive scientists, as well as highly respected philosophers, poets, and warriors, all we have to set us above the savages is the perfection of a knot in a length of linen?"

There was a cough from one of the numerous uniformed servants that were crowded into the room until Lord Bidwell's unnerving gaze fell upon the hapless man.

"Leave us," he commanded. "I will speak with his lordship alone."

As one the servants anxiously filed out of the room, all too pleased to be away from the dandy's sharp tongue and habit of flaying those who dared to interfere in his torturous lessons. Only the well-trained valet was daring enough to linger a rebellious moment to pluck a tiny thread from the shoulder of Edward's mulberry jacket before he too joined the mass retreat.

Once alone with his friend, Edward strolled to glance at his form in the floor-length mirror. He grimaced at the satin white pantaloons and silver waistcoat. Such elegance might be *de rigueur* for an evening in London, but he felt a dashed fool.

Gads, he had seen trained monkeys who looked more comfortable in satin and diamonds than he did.

What did he know of society? He had not been raised to take his place among the upper ten thousand. Indeed, during most of his eight and twenty years he had been only vaguely aware of any connection to the aristocracy. The knowledge that he had become heir upon the death of the old Earl, followed swiftly by the death of his son and two nephews, came as much of a shock to him as to the horrified Harrington family, which viewed him as little better than a puffed-up encroacher.

The sudden slap of the fan upon his shoulder had Edward reluctantly turning to meet the glittering gaze of the elegant gentleman.

"Edward, there are few who are as well versed in traversing society as I," Biddles warned in stern tones. "Which, I flatter myself, is precisely the reason that you requested that I be the one to introduce you to society. I am quite as cognizant of the ridiculousness of the *ton* as you. Perhaps more so. But while I might secretly find the shallowness and too-common lack of intelligence a source of amusement, I have never made the mistake of underestimating the power that society wields. Never."

Edward heaved an inward sigh. His friend was right, of course. Even if he did not care a fig for the opinion of society for himself, he could not forget that he now possessed a far-flung family that depended upon him to maintain a certain dignity. One of the many burdens that had come with the title.

More importantly, however, was the knowledge that if he hoped to use his newfound position to help those he had left behind, he would have to win the confidence of his fellow noblemen. His seat in the House of Lords would be meaningless if he were seen as a bumbling simpleton without the necessary skills to move through society.

Or to demand entrance to the various gentlemen's clubs, which, of course, were where the true power was hoarded.

"Forgive me, Biddles." He offered a faint bow of his head. "I do not mean to make light of my entrance to society. It is only that I feel awkward and not at all confident that I shall not make an utter ass of myself."

The thin features abruptly settled back into the familiar sardonic amusement.

"Do not fear, Edward. You may not be the most dashing or elegant of gentlemen, but you are intelligent and you do possess a measure of charm when you choose to exert yourself."

"Thank you . . . I think."

The pale blue eyes glittered. "And with a bit of luck, you will not be a complete ass."

He tilted back his head to laugh at the tart compliment. Biddles would never be considered a comfortable companion. He could play the buffoon to perfection or suddenly reveal the razor-edged brilliance that had once made him the most successful spy the Crown had ever possessed. But Edward did not regret his choice in seeking help.

Despite the fact that Biddles was currently the proprietor of Hellion's Den, an elegant gambling establishment, he was undoubtedly a leader of society and the perfect companion to introduce Edward to the more fastidious *ton*.

"Well, I may wound several maidens unfortunate enough to be my partner upon the dance floor and forget which fork to use, but at least my cravat is glorious perfection and my coat cut so tightly I can barely breathe. I trust no one shall mistake me for the gardener."

Biddles offered a condemning sniff. "As if any gardener could afford a coat cut by Weston."

"Or would be ridiculous enough to want one." Edward sucked in a deep breath. As much as he might long to remain in the dubious comfort of the drafty house, he knew that it was impossible. It was time to take his place as Earl of Harrington. Whether he desired the position or not. "Shall we be on our way?"

Lady Bianca, daughter of the Duke and Duchess of Lockharte, was in a towering fury.

Not an uncommon event.

Despite the endless parade of governesses who had tried to coax, coerce, and downright bully her into becoming a properly modest lady, she possessed a fiery temper and habit of speaking first and thinking later. Often much later.

In her defense, however, she was always swift to admit when

she was in the wrong and never took her ill humor out upon servants or staff who were in no position to defend themselves.

Not that any servants willingly lingered when Lady Bianca pitted her will against her father. It was said below stairs that it was preferable to stick a hand into a hornet's nest than to stumble into a blue-blooded battle.

Even the butler, who was well known to consider himself just a step below royalty, was swift to scamper toward the servant's quarters when he heard the first of the delicate Wedgwood plates launched against the door.

Unaware of the household exodus to safer grounds, Bianca stomped angrily from one end of the vast library to the other. She briefly considered hefting a few of the rare, leather-bound books at the door. They would make a much nicer thud than the china she had tossed. But while she was furious enough to throttle something, or better yet someone, she had not plunged into utter stupidity.

The large, silver-haired duke with a powerful, handsome countenance could be astonishingly indulgent toward his only daughter. Most would say too indulgent. But he would have her head on a platter if she so much as touched one of his beloved books.

As if sensing her smoldering need for destruction, her father settled more comfortably upon the elegant damask sofa and waved his hand toward the shelves of painted china.

"I do believe that you missed one of your mother's Wedgwood plates, Bianca, in case you are still in the mood to act like a petulant child," he drawled.

Bianca came to an abrupt halt to glare at her father. She could actually feel the hair on the nape of her neck stand upright, like the hair of a bristling cat.

"This is unacceptable. You had no right to refuse Lord Aldron's offer of marriage," she gritted between her clenched teeth.

A silver brow arched at her scathing words. "As a matter of fact, I had every right. Despite your oft-stated belief that you are in charge of the world and everyone in it, I am still your father and I will not have you toss away your future upon a practiced rogue. Certainly not one who would make you miserable within a week."

Bianca sucked in a sharp breath. She had known that the duke possessed no great fondness for Lord Aldron. How could she not? The two men had only to be in the same room for the ice to begin to form. But she had not thought he would sink to tossing about such slanderous insults.

"Lord Aldron is not a rogue."

"Bah. Only an innocent such as you would not know of his infamous reputation." Her father's expression hardened with an unfamiliar disgust. "For God's sake, he is a hardened rake, a gambler, and an adventurer who has been mired in scandal from the day he stepped foot into London."

Bianca resisted the urge to roll her eyes. Innocent or not, she was perfectly aware of Stephen's reputation. It was that hint of danger that had attracted her to him in the first place.

Well, that and his delicious blond hair and deep blue eyes, she acknowledged with a faint shiver.

For a young maiden who had been kept ruthlessly protected her entire life, what could be more fascinating than a gentleman who dared to ignore the tedious rules of society?

He was fiery, unpredictable, and most of all perfectly willing to teach her of the world outside her pampered existence.

Quite simply irresistible.

"You are hardly one to throw stones, Father," she retorted, her dark eyes flashing fire. "From all I have heard, you indulged in your own share of scandals when you were young."

"My scandals did not include fighting duels, hosting Cyprian balls in my home, or leading innocent young females into danger."

Her brows snapped together. "Danger? That is absurd."

One of the very few who did not fear her temper, the Duke rose to his feet and regarded her with a somber expression.

"I am not a fool, Bianca. I am well aware that the scoundrel has lured you from the house so you could attend boxing matches and horse races, as well as a bawdy pantomime that was not fit for the eyes of a harlot, let alone an unwed lady," he interrupted in stark tones.

Her breath caught in shock.

Oh . . . botheration. So much for her carefully elaborate schemes to hide her exhilarating outings.

Obviously being a Duke included knowing every damnable thing that happened in London.

It was with an effort that she met his accusing gaze. "Do not hold Stephen to blame. It was upon my urging that he escorted me to such places."

"Which is the only reason I did not take a horsewhip to him, I assure you."

"And I only urged him to do so because I am sick to death of being treated as if I am a witless idiot without the ability to think for myself or to make even the simplest of decisions."

His eyes narrowed at her sharp words. "You are my daughter. It is my duty to protect you."

Bianca nearly screamed in frustration. On how many occasions had she heard the familiar lecture?

A hundred? A thousand?

Certainly it was trotted out whenever she happened to be in danger of having a bit of fun.

"I am not your daughter. I am a pretty doll you put on display and then tuck away when I am not of use. At least Stephen realizes that I am a woman perfectly capable of knowing something of the world."

"Oh, no doubt Lord Aldron has played his role well. He is, after all, a highly successful seducer and quite accustomed to doing whatever necessary to please a lady." He lifted a deliberate brow. "I wonder, however, if you have considered why the gentleman has shown such a marked interest in you after so assiduously avoiding debutantes?"

Bianca had a sudden vision of a cat toying with a mouse.

And she wasn't the cat.

"He finds me . . . fascinating."

"No, my child. What he finds fascinating is your rumored dowry."

She blinked in shock. Then blinked again.

"Father."

"The man is without a feather to fly with," the Duke retorted in hard tones. "Despite having hocked every belonging he possesses, he is still mired in debt. There is not a gambling house in town that will allow him across the threshold, and his clubs have long since turned him away. His only hope to avoid fleeing to the Continent is to snatch a bride too naïve to see beyond a handsome countenance and shallow charm."

Bianca gritted her teeth. She would not listen to her father. She could not. To do so would mean that the gentleman who had stolen her heart, the one who had offered her the promise of a glorious future without tedious rules and expectations, was nothing more than a lie.

The servants had been wise to go into hiding.

"I will not listen to such slander. Stephen loves me."

The Duke curled his lip in disgust. "Lord Aldron loves no one but himself."

"You do not know him as I do."

"I know him far better than you, Bianca." There was a brief pause before her father lifted his chin to a stubborn angle. "Which is precisely why he will never be your husband."

Her chin tilted to match his own. Damn and blast but she was weary of being dictated to as if she were a mindless dolt.

At least Stephen made the pretense of listening to her desires.

"I am two and twenty, Father, and quite at liberty to do whatever I please. You cannot halt me from wedding Stephen." Her hands were planted on her hips just in the unlikely event the Duke did not realize the extent of her resolution.

The Duke calmly adjusted the cuffs of his elegant coat. Her teeth snapped together at his deliberate nonchalance.

"Perhaps not, but do you truly believe that either of you will be content living in some decrepit cottage or renting rooms in the stews?" He smiled without humor. "I assure you that it might seem charming enough in storybooks, but there is nothing pleasurable in scrubbing your own floors or freezing before an empty grate. Besides which, Lord Aldron would barter off his own mother before becoming a pauper."

"Pauper?" Her momentary bravado faltered with stunning speed. "You would disinherit me?"

Without warning, her father's eyes darkened with what seemed an emotion strangely close to regret.

"There would be no need for such drastic measures. I simply have nothing to offer as a dowry."

"But . . . that is absurd."

"It is the simple truth."

"I do not understand."

"Because I never intended you to understand," her father admitted with a harsh sigh. "With your beauty and position, I simply assumed that when you chose your husband you would have the good sense to select one with a large fortune. It is after all what most maidens do."

Her brows snapped together. Most maidens were not the daughter of a duke, she thought with a tingle of panic. For God's sake, she had never devoted a moment to considering something so tedious as wealth.

"But what of my dowry?" she demanded.

"What do you think has funded your very expensive Seasons for the past four years?"

For perhaps the first time in her young life, Bianca's swift wits deserted her. Her brain froze and she was forced to open and close her mouth several times before she at last managed to speak.

"Are you telling me that we have no money?"

There was a moment of silence before her father turned to stroll toward the large bay window. He kept his back turned as he at last cleared his throat.

"Being a duke is an expensive business, my dear. I have estates that need constant upkeep, a near battalion of servants to keep paid and pensioned, tenants to keep housed, your brothers schooled, and of course you and your mother properly clothed and bejeweled."

"But what of your rents and investments?"

His gaze remained trained upon the Mayfair street below him. "They would be adequate as a rule, but while London has devoted itself to pleasure, war has ravaged the world. Trade has all but disappeared, and not nearly enough able-bodied men remain to tend to the lands." He gave a frustrated shake of his head. "These are troubled times for all landowners. Would you have me stand aside and watch my tenants starve?"

Well, for goodness' sake. Of course she would not wish for anyone to starve.

Still, she found it difficult to accept that matters had come to such a desperate quagmire. Surely being a duke must count for something?

"But the war has ended," she lamely pointed out.

"That does not bring young men back from the grave to plant my fields, nor fill empty pantries. Such devastation will take years to repair."

"Why have you not said something before?" she rasped.

Slowly he turned to regard her with a somber expression. "As I said, I simply assumed that when you chose to wed, it would be to a gentleman of means."

The sickness in the pit of her stomach became outright nausea. The glorious future she had dreamed of for months was crumbling into dust.

"My God . . . this is horrible."

"Not so horrible." Her father moved to gently pat her shoulder. "There are any number of suitable gentlemen who will be eager to wed the daughter of a duke. Especially one who happens to be as lovely as an angel."

She abruptly pulled away from his comforting touch, her eyes glittering with suppressed tears.

"Do you have no feelings at all? I love Stephen. I do not want any other gentleman." Her expression became one of deepest scorn. "Especially not one who only wishes to wed me because I happen to be your daughter."

With an insulting lack of sympathy for her wounded heart, her father gave a vague shrug. "Then approach Lord Aldron and tell him that you wish to wed without dowry or a prospect for an allowance from me. Let us see precisely how quickly he leaps at the opportunity to have you for his wife."

Bianca did not even consider the notion of approaching Stephen. Not because she feared he would slither away the moment he discovered she was penniless, she hastily reassured herself. But simply because she would never wish for him to sacrifice himself in such a manner.

No matter how much it might hurt.

Knowing she could not hold back her tears for much longer, she glared at the gentleman who had managed to ruin her life in a few short minutes. Unwittingly, her hand lifted to clutch the silver locket that lay against her pounding heart. The necklace had been a gift from Stephen and held his precious portrait.

"I will never forget Stephen. Never," she announced in dramatic tones. Then, turning on her heel, she flounced from the room and headed for her private chambers to cry out her misery.

CHAPTER TWO

The seeking female fingers crawled over Edward's thigh with all the subtlety of a charging bull.

Nearly choking on the delectable morsel of game hen that he had just placed in his mouth, Edward shot a covert glance at the woman seated next to him.

Hell's teeth.

As hostess of the vast London townhouse, Lady Beauvaille was no doubt a beauty, he grudgingly conceded. Though she was past the first bloom of youth, there was a lush sensuality to her full curves and a smoldering hunger in her dark eyes.

And yet, while he enjoyed being groped beneath the table as much as the next gentleman, he preferred that the woman seducing him did not possess a husband who was renowned for his marksmanship. Or one who just happened to be sitting across the table.

Sedately sipping her wine while pretending an interest in the elderly general at her side, the woman boldly continued her exploration of his lap. The nimble fingers squeezed and stroked with undeniable expertise. Then, shockingly, they began honing in with ruthless intent.

Edward hastily swallowed the piece of game hen lodged in his throat as he shifted from the determined attack.

Was the woman demented? Biddles had not warned him that the wealthy matron was in any way out of her wits, but then perhaps it was simply the way of London society. Perhaps all hostesses made a habit of fondling their dinner guests.

Denied of her quest, Lady Beauvaille swiftly turned to regard him with a faint pout.

"Why, my dear Lord Harrington, is there anything amiss?"

Carefully wiping his fingers upon a linen napkin, Edward swiftly considered his options. He did not desire to cause an unpleasant scene. Not when it was bound to create a scandal. On the other hand, he did not wish her to believe he had any interest in a more . . . intimate relationship.

The mere thought was enough to send a shudder through his body. He happened to be extremely fastidious when it came to his mistresses. And besides which, he possessed a healthy dose of self-preservation. Banal sex with a woman who had no doubt spread her legs for any number of gentlemen was hardly worthy of a lead ball through the heart.

Hoping to soften any sting of his rejection, he conjured a polite smile. "What could possibly be amiss, Lady Beauvaille?" he murmured. "The rumors of your extraordinary skills as a hostess have not been exaggerated."

The dark eyes restlessly studied his carefully bland expression. They lingered upon the rich hazel of his eyes and the chestnut locks. Then deliberately they moved down to take a slow and shockingly thorough inventory of his broad shoulders and flat waist.

For the first time in his twenty-eight years of life, Edward comprehended what a woman must feel like to be mentally stripped bare.

Oddly, it was not nearly as pleasant as he had assumed it to be.

"I hope, my dear Lord Harrington, that it was more than my skills as a hostess that attracted you to my small gathering?" she said in a throaty voice.

Edward resisted the urge to tug at the cravat that was suddenly choking him. If he were a hare, he would be bolting for the nearest hole.

"Well . . . yes, certainly."

She licked her full lips in a predatory gesture. "It seems that we are of the same mind. Perhaps we should discuss our common interests later in the conservatory? After the dancing begins?"

There was a muffled noise from across the table, and Edward shifted to glare at the suspiciously innocent expression of Biddles. Damn the sneaking rat, he silently seethed. His friend had been perfectly aware of Lady Beauvaille's penchant for accosting her gentlemen guests and had done nothing to warn him. Indeed, he was clearly taking inordinate pleasure from his discomfort.

Never one to allow such a fine jest to go unrewarded, Edward leaned to grab his wine glass and at the same moment gave a sharp kick to Biddles's shin. He had the satisfaction of a muffled grunt but no ready escape from the woman regarding him as if he were a tasty morsel.

"I must admit that it is a tempting offer, my lady. However . . ."

Like a blessing from above, the awkward moment was interrupted as Lord Beauvaille loudly cleared his throat to indicate it was time for the women to depart the table.

With a last, shameless squeeze of Edward's leg, Lady Beauvaille rose grandly to her feet and led the handful of ladies from the dining room to the nearby salon. Reprieved for the moment, Edward heaved a silent sigh of relief.

Gads. He had imagined any number of pitfalls when he had traveled to London. Embarrassing gaffs, naïve blunders, and disapproval from the overabundance of puffed-up prigs. But . . . being accosted by a randy lady of the realm at her own table? Never. And now the bold hussy would be expecting him to join her in the conservatory.

With a pang of longing for the simple, quiet existence that

he had left behind, Edward sipped his port and dutifully laughed at the bawdy jokes that were tossed about the table. He even indulged in a small cigar without coughing upon the vile smoke. Any hope for an intelligent discussion of the current laws being argued in the House of Lords or discovering the latest news from the Continent had long before been crushed. It was obvious that nothing but the most frivolous conversations were allowed at such events.

They lingered until the sound of arriving guests marked the beginning of the ball. Hoping his impatience was not noticeable, Edward followed the gathering herd up the stairs to the ballroom. Once within the depressingly opulent gold and ivory room, he stepped to one side and waited.

It took several moments, but at last the slender, brilliantly attired gentleman entered through the door and paused to peer about the crowd with his quizzing glass. Edward did not hesitate. Reaching out, he grasped the nefarious rat by the scruff of his neck and plucked him into the shadows at his side.

"Going somewhere, Biddles?" he murmured with a glitter in his eyes.

Smoothing his hand over his peacock blue coat, Biddles smiled with a guilelessness that was at utter odds with the sly amusement in his pale eyes.

"Oh, here you are, Edward. I feared you might have bolted."

Edward planted his fists upon his hips in a decided threat. "Believe me, the notion has crossed my mind more than once this evening. Unfortunately, my desire to throttle you overcame my sensible urge to return to my home and pack my bags."

Biddles produced a lacy handkerchief to dab at his nose with a wounded air. "Really, Edward, there is no cause to be in such a twit. Granted the game hen was shockingly overcooked and the vegetables as limp as Lord Beauvaille's manhood is rumored to be, but even you must admit that the pastries were divine."

Edward rolled his eyes heavenward in a silent plea for patience. This was not at all what he had agreed to.

"Quite amusing, my friend. However, you are well aware my annoyance has nothing to do with Lady Beauvaille's chef."

"No?"

"No." His eyes narrowed in an ominous manner. "Why did you not warn me?"

"Warn you of what?"

"Biddles."

The thin lips twitched, but at last, conceding he had pressed the larger man's temper as far as he dared, Biddles offered a small sigh.

"Oh, very well." He met Edward's glittering gaze squarely. "I did not warn you because I knew you would flinch like a terrified virgin the moment Lady Beauvaille approached you."

Terrified virgin? Edward stiffened in outrage. He had been called many names, but that was certainly not among them.

No doubt because most gentlemen preferred not to be thrashed within an inch of their life.

"Ridiculous," he growled.

"Now, now." Biddles held up a slender hand. "Do not be angry. 'Tis not my fault that, for all your fine qualities, deception is not among them. Your every thought is written upon your countenance."

He offered an impatient snort. "Thankfully deception has never been a much-needed skill in Kent. There a gentleman is judged upon his honesty and integrity."

"Good gads, what a tedious notion."

Edward smiled wryly. "I happen to find it quite refreshing."

"No doubt." Biddles gave a flutter of his handkerchief. "However, you are in London, not Kent, and here you will discover your refreshing honesty does not serve you well."

A pang of sharp longing rushed through Edward. Damn.

He wanted nothing more than to be back in his shabby home with a good book and a glass of brandy. Now, that was his notion of a perfect evening.

Unfortunately Biddles was correct. He was in London and trapped into playing the ridiculous games of the *ton*.

"You mean I must endure being groped under the table by an aging jade with a smile upon my lips?" he said dryly.

Biddles did not even blink. "Precisely. Lady Beauvaille is a powerful figure among society. Had you deliberately avoided her advances or revealed your distaste for her peculiar habits, she could have made your introduction to the *ton* unbearable."

"Lovely."

There was a moment's pause as the humor became more pronounced in the pale eyes. "Besides which, watching you choke upon your game hen was utterly priceless."

Edward could not halt a strangled laugh. Really, the outrageous rogue was without shame.

"I am happy I could be so entertaining."

"Think nothing of it."

Edward snorted, crossing his arms over his chest. "Now, while you are enjoying your little jest, perhaps you will be so kind as to reveal how the devil I am to avoid meeting the doxy in her conservatory. She expects me as soon as the orchestra begins."

"Do you truly wish to avoid the encounter?" Biddles demanded with a speculative glance. "Lady Beauvaille may not be fresh out of the nursery, but her beauty remains, and it is said that she is quite talented."

Edward did not attempt to conceal his shudder. "She is also wed. Even if I did not find her utterly repellent, I do not dally with other gentlemen's wives."

"Honest and principled." Biddles gave a world-weary sigh. "Gads, you will never survive among the natives, old chap."

Edward merely arched a dark brow. "It is your duty to ensure that I do."

Biddles grimaced as he glanced toward the full-blown matron who was even now regarding Edward with a hungry smile.

"Oh, very well. I shall go and attempt to distract Lady Beauvaille. You remain here and try to avoid bewitching any other desperate ladies."

Unable to resist a measure of revenge for his friend's taunting, Edward conjured a sweet smile.

"Thank you, Biddles. I shall be certain to tell Anna of Lady Beauvaille and the terrible sacrifices you have been forced to bear for me."

Not surprisingly, the slender gentleman abruptly froze to regard him with a narrowed gaze. There were few in London who did not realize that the one-time rake and scoundrel was now firmly under the authority of his spirited wife.

"Breathe one word of this to Anna and I will have you trussed up in a corset before you can blink," he muttered in low tones.

"Only if your sweet wife doesn't murder you first. My bet is on Anna."

Biddles cast him a sour glare. "So is mine."

With a loud sniff, the flamboyant dandy turned on his heel and threaded his way through the growing crowd.

Still smiling, Edward moved deeper into the shadows and leaned his large form against the wall. He did not doubt that Biddles would somehow manage to divert Lady Beauvaille. There were few who could resist his charm. That, however, did not completely ease his discomfort.

His smile faded as his gaze idly roamed toward the dance floor. Despite the vastness of the room, he felt suffocated by the growing crowd and all too aware of the sneering glances cast in his direction.

Gads, the evening had only begun and already he was

wishing himself miles away. How the devil was he supposed
to endure another three months of such torture?

Absently lifting a hand to tug at the demon-spawned cravat
that dug into his throat and tickled his jaw, Edward was counting the hours before he could reasonably offer his excuses to
leave when his gaze was abruptly captured by an exotic beauty
as she stood in a distant corner.

Good God.

Edward forgot to breathe. He forgot to blink. And even
how to swallow.

Hell's teeth, but she was exquisite.

In the candlelight her hair appeared as dark and glossy as
polished ebony. It had been elaborately arranged in curls atop
her head, with a handful left to brush the ivory of her cheeks.
Her dark eyes were heavily lashed and so large they seemed
to dominate the perfect oval of her face, while the curve of
her lips was full and a delicate shade of pink.

Slowly his stunned gaze lowered to the slender form currently attired in a shimmering yellow gown. His body instantly heated in awareness, and he clenched his hands at his
side.

It was not just that she was a brilliant peacock among the
pale doves that caught and held his attention.

It was more the vibrant force that seemed to crackle in the
air about her.

This was not a woman who would drift through life. Oh, no.
She would blaze her own path and damn anyone in her way.

A startling, near-overwhelming urge to charge across the
room and claim her as his own shuddered through him.

Thankfully he had not lost his wits entirely.

Even if he were to toss himself at her dainty feet, it would
accomplish no more than to embarrass the poor woman and
make a fool of himself.

Edward was painfully aware that he was a source of mocking amusement among society. He was bourgeois, unsophisticated, and lacking the smooth charm that ladies admired.

It would take a great deal more gloss before he could hope to approach a young woman of breeding. For now she was just as likely to take him for a servant as for a nobleman.

Without allowing himself the opportunity to do something ridiculous, Edward pushed from the wall and headed firmly toward the French doors.

The cloying air was beginning to make his head ache, not to mention the god-awful screech of the violins tuning in a distant corner. If he were to survive the night, he needed fresh air.

And perhaps a healthy dose of arsenic.

Lady Bianca was in a glorious fury as she stood in the corner of Lady Beauvaille's ballroom.

Again.

It was so glorious, indeed, that none but the very dense or very desperate had possessed the courage to even smile in her grim direction.

How dare her father, she had brooded with a great deal of self-pity.

It was surely horrid enough that he had devoted the afternoon to ruthlessly breaking her heart and laying waste to her future. One would think that even the most dastardly of sires would be satisfied with such a feat.

To insist that she attend this tedious gathering while she was still in shock went beyond the pale. She needed time to compose her shattered nerves. A few days to accept the unacceptable.

For the first time in her young existence, however, she had discovered that neither her tantrums nor her tears had made the least impression upon her father.

Indeed, when she had adamantly proclaimed nothing could halt her from spending the evening alone in her chambers, the

Duke had brutally threatened to toss her over his shoulder and haul her to the Beauvailles's ball, in her unmentionables if necessary.

It was enough to make the most docile maiden smolder in frustration.

And Bianca had never been mistaken for docile.

Unfortunately, for all her desire to stomp and pout and toss about breakable objects, she could do no more than endure her aggravation in stoic silence. God knew there would be enough gossip when it was discovered her father had turned Stephen away. She would not add to the fodder by behaving as an ill-tempered shrew.

At least not in public.

Once in private, however, well . . . that was an entirely different matter, she acknowledged as her father nonchalantly moved to her side.

"I must admit, my dear, you appear delightfully tragic standing alone in this corner," her father murmured in low tones. "Quite the Joan of Arc, in fact. However, playing the martyr is hardly the best means of attracting a prospective husband."

Bianca snapped open her fan as she glared at the hapless guests twirling about the ballroom.

"Luckily for me I have no interest in prospective husbands. You have seen to that."

She thought she heard a muffled sigh, but when her father spoke there was nothing but sardonic amusement in his voice.

"Ah, so you intend to remain a heartbroken spinster. No doubt you'll live with your brother as he struggles to keep the estate from falling into shambles and become one of those bitter old aunts that frightens away all the children?"

Bianca stiffened, battling back the ghastly image her father had painted.

Egads . . . it did not even bear considering.

The fan fluttered until her curls bounced in the breeze. "What does it matter to you?"

"Beyond my intense dislike for a sulky child, there is the undeniable fact that you could ease the burdens that currently plague us." There was a strategic pause. "It seems I shall have to take matters into my own hands."

With mounting unease, Bianca shot her father a suspicious glare. "And what does that mean?

"If you do not choose a husband, I will."

The blunt statement was as shocking as if he had slapped her in the face. Perhaps more so. For a moment Bianca struggled to simply catch her breath.

"You must be jesting."

"Not at all. A wealthy husband would no doubt be generous to his newest family members. Especially if you are wise enough to please him."

"No." She gave a shake of her head. "You cannot force me to—"

"I believe we have already established that as your father, I can force you into almost anything, including marriage." He smoothly overrode her furious words, blithely lifting his quizzing glass as he turned to regard the passing crowd. "Let me see. . . . What of Lord Stackhouse? He is old enough to endure your tempers with patience and rich enough to keep you in style."

The fan dropped from her fingers in horror. "Have you taken leave of your senses?"

"Not at all."

"For heaven's sake, he is ancient enough to be my grandfather. Not to mention the fact that he smells of cabbage."

Unperturbed, the Duke shifted his attention to a lumpy baronet with a florid countenance and unsteady gait.

"Very well. What of Sir Hewitt? He is only a few years older than you and has inherited a tidy fortune."

"He is also an incurable drunk and stupid beyond bearing."

"Which only means he would be easily swayed by a beautiful young maiden."

Blankly wondering if her father was as bosky as the baronet, she glared at him in disbelief.

"You wish me to produce a herd of beef-witted offspring who are overly fond of the bottle?"

"Perhaps not," he reluctantly conceded. "Hmm . . . there are not so many eligible bachelors as one would wish. Lord Carlfield is rumored to be on the dun, and Mr. Summers has already managed to bury three wives. Not at all seemly."

She nearly gagged, all too aware of the rumors that Summers was queerly attached to sickly females.

"I would rather toss myself from the nearest cliff."

"Ah, well, I fear the pickings are dismally slim. But never fear—there is still Lady Talford's soiree."

Grinding her teeth until she feared they might crack, Bianca clenched her hands at her sides.

"Surely, you must have overlooked the gentleman in the corner? He appears to possess a heartbeat, which seems to be your only prerequisite for my husband."

Her father glanced toward the decidedly large gentleman who stood in the distant shadows. Astonishingly, he seemed to stiffen in horror.

"Lord Harrington? Absolutely not."

Bianca was instantly intrigued. If her father disapproved of the man, then she was certain to desire a closer acquaintance.

At the moment nothing would please her more than to tweak the Duke's arrogant nose.

"Why? Is he wed?"

"No."

"Are his pockets too shallow to haul us out of the hatches?"

"His fortune is more than respectable."

Bianca gave a lift of her brows. "A heartbeat and a fortune? What more could you possibly demand?"

"He is the Peasant Earl."

It took a long moment before Bianca at last placed the contemptuous title with the newest member of society.

A member that had been greeted with a decidedly cold shoulder by most of the *ton*.

"Lord Bidwell's acquaintance?" she murmured.

His nose flared in disapproval. "A most peculiar connection, I must say. I had no notion Biddles possessed a taste for trumped-up farmers."

Bianca frowned in bewilderment. For all his faults, her father had never been a prig. Powerful, assertive, and arrogant . . . but never a prig.

"I have never known you to condemn a man for having worked with his hands, Father. Were you not the one to claim that one loyal tenant was worth a dozen mincing dandies?"

"For my estate, not for my daughter," the Duke retorted in haughty tones. "And I will expect you to take care to avoid any unnecessary introductions, Bianca. There is no telling but that he might very well be toadish enough to presume he would be free to call upon you."

"Indeed," Bianca murmured, her gaze returning to the Peasant Earl.

Oddly, she found herself fascinated. There were few members of society she was not familiar with. Overall the *ton* was a small and exclusive membership, rarely changing or admitting new members.

And never a stranger such as the Peasant Earl, she acknowledged, gripped by an unfamiliar sensation as her gaze ran boldly over the intruder.

He was larger than most gentlemen of the *ton*. Perhaps not taller, but broader through the shoulders, with heavy muscles that rippled with a fluid ease. Muscles that ensured there was no need for padding . . . anywhere, she noted with pure feminine appreciation. Nor for any of the lace and baubles that many dandies used to distract from narrow chests or weak chins.

Ornamentation would only distract from the raw male perfection.

Her heart gave an odd hitch as her gaze inched higher, encountering the countenance that was startlingly bronzed.

He was not traditionally handsome, she concluded. There was nothing elegant or pretty in the fierce Roman nose or prominent cheekbones and full lips. They were brash and bold and unrelentingly male. But combined with the heavily lashed hazel eyes they formed a compelling beauty that was nicely framed by thick chestnut locks that brushed his collar and tumbled onto his brow.

All in all he was a gentleman who would command attention no matter where he might be.

And best of all, the sort of gentleman who would not allow himself to be intimidated by anyone.

Not even a duke.

Bianca felt a smile curve her lips.

Perhaps sensing the direction of her rebellious thoughts, her father regarded her with a gathering frown.

"Bianca, what are you about?"

With perfect timing, the mysterious gentleman detached himself from the shadows and strolled toward the nearby French doors and onto the terrace.

Tossing her father a defiant smile, Bianca was swiftly following in his path.

"I have decided that I wish to discover more of this Peasant Earl."

"Absolutely not," her father growled, remaining doggedly upon her heels. "Bianca, I forbid you."

She did not miss a step. "If he possesses the funds that you claim he does, then I have no need for your approval, Father."

"Bianca . . ." The Duke halted at the French doors even as Bianca swept determinedly forward, not halting until she was standing directly before the startled Earl.

She felt a moment of trepidation as she glanced up the long distance into the starkly male countenance. Something warned her that this man was like no other that she had encountered.

But, still seething with a mixture of pain and frustrated rage, she ignored the tiny bells of warning.

For the moment all that mattered was punishing her father.

"My lord, we have not been properly introduced, but I wished to . . ." Her nerve briefly faltered.

The chestnut brows arched as the Earl of Harrington regarded her with a quizzical smile. "Yes?"

"Bianca, return to me this moment," her father commanded, for all the world as if she were his faithful hound.

That was precisely all that was needed to goad Bianca beyond the point of reason.

Without further ado, she stepped indecently close to the gentleman before audaciously smiling into his hazel eyes.

"I wish you to know that you are soon to be my husband."

There was a strangled groan from behind Bianca as her father fled in either fury or horror.

Or more likely a combination of both.

A flare of satisfaction at having bested the Duke at his own game raced through her.

Later she would excuse her behavior as that of a madwoman. A stark raving lunatic. At the moment, however, she was too enwrapped with her childish need to strike out to care.

A smug smile had just begun to curve her lips when, without warning, strong arms lashed about her waist and hauled her against a granite-hard chest.

Startled, she opened her lips to protest the shocking treatment. A breath too late as her words were smothered by a pair of warm, wickedly talented lips.

The kiss seared through her body.

Her toes curled, and the protest died a swift death.

Oh . . . my.

CHAPTER THREE

Edward shuddered in pleasure as he gathered the slender female form even closer to his stirring body.

He did not need Biddles's strictures to realize he was not behaving in a gentlemanly manner. Hell, he was not even skirting close to gentlemanly manners.

Even a country oaf like himself knew that one did not haul unknown maidens off their feet and kiss them senseless.

Thankfully, he possessed no interest in being a gentleman, mannerly or not, at the moment. Not when it was perfectly obvious that society ladies were determined to view him as no more than some ridiculous sport.

First had been Lady Beauvaille and her obnoxious groping. And now this chit.

He could only presume that London females considered it a grand jest to trifle with the peasants.

Oddly, the notion had not troubled him with the older matron. At least not beyond sheer annoyance. But there was no mistaking a hint of wounded pride at the antics of the young and beautiful woman in his arms.

Dammit all. He had been enchanted by her raven-haired beauty. Even at a distance. And while he had known such a female was well beyond his touch, it had not lessened his artistic appreciation.

To now realize she considered him as no more than a source of amusement was enough to bring out any man's more barbaric nature.

Perfectly understandable.

Just as understandable as the sharp desire that urged him to nibble at the soft, satin lips until they hesitantly parted to offer him entry into the warm heat of her mouth.

Sweet Christ, but she was a tasty morsel, he acknowledged, his hands sliding over the curve of her hips. Perhaps she was rather slender, but there was nothing lacking in the gentle curves that pressed against him.

And nothing lacking in the way she arched closer, her hands clutching his coat in a manner certain to bring the wrath of his valet down upon Edward's head.

What had begun as a punishment for the teasing minx was swiftly becoming a far more interesting game.

Taking care not to startle his prey, he nipped at her full lower lip, gently sucking it into his mouth as she gave a strangled moan. With his boldness readily rewarded, he outlined her mouth with the tip of his tongue, savoring her taste as a connoisseur might savor a fine vintage.

"Such sweetness," he murmured. "You are surely meant to bring a man to his knees."

"Sir . . ." What might have been the beginning of a protest ended in a soft sigh as Edward swept his lips along the line of her jaw to nuzzle a tender spot just beneath her ear. "Oh."

Edward smiled as delightful licks of flame raced through his blood.

Who could have suspected that when he had reluctantly forced himself to attend Lady Beauvaille's ball he would tumble into such a delightful encounter? He could only hope every social gathering provided such wicked entertainment.

As he stroked his tongue over the warmth of her skin, his fingers tightened upon the curve of her hips.

She fit against him perfectly. The soft swell of her breasts, the long length of her legs, and the narrow waist that hovered tantalizingly close to his rising erection.

And that scent . . . warm honeysuckle.

It was enough to enflame any poor gentleman.

Tracing a path of kisses down the arch of her neck, Edward lingered as she gave a sudden shiver of excitement.

Ah, she liked that.

Nearly as much as he did.

Brushing his lips over the sensitive pulse, Edward choked back a groan. No woman should feel so wonderful in his arms. Not when he was in no position to bring a satisfying conclusion to the unexpected encounter.

Bloody hell. He was hard and aching and wishing they were anywhere but upon a terrace where anyone might happen upon them.

Her head tilted backward, and Edward urgently shifted to scatter delicate kisses down the plunging line of her bodice.

God bless the latest fashion, he silently applauded.

There was an ample-enough amount of exposed bosom to please any man.

Taking care to inspect every silken inch, Edward was tasting of the sweet valley between her breasts when the woman gave a shuddering moan and pressed her hands against his chest.

"Please," she whispered. "You must halt."

Thwarted in his desire to continue his exploration of her half-bared breasts, Edward contented himself with nuzzling the lobe of her ear.

"Not yet."

There was another breathless shiver. "My lord."

His tongue lightly traced the curve of her ear. "If we are soon to be wed, muirnin, then I wish to assure myself that we are utterly compatible. It would be unfortunate to tie the knot and discover we could not . . . complete the deal, so to speak."

"Oh," she breathed, briefly leaning close before she was reluctantly wrestling herself from his lingering grasp. "No. No. There will be no . . . completing of deals. And most certainly not on a terrace in the midst of a ball."

Edward was struck by an odd sense of loss as she stepped backward.

Well, perhaps not so odd, he conceded as he gazed down at the flushed features and flashing midnight eyes.

By gad, she was a bewitching minx.

One who would make any gentleman long to capture her interest.

And one who was quite likely out to make him appear a buffoon, a cynical voice whispered in the back of his mind.

Fiercely squashing the renegade flare of fascination that was clouding his senses, Edward leaned forward to scoop her off her feet and cradled her against his chest.

"You are right, of course." Ignoring her gasp of shock, he easily crossed the terrace and moved down the stairs to the vast garden beyond. "Such a wicked pastime demands privacy."

She frowned as she instinctively clutched at his arms. "Good God, are you mad?"

"Only during the full moon." He cast her a faint smile. "Do not fear. My valet is trained to tie me to my bed, and I rarely foam at the mouth for more than a few hours. In a few years you will barely notice my lunacy."

"Barely . . . notice?"

"Oh, and I suppose you should know that I tend to gnaw on the furniture and insist on sleeping in the stables, but I assure you that it has been years since I was afflicted with fleas."

She gave a choked sound. "Are you attempting to be amusing?"

He paused in the shadows of a large gazebo to stab her

with a sharp gaze. "Would you rather I put you over my knee and paddle you as you deserve?"

In the perfumed silence of the garden, he heard her breath catch, her lashes lowering almost as if she were properly shamed.

"I will admit that I behaved badly. But there were reasons . . ."

"Such as making a mockery of the Peasant Earl?" he rasped. Her gaze flew upward, her lips parting at his direct accusation. "What? No, of course not."

"I am not such an idiot as you might have suspected."

"I never thought you an idiot."

"So you approach every strange gentleman on verandas and announce your intent to have them as a husband?" he demanded in measured tones. Inwardly he battled his reaction to having her so near. His treacherous body was blithely unconcerned with the reason she was in his arms. Only that he do something about it. Something that would include heated kisses, raised skirts, and sweet moans of feminine pleasure. *Dammit, Edward, concentrate.* "Either you are frighteningly desperate or you thought it some delightful joke to play on the yokel."

"I . . ." She bit her lip before sucking in a deep breath. "Please, will you put me down?"

"So that you can scamper back to have a good giggle with your friends?"

"No, I wish to apologize," she shocked him by admitting in strained tones. "And to offer an explanation, if you are willing to listen."

Still far from certain that this was not just some ploy to escape from his clutches, Edward slowly lowered her to her feet, once again experiencing that pang as she stepped from his arms.

He sternly folded his arms over his chest, as much to keep

himself from reaching out to tug her close as to appear threatening.

"Very well." His eyes narrowed. "Explain."

Bianca discovered her entire body shaking as she smoothed her hands over her rumpled skirts.

She had behaved badly.

There could be no mistake about that.

Not only had she managed to make an utter fool of herself, but she had unintentionally touched a vulnerable nerve within the large gentleman who was currently regarding her with a disdainful expression.

Still, if she were being perfectly honest with herself, she would have to admit that her shaking had little to do with her well-deserved embarrassment and everything to do with having been so expertly and thoroughly kissed.

Oh . . . blessed saints.

The gentleman might be fresh from the country, but he possessed skills the most hardened rake might envy.

Even now her skin still tingled from the warm brush of his lips and feel of his hands so intimately holding her close. Worse, she could not deny that a tiny ache of frustration remained lodged deep within her.

Oh, it was not that she was a prude. She fully understood that a woman need not be in love to enjoy the touch of a man. After all, women throughout the ages had allowed themselves to be seduced by the most disreputable sorts of scoundrels.

But knowing in theory it was possible to respond to the touch of a stranger was considerably different from nearly melting into a puddle at his feet.

Shifting beneath his steady gaze, Bianca nervously cleared her throat. *Stop it,* she firmly commanded herself. Now was not the time to brood on wicked kisses, dash it all.

Not when a very large, very angry earl was hovering over her.

"I . . ." Her voice came out as a croak, and with an effort

Bianca sucked in a deep, steadying breath. "I meant no insult when I approached you, Lord Harrington."

His eyes narrowed. "But you knew my identity?"

"Yes."

The dark, handsome features tightened with what might have been disappointment.

"And that was the reason you sought me out?"

Her heart gave a sharp squeeze. She could offer a lie, of course. She was not above a bit of deception. Especially when it might protect the feelings of another.

Unfortunately, there was a fierce intelligence in those hazel eyes that warned he would not be easily deceived. Nor would he take kindly to any attempts to spare his sensibilities.

"Only in part," she grudgingly confessed.

"And what part would that be?"

She winced at his clipped words. He was certainly . . . blunt. A quality she was not yet certain she admired or not.

Needing a moment to collect her rattled thoughts, Bianca settled on a bench beside the gazebo.

"This is not simple to explain." She gazed the long distance up to his shadowed countenance as she patted the seat beside her. "Will you join me?"

His deliberately glanced about them. "That all depends."

"Depends upon what?"

"You do not have a vicar lurking about the hedges who is about to leap out and join us as man and wife?" he demanded dryly.

Her eyes widened before her lips gave a reluctant twitch. Good heavens but he was the most unexpected of gentlemen.

"To my knowledge the hedge is without vicars, parsons, or even monks, although I would not lay odds upon a stray bishop or two."

The hazel eyes glittered in the moonlight. "I suppose I shall take the risk."

"Thank you."

There was a pause before he seated himself on the bench next to her. Bianca nearly gasped as a startling rash of awareness blazed through her.

Aye, aye, aye.

The man was a menace to any woman under the age of eighty. Herself included.

"Perhaps before we go much further you should tell me your name," he drawled, seemingly unaware of her tiny shiver. "I should hate to discover myself tied for an eternity to an Esmeralda or Bertie."

She gave a distracted blink. "What is the matter with Esmeralda?"

"I possess a particularly loathsome Aunt Esmeralda who used to descend upon us every Sunday for the specific purpose of lecturing me on my lack of piety and prophesizing that someday I would find the path that would lead me straight to hell."

"And did you?"

"Did I what?"

"Find the path to hell?"

He shrugged, his expression unreadable. "I am still searching."

"Ah." She tilted her head to one side. "And Bertie?"

"The name of my mule."

Her gaze narrowed at his smooth retort. Was he teasing her? Impossible to tell.

A strange sensation for a woman who had been wrapping gentlemen about her little finger since the cradle.

"Well, I can safely assure you that my name is neither Esmeralda nor Bertie. It is . . ."

"Yes?"

"Lady Bianca Carstone."

"Lady?"

"My father is the Duke of Lockharte."

There was an ominous silence before his lips twisted in a humorless smile.

"Ah. Of course he is."

Bianca stiffened at the edge in his voice. "What is that supposed to mean?"

With a smooth motion he was back on his feet, his face adverted to reveal a perfectly chiseled profile.

"You have yet to explain your little charade on the terrace."

She pressed her hands together at his suddenly cold tone. "I have no real excuse but that I was furious with my father and hoping to punish him."

"By being seen in the company of the Peasant Earl?"

Put like that, it did sound horrible.

Selfish, insensitive, and horrible.

"Yes."

His gaze swung toward her at the soft admission.

"Well, at least you're honest. A rather rare commodity here in London."

She grimaced as she rose to her feet and lightly placed her hand on his sleeve. "I am sorry."

He stiffened beneath her touch but did not pull away. "You are not the first woman to find amusement in seeking my attention. If I were a vain man I would simply presume it was my masculine charms that stir such unexpected interest. As it is, I am well aware it is the fact that I am an odd bit of dross among the glittering gold."

She frowned. Not at the thought of women throwing themselves at him. She had already accepted that he possessed an indecent appeal for the opposite sex. But that he could be unaware of that appeal.

"That is ridiculous. You are an earl."

His jaw tightened, almost as if her words had managed to offend him further.

"I am a common farmer, as all are swift to remind me. Having a dozen titles dropped on my shoulders does not change who I am or make me more welcome in society." He smiled, on this occasion without humor. "As I am certain your father must have warned you before you flounced onto the terrace in a snit."

Her cheeks flared at his all-too-accurate thrust. "Rather more than a snit."

"What was it? Did your father refuse to purchase you a pretty diamond? Or perhaps you had your heart set on a matching pair to pull your golden carriage?"

Despite the knowledge that she was in the wrong, Bianca felt a shaft of annoyance flare through her. He condemned her as shallow and spoiled without knowing the least thing about her. Just as all of society did.

"What I had my heart set on was a marriage based on love. Instead my father has recently informed me that I am to be bartered off to the highest bidder in an attempt to salvage the family's failing estates." Her chin tilted. "Since the lands and estates are entailed, it appears I am the only property he has left for the auction block."

He paused, as if she had caught him off guard. "A marriage of convenience?"

"Convenient for my father, not for me."

In the shimmering moonlight his brow furrowed and he reached out a hand as if to touch her.

"Lady Bianca . . ."

Bianca took an abrupt step backward.

Blast it all, what was she doing? She sounded as if she were begging for his sympathy like some soppy milquetoast.

Something she detested above all else.

"I have apologized, my lord, and I sincerely hope that you will forgive me for entangling you in my ridiculous troubles. I assure you that I will not bother you again."

Sweeping an elegant curtsey, Bianca set a determined path toward the townhouse only to be halted by the soft sound of his voice.

"You have told me why you approached me on the terrace," he murmured. "But that does not explain why you allowed me to kiss you."

Bianca bit her lip before forcing her feet to carry her forward.

The day from beginning to end had been an utter disaster.

Tomorrow, by God, she intended to spend the entire day in bed.

CHAPTER FOUR

For the first time since his arrival in London, Edward discovered himself arising from his bed with a surge of anticipation.

He could attribute his eagerness to begin the day to the rare spring sunshine that shimmered through his window. Or to the fact that his valet had managed to inflict only a handful of bruises as he washed, shaved, and wrestled him into the skintight buff breeches and sapphire blue coat. Or even to the hot coffee that his cook had at last been convinced to include with his breakfast tray rather than the insipid tea he detested.

Unfortunately, he had never been one to hide from the truth.

However pleasant he found the sun and coffee and a lack of broken limbs, none of them could have him hopping from his bed and humming beneath his breath.

Humming, for God's sake.

A wise man would no doubt crawl back into bed and pull the covers over his head.

Humming was never a good thing.

Especially not after a night filled with delicious dreams concerning a raven-haired minx with the most kissable lips in all of England.

Instead he meekly allowed Hallifax to fuss to his heart's

content over the ridiculous knot in his cravat. He didn't even attempt to flee when his servant was interrupted by a discrete tap on the door.

There was a low murmur as a uniformed footman passed his message to Hallifax and the sound of the door once again being shut. Returning to his interrupted work of art, the valet met Edward's curious gaze in the mirror.

"It seems that Lord Bidwell has called, my lord."

"At this hour?" Edward grimaced.

He had already endured a sharp lecture from his friend when he returned to the ballroom last evening. It appeared all were aware that he had spent several moments alone with Lady Bianca, and Biddles had wasted no time in assuring him that only the worse sort of clod willingly made an enemy of the powerful Duke of Lockharte.

A wise warning, no doubt. But Edward had been in no mood to listen to reason.

Lady Bianca had fascinated him in a manner he could not fully explain. And while every instinct assured him that she was firmly out of his reach, he could not force himself to put her from his mind.

Not after the kiss they had shared.

"Sir?" his servant prompted as Edward remained lost in his thoughts.

"Oh, for heaven's sake, tell him . . . tell him that I was attacked by a pack of wild dogs and even now hover upon the brink of death."

The thin, sour face remained stoic even as he lifted a disparaging brow. "Dogs, my lord?"

"You think pirates a better choice?"

"Far more distinguished."

Edward gave it a moment of consideration. "Yes, but surely a gentleman trained in the sporting arts should not be so faint-hearted as to be bested by ruffians?"

"You were rescuing a poor maiden and as such unable to

toss yourself fully into the fray for fear of disturbing her delicate sensibilities."

"Ah . . . a nice touch."

Hallifax gave a faint nod as he twisted the linen into a perfect knot.

"You may depend upon me."

"Arrgg." Edward glared at his valet as he struggled to breathe. "You do know if you wish to be done with me, Hallifax, it would be much less painful to simply slash my throat with your razor."

"I could never abide the sight of blood, sir."

"And a slow torture is so much more rewarding?"

Hallifax offered a bow. "There is that."

"Damn." Rising to his feet, he reached to slip on the heavy signet ring that had come with the equally heavy title. "I suppose you might as well send Biddles up, although I must insist you take away his walking stick. 'Tis bad enough to be whacked by his ridiculous fan; I will not be beaten with a cane."

"I shall do my best."

Gliding from the chamber with his superior silence, Hallifax left the door open, and within moments the slender, flamboyantly attired Biddles made his entrance.

"Ah, Edward, my dearest friend," the nobleman purred with a deep bow.

Edward could not halt the warm smile that touched his mouth. Whatever their differences, he counted the roguish rat as one of his closest friends.

"Good morning, Biddles." He motioned toward the breakfast tray. "Coffee?"

"Gads, no." With a shudder, Biddles withdrew a flask from his coat to take a swig of the no-doubt-excellent brandy. "'Tis horrid enough to be up and about at this unsavory hour without being forced to consume something so akin to tar."

"And may I ask what has you up and about at such an unsavory hour?"

"You, of course." Returning the flask to his pocket, Biddles regarded him with a searching gaze. "I wish to assure myself you do not intend to do anything foolish."

Edward gave a lift of his brow. "By 'foolish,' do you mean running naked through Hyde Park? Or, horror of horrors, scuffing the gloss upon my boots?"

The pointed nose twitched with annoyance. "I mean by allowing your little tryst with the Ice Princess to lead you to waters too dangerous to swim."

Edward discovered his jaw tightening. "I presume you are referring to Lady Bianca?"

Biddles took a step closer, his expression somber. "Listen, Edward, I will be the first to admit that she is a rare beauty with enough charm to make the most hardened rake toss his heart at her feet. But she has also proven to be a callous flirt who has devoted four seasons to luring susceptible men into her trap and tossing them aside when she becomes bored with their adoration."

Edward considered the warning for a long moment. Not unusual. He was not a gentleman to leap to swift conclusions or made decisions in a blink of an eye. There were those, of course, who thought his habit of careful consideration a sign of slow wits, which suited him just fine. To be underestimated always ensured he had the upper hand.

"You think her a *femme fatale*?"

"Of the first order."

"And you fear she desires to break my heart?"

"Only if you are naïve enough to allow her." Biddles gave him a look that indicated his opinion of anyone so hideously stupid. "Take my advice and avoid Lady Bianca like the plague. There are any number of debutantes who would not only be eager to become your countess but have been trained to ensure your household is a haven of peace and comfort."

Edward could not halt the twitch of his lips. "And is that what you searched for in a wife, Biddles? Comfort and peace?"

The pale eyes held a sudden glint. They both knew that comfort and peace were two words that would never be applied to Lady Bidwell.

"Perhaps not," he conceded wryly. "Still, I do not wish to see you hurt, old friend."

Edward gave a tug of his cravat. "If that were true, then you would never have hired a valet for me who is obviously determined to slowly strangle me to death."

"Edward."

"Forgive me, Biddles." Reaching out, he placed his hand upon the nobleman's shoulder. "You must know that I am deeply appreciative of all you have done for me."

"And you will heed my warnings?"

A beat passed before Edward gave a lift of his shoulder. He better than anyone knew that appearances could be deceiving. Had he not already been judged by a society that knew nothing of him?

Whatever Biddles's opinion, he suspected there was more to Lady Bianca than just a heartless jade.

Or at least he had hopes there was.

And there was only one way to discover the truth.

"I am more than willing to heed your warnings when it comes to matters of etiquette, fashion, and society, Biddles. They are, after all, a complete mystery to me. In affairs of politics and the heart, however, I must insist on following my own desires."

Biddles narrowed his gaze. "Even if they lead to disaster?"

"A life without a few risks is a life not worth living."

"Gads, if you are to sink to homilies, I shall leave you to your fate." Biddles gave a violent shudder. "It is far too early in the day for such trite nonsense."

Edward chuckled. "More likely you cannot bear to be away from your wife."

A sly expression touched the narrow countenance. "You know, old chap, it is not too late for me to order that corset."

"Egads." Edward stepped back and pointed toward the door. "Go away and pester poor Anna."

Biddles readily strolled toward the door, although he could not resist a last glance over his shoulder.

"Stay away from Lady Bianca, my friend. She is nothing but trouble."

Edward smiled blandly.

He fully intended to stay away from Lady Bianca.

At least for the moment.

It simply would not do to call before the appropriate hour.

Despite her vow to remain abed throughout the day, Bianca discovered herself rising with the sun.

She had always been plagued with an excess of energy. A fault pointed out with tedious regularity by her mother, her governesses, her pianoforte instructor, and even her dearest friends.

The mere thought of devoting the day to lying upon the sheets in melancholy splendor was enough to make her break out in hives.

No, it was far better to keep occupied, she had told herself. To simmer and stew upon her troubles would only lead her to another disaster.

And after last eve she had a stomachful of disasters.

At least for the week.

Unfortunately, once she had enjoyed her breakfast and allowed her maid to attire her in a muslin gown in a pale shade of peach and had her raven curls tucked in a tidy knot, she discovered herself at a loss.

There were certainly any number of activities to tempt her interest.

A visit to her dressmaker, an al fresco breakfast at Lady Marrow's, an Egyptian mummy being displayed at the museum, a charity meeting to assist wounded soldiers returning from the war, and any number of friends who would be delighted to have her call upon them.

Under normal circumstances, any one of the events would have captured her interest. This morning, however, she discovered herself tossing aside the gilt-edged invitations with a frustrated sigh.

Toying with the silver locket hung about her neck, she realized she desired something far more distracting. Something . . .

With exquisite timing, the door to her chamber burst open and the downstairs maid rushed in with a flutter of sensible wool-and-lace-fringed apron.

Rising to her feet, Bianca regarded the servant with a lift of her brows.

"What is it, Molly?"

"Oh heavens, Lady Bianca, you must come and see."

"See what?"

"Ach, never did I see such beautiful flowers," she breathed, her round cheeks flushed with excitement. "Roses and tulips and the sweetest daisies. Why, the entire house is nearly filled, and the door never silent for a moment as more arrive."

Bianca's brief spurt of interest swiftly dissipated. After four seasons, she had long ago grown accustomed to the bevy of flowers that arrived each morning. After all, they were far more a tribute to her wisdom in being born the daughter of a duke than to her own charms.

"Indeed."

Undeterred by her lack of enthusiasm, the maid pressed her hands to her ample bosom.

"And not just flowers. I seen a half a dozen boxes of them marzipan you so love and the dearest ivory fan with ribbons. Why, there was even a beautiful locket with a miniature of Lord Cassel."

A tiny chill inched down Bianca's spine.

Fans? Lockets?

Even she had to admit it sounded more than a tad excessive.

And there could be only one reason for the sudden bounty of admiration.

"It seems that Father has lost no time," she muttered beneath her breath, realizing that the Duke had used her absence from the ball last eve to his own advantage.

Oh, it would all have been exquisitely discrete. A word dropped here, a knowing smile there. Nothing would have been said outright, but by now all of society would know that the Duke of Lockharte had turned away the encroacher Lord Aldron and once again Bianca was firmly upon the Marriage Mart.

Blast the devil.

"Beg pardon?" Molly questioned with a frown.

"Nothing of importance, Molly." Grimly keeping her temper in check, she managed a tight smile. "That will be all for now."

"Oh, but . . ." A sudden flush stained the round countenance.

"Yes?"

"Surely you'll be wanting me to join you in the drawing room? Your callers have already begun arriving, and it wouldn't do to keep them waiting too long."

"They can wait until doomsday as far as I am concerned. I intend to spend the afternoon reading."

"But you cannot," the maid unexpectedly burst out, only to bite her lip at Bianca's startled frown. "What I mean to say is that the gentlemen are all atwitter to visit with you. They would be sorely disappointed if they were not so much as to catch a glimpse of you."

That warning shiver once again made a brief appearance.

Molly would never be so persistent without cause. A large, interfering, ducal cause.

Blast her father.

"You may inform His Grace that I have no intention of

coming down to be fawned over by a pack of social-hungry jackals," she stated in grim tones.

The maid's eyes widened in sudden horror. "You are not coming?"

Realizing that Molly was genuinely frightened of confronting the Duke and confessing she had been unable to lure his mulish daughter down to the waiting herd, Bianca reached out to lightly touch her arm.

"Perhaps it would be best if you assisted Mrs. Felton in the kitchen today," she murmured.

"Yes . . . oh yes, thank you," Molly breathed in relief.

"You may go now."

With a hasty dip, the servant scurried from the room and Bianca angrily paced toward the window overlooking the garden.

Did her father possess no scruples whatsoever?

Did he not realize that her heart was still aching?

She did not wish to be in the company of another gentleman, let alone choose one for a husband.

Not any gentleman.

Against her will the memory of a dark, fiercely handsome countenance rose to mind. Along with the startling realization that it had not been Stephen in her thoughts when Lord Harrington had held her in his arms and kissed her.

Her heart gave an odd leap before she was ruthlessly thrusting aside the dangerous thought.

No. Not now.

At the moment, she had to concentrate on some means of evading the horde of husband hopefuls that filled the drawing room.

And teaching her father she would not be so easily manipulated.

Squaring her shoulders, Bianca moved to place a pretty chip bonnet on her curls and wrapped a light shawl about her shoulders.

Let her father entertain the callers.

They were only here to please him anyway.

Leaving her chambers, she took the precaution of using the servants' staircase to slip out of the house and into the garden. For all her bravado, she was in no mood for yet another argument with her father.

Not one she was bound to lose.

Thankfully, the townhouse was vast enough to allow her to slip through without note, and once in the gardens she headed directly to the mews. She would collect her carriage and groom and call upon her cousin Alexander. The sardonic dandy would be just the person to take her mind off her current troubles.

Sensing that her father would soon come in search of her, Bianca left the graveled pathway and angled through the rose garden that would take her directly to the back gate.

A fine notion until her hurried flight was brought to an abrupt halt as her fluttering skirts tangled on a large rose-bush.

"Oh . . . blinking, blooming, bloody hell," she muttered as she turned to glare at the offended bush. "Damn you to the netherworld."

Her words rang through the silent garden, and without warning there was a soft chuckle from the gate.

Bianca froze in wary suspicion. "Who is there? Reveal yourself."

A beat passed before a solid, now-familiar form stepped through the gate. Lord Harrington. Even larger than she remembered and startlingly handsome in the slanting sunlight.

Her breath caught. He was so . . . gads, what was the word? Earthy? Male? Virile?

His presence filled the air with a powerful force that was nearly tangible. A force that seemed to wrap around her with a tingling excitement she felt all the way to her toes.

More than a tad alarmed by the unfamiliar sensations,

Bianca forced herself not to fidget beneath the amused hazel gaze.

Daughters of dukes did not fidget.

Not even when confronted by the near stranger who had kissed her witless the night before.

"Whatever are you doing hiding in the mews?" she demanded.

A startling pair of dimples danced about his lips.

"Actually, I was just admiring your rather . . . colorful vocabulary," he murmured in deep, rich tones. "I had no notion that governesses were teaching such language in the schoolroom these days."

Against her will, her lips twitched. Most gentlemen would have pretended that they had not heard her less-than-ladylike curses.

Or else chastised her.

Few if any would have found it a source of amusement.

"If you must know, my governesses were always quite prim and proper. It was my groom who taught me the more interesting words of the English language," she corrected in pert tones.

"Ah." He stepped close enough for Bianca to catch a faint whiff of warm male skin. Delicious. "I should have guessed as much. There is a certain cadence to a groom's turn of phrase that I particularly enjoy. However, if you desire a truly spectacular vocabulary, then you must spend time with a sailor. They can curse in nearly a dozen different languages and possess several hand gestures that add a distinctive charm."

"I shall keep that in mind." Her lips twitched again. "However, I must point out that I am unlikely to have the occasion to be in the company of a sailor. Certainly not one willing to school me in curses."

"Ah well, if that is your desire, I stand ready to introduce

you to any number of sailors. I am always happy to be of
service to a beautiful maiden."

"A charming invitation, but one I fear I must decline."

His soft chuckle sent an astonishing shiver down her spine.
"As you wish."

Bianca was momentarily bewitched by his engaging grin
before she gave a shake of her head. Oh, for heaven's sake.
How the blazes did this gentleman manage to lull her into
such a sense of ease?

She should be discovering why he was creeping about her
mews like a common thief, not treating him as an old and
treasured friend.

Conjuring as much dignity as possible considering she was
currently attached to a rosebush, she regarded him with a suspicious expression.

"You still not have told me what you are doing here."

He shrugged. "In truth I was on the point of collecting my
carriage when I heard your . . . intriguing mutterings." His
lips twisted. "It seems your butler has taken an exception to
my presence and refused to accept my calling card."

Bianca blinked in confusion. "Harrison?"

"Thin, beak-nosed chap with a face that could sour milk?"

There was no mistaking the description of the ancient
butler. Still, it did not make the least amount of sense.

"That is absurd. Why would he turn you away?"

"Well, I have it on excellent authority that it cannot be the
cut of my coat or the gloss of my boots." He gave a shrug. "So
I can only assume that he was either convinced I might nip
the silver or was told by your father I was unwelcome within
the ducal townhouse."

A sharp, painful wave of embarrassment flared through her
at his unruffled manner. He had every right to be furious at
being treated in such a boorish fashion. For God's sake, he was
a peer of the realm. An earl with impeccable lineage despite
his more humble beginnings.

More importantly, he possessed an air of solid decency that was all too rare among noblemen.

Certainly none of the rakes, rogues, scoundrels, and decrepit roués currently littering her drawing room could make such a claim.

"I am beginning to suspect that he has become completely doddy," she muttered.

"Your butler?"

"No, my father."

His glance was quizzical. "Why? Because he does not wish you to associate with the Peasant Earl? He is not alone."

The very fact that he seemed so indifferent to the insult delivered to him only made Bianca feel worse.

"He has never cared for such things before."

"Then perhaps Biddles is wrong and it is my coat," he retorted with a small smile, abruptly lowering himself to begin untangling her skirt from the devilish thorns that held it captive. "It could be your father possesses an aversion to Weston."

Watching as he gently worked the delicate fabric loose, Bianca found her gaze lingering on the strong hands that had been bronzed by the sun.

Her heart skipped a beat. Those hands had been warm and powerful as they had held her in the darkness. Strong in a manner not found among noblemen. Even now she could swear she could feel the lingering pleasure of his touch.

She resisted the urge to fan her hot cheeks and hurriedly sought to distract herself.

"Does it bother you?"

"The foolishness of society?"

"Being called by that ridiculous title."

His head lifted, the sun shimmering in the thick strands of his chestnut hair.

"Why should it? Some of my closest and most trusted friends are peasants."

"Yes, but . . ."

"But I should never confess to such shameless connections?" His jaw hardened to a determined jut. "I fear I am too old and too set in my ways to begin pretending superior ways, even if I desired to."

"It would make your entrance to society considerably easier," she pointed out softly.

"Perhaps. But while I am willing to endure London and the silliness of the fashionable world, I cannot change who I am."

Bianca did not miss the tightening of his jaw, nor the edge in his voice. The Earl of Harrington clearly was not without his own share of pride.

"Or are too stubborn to change," she murmured.

There was a moment before his features softened with that disarming sense of humor.

"Touché, muirnin."

Her brows drew together. "What does that mean?"

"Muirnin?"

"Yes."

He offered a faint shrug. "Just a term of endearment. My mother was from Ireland." Having rescued her skirt from the thorns, the gentleman rose to his feet. "I have answered your questions as to my presence here. Now it is your turn."

"My turn?"

He shot a deliberate glance toward the nearby townhouse. "I am well aware that there are near a dozen gentlemen awaiting your presence. Why are you attempting to slip away?"

Her features unwittingly hardened. Had he been anyone else, she would never have confessed the truth. In London one did not reveal sordid family secrets.

But there was simply something in that steady hazel gaze that lured her to unburden the frustration that seethed like a cauldron within her.

"What does it matter if I make an appearance or not?" she demanded. "My father is perfectly capable of discovering which of the fools possesses the largest fortune."

His brows arched although he thankfully resisted the urge to point out she sounded like a petulant child.

"And you are content to allow him to choose your husband in such a manner?"

"Content?" Her heart gave a sharp twist at the memory of Stephen's handsome countenance. "Of course not. Unfortunately, I seem to have no say in the matter."

"You do know he cannot force you to wed?" he questioned softly.

She wrapped her arms about her waist. "Perhaps he cannot force me, but he well knows that I would never stand aside and allow my family or our tenants and staff to suffer. If I must wed a fortune, then that is what I will do."

He absorbed her words with a silent nod, seeming to consider his words before he spoke. A habit she was beginning to expect from him.

"Duty to family."

"Yes."

"That I understand." Without warning his hand reached up to brush a stray curl from her cheek. It was a casual gesture, but there was nothing casual about the sizzle of heat that arrowed toward the pit of her stomach. "I also understand that duty can be near unbearable. It seems to be something we have in common."

Her eyes widened. "You consider your inheritance a duty?"

"Does that surprise you?"

"I would think that it would surprise anyone."

His hand dropped from her cheek, and Bianca struggled not to reach up and ensure her skin had not been singed. Oh lordy, but the man was lethal.

"As hard as it might be to believe, I was quite content with my life as a gentleman farmer. I possessed a comfortable home with enough staff to suit my purposes, loyal friends, and the satisfaction of turning a neglected manor into a flourishing estate. Now I spend my days mincing about like a buffoon and never come closer to my lands than a handful of letters from my stewards."

Bianca opened her mouth to protest. Being blessed with an unexpected title and vast fortune was hardly some gruesome duty. In fact, it had to be the secret fantasy of every commoner in England.

But before the thoughtless words tumbled from her lips, she abruptly bit them back.

Certainly his inheritance had been a windfall. But it had also thrust him into a society that had been far from welcoming and burdened him with responsibilities he had never been trained to carry.

Even worse, he obviously yearned for the quiet life that had been his before being thrust into his earldom.

"Perhaps we do have something in common," she reluctantly agreed.

"It is a beginning," he murmured with a rather mysterious smile.

A beginning to what?

Before she could inquire, she was distracted by the unmistakable sound of her father's voice.

"She must be here somewhere. Inform her that I expect her to make an appearance in the drawing room without delay."

"Yes, Your Grace," a decidedly nervous servant replied.

"And I do mean without delay," the Duke growled. "Even if that means dragging her in by her hair."

"I . . . of course, Your Grace."

Clenching her hands, Bianca allowed her gaze to collide with the amused hazel eyes. Blast, but she should never have allowed herself to be distracted. Now it was too late to escape.

With unnerving ease, Lord Harrington read the emotions flitting over her countenance and stepped forward to whisper directly in her ear.

"Do you desire a knight in shining armor?"

She tensed, more at the feel of his warm breath stroking over her skin than his odd question.

"I beg your pardon?"

"My carriage is awaiting me just beyond the gate. I could whisk you away before you are discovered."

Whisk her away?

Away from the yammering fools who cared for nothing for her? Away from her father, who had somehow become the enemy?

Away from the terrified footman who was even now scurrying in her direction to pull her into the townhouse by her hair?

It sounded like paradise.

Still, she was not about to escape from one marriage trap to tumble into another.

"I cannot be alone with you in a carriage," she protested.

"Ah, it is a Tilbury, which Biddles assures me is all the crack, not a closed carriage. Besides which, we would hardly be alone. I have a groom as well as a footman with me."

That did indeed change matters.

There was certainly nothing scandalous in a drive through the park in an open carriage and in the companionship of servants.

Still, she hesitated.

Not that she did not trust Lord Harrington. Everything about him inspired trust.

It was more those tiny shivers inching down her spine she did not trust.

There was the heavy crunch of footsteps on the graveled path, and Bianca frankly panicked.

God almighty. Anything was preferable to the horror of an afternoon being trapped in a room with a group of spineless toadies.

"I . . . yes," she muttered before she could come to her senses.

"Then, one knight in shining armor to the rescue," he breathed before taking her arm and wrapping it firmly through his own. "This way, my damsel in distress."

CHAPTER FIVE

He had taken complete leave of his senses, Edward acknowledged as he assisted Bianca onto the bench seat of the Tilbury and vaulted up beside her. Taking the reins from the groom, he set the horses into motion.

He had come to London with every intention of establishing his place as Earl of Harrington.

Among society.

Among his pompous, appallingly priggish extended family.

And, most importantly, among those powerful gentlemen who would be necessary to begin the various reforms he knew were so desperately needed for the common laborer.

And yet here he was endangering it all because of a pair of midnight eyes and a smile that made his toes curl in his glossed boots.

One did not need to have been born and raised among society to realize that angering the Duke of Lockharte was very much akin to pointing a loaded pistol to one's own head.

Should the gentleman choose, he could see that Edward was all but shunned by society. And that any legislation he might wish to bring before the House of Lords would be squashed before the ink dried upon the parchment.

Could a few stolen moments alone with a female, no matter how delectable, be worth such a fate?

He slanted a sideways glance at the perfect porcelain countenance and slender form settled close enough for him to feel her feminine heat. A smile curved his lips.

Oh . . . yes.

She was worth it.

And if that made him a loon, well then, so be it.

Turning his attention back to the heavy traffic, he easily weaved his large bays onto Westminster Bridge. His skill with the ribbons was at least one asset since coming to London, he wryly acknowledged. A skill direly needed considering the number of dandies and drunken asses who littered the streets.

They had reached Newington and turned onto High Street when his companion shifted to regard him with a faint frown.

"You do know that you have gone far past both Green Park and St. James's?" she demanded.

Avoiding a pack of filthy urchins that darted from a narrow alley, he flashed her a quizzical glance.

"Did you particularly desire to visit one of the parks?"

"It is the customary destination for a drive."

He smiled with wry amusement, recalling his few tedious turns through Hyde Park. He had witnessed snails clipping past him as he had been forced to crawl through the narrow lanes. And then there had been the barely concealed sneers and snubs along the way.

Not a pleasure he was anxious to repeat.

"I believe we can safely say that I rarely do what is customary," he murmured.

"So I am beginning to realize."

He lifted his brows. "Does that trouble you?"

"I suppose it all depends."

"Depends upon what?"

She met his gaze squarely. "Upon where you are taking me."

"Ah." His smile became teasing. "I assure you that it

does not include the docks or any ship involving the white slave trade."

She rolled her eyes at his teasing. "I cannot express the depths of my relief, but you still have not answered my question."

Slowing his massive bays, Edward gave a shrug. "I have a few errands that I must complete."

There was a faint pause. "In this neighborhood?"

Edward cast a swift glance over the narrow, shabby buildings and even shabbier inhabitants who shuffled along the street.

Certainly not the most romantic of locations, he ruefully acknowledged. Hell, it barely scraped the edge of respectable.

Who could blame the woman for regarding him as if he had taken leave of his senses?

Still, he calmly pulled his carriage to a halt before a nondescript building and handed the reins to the waiting footman.

What was the purpose in pretending to be something he was not?

Turning, he regarded her with a searching gaze. "Does it trouble you to be here?"

She unconsciously wrinkled her nose at the foul smells that drifted from the gutters.

"It is hardly an area that I frequent."

"I thought all society ladies devoted themselves to charities and those less fortunate?"

"Not by personally visiting them."

Edward found himself puzzled by the genuine shock in her voice. He had been raised by a mother who took a personal interest in all about her. From the lowest tenant to the local squire, she had clucked and fussed and commanded them with equal concern.

And not from a tidy distance.

"Then how do you assist?"

"By donating money and clothing and other items they

might need. We also have luncheons to bring their needs to the attention of those in the House of Lords."

Her chin tilted to a defensive angle, and Edward battled his amusement.

"Ah."

The dark eyes sparked with a sudden fire. "What?"

"Nothing."

"I believe there is something upon your mind."

His lips twitched. "Where it most definitely should remain. It will only make you angry."

The fire smoldered. "You have already succeeded at that."

Edward considered a long moment before he lifted a shoulder in resignation. For such a tiny thing, Lady Bianca possessed an inordinate amount of determination.

Some would say mulish obstinacy.

But not him. At least not when she was close enough to take a poke at him.

"Very well." Leaning against the back of the padded bench, Edward chose his words with care. "I was about to suggest that society ladies seemed happy to support charities so long as it does not risk getting your hands dirty."

She gave a small jerk, as if caught off guard by his charge.

"You believe I should come down here to sweep floors and empty chamber pots?"

He ignored the edge in her voice. "I think I would wish to know that the money I donated was being used to assist those in need and not to line the pockets of the directors," he said in reasonable tones. "The only means to do that is to personally speak with those in need."

Her lips thinned, as if she wished to argue his logic. Then, glancing toward the nearby building, she gave a loud sniff.

"Is that what you are doing here today?"

"In part. I also have a task from one of my tenants in Kent."

He had once again managed to catch her off guard. Not surprising. He managed to shock and bewilder most of society.

"A tenant?"

His expression became somber as he recalled his brief meeting with Joseph before leaving for London. The poor man had been nearly beside himself with worry.

"His sweetheart was . . . lured from her home by a scoundrel near two months ago. He fears that she was abandoned here in London and that she may be found at one of the almshouses."

She turned with a frown. "He wishes you to take her back?"

"Not against her will," he retorted. "But without family or friend in town, it may be that she is unable to make her way home. He has sent his entire savings to assist in her return."

The soft lips parted in surprise. And jolted Edward with a shaft of sudden heat.

God almighty.

Too easily did he recall the searing delight and the precise taste of those lips. The manner in which they had moved beneath his own. The satin heat that had left him hard and aching the entire night.

"He wishes her return even if she has been with another?" she demanded.

With an effort, he wrenched his thoughts away from such dangerous sensations.

Not that his stirring body was entirely cooperative.

He cleared his throat. "Joseph loves her."

"Indeed, he must," she murmured.

Needing to put a measure of space between him and her warm scent, Edward leaped gracefully onto the street.

"Remain here. I shall only be a moment."

Without warning she was on her feet. "You do not imagine I intend to remain here, do you?"

He blinked in surprise at her vehement tone. "I will leave my servants with you. You will be perfectly safe, I assure you."

In a flurry of muslin, she was launching herself from the

carriage to stand at his side. With her hands planted upon her hips, she regarded him with a tight expression.

"This almshouse happens to be one of those charities that I support," she informed him in clipped tones. "Obviously I am in need of inspecting the premises."

He gave a soft chuckle as he met her defiant expression. Surely such a spirited lass must have some Irish in her.

"You flounce very well, muirnin," he complimented. "No doubt you've had a great deal of practice?"

"Flounce? I take leave to tell you, sir, that the daughter of a duke does not . . . ," she began, only to halt as she encountered his glittering gaze. She threw her hands in the air. "You are a horrible man."

"So I have been told," he readily agreed, holding out his arm. "Are you prepared to discover how the truly poor are forced to suffer?"

She glanced toward the large, brooding building that had nothing in common with her usual haunts.

Half expecting her to balk, Edward found a flare of admiration racing through him as she tilted her chin and firmly laid her fingers upon his arm.

"Yes."

It was a distinctly subdued Bianca who returned to the pristine streets of Mayfair.

As much as she would have liked to claim it had been courage or generosity that had led her into the almshouse, inner honesty forced her to admit that it had been sheer pique.

She did not care at all for that hint of condescension in Lord Harrington's manner when he had discussed her charities.

As if she were some worthless ninny playing at helping others.

Now she was forced to admit that he had not been far from the truth.

A shiver inched down her spine as she recalled stepping

into the dark, musty building. Suddenly she was not witnessing poverty from the safe distance of her carriage or tidily reading about it in the *London Gazette*.

It had been as tangible as the stale air that was rank with unwashed bodies and festering disease. As tangible as the sight of frail women clutching their precious children as if in fear they might be yanked from their arms. As tangible as the stoic composure of the wounded soldiers left in corners like broken toys that had been tossed in a rubbish heap.

Gads, never had she seen such need. Such hunger. Such bleak desperation.

And yet the worst thing of all had been the sudden glimmer of hope in the eyes that had followed her. As if they believed she could somehow offer them salvation. As if they expected her to do . . . something.

Anything.

She had been playing at helping others.

Oh, no doubt her money helped to feed some. And to keep a roof over others.

But did it truly change lives?

Did it offer a future for those poor, wretched children?

Still pondering her dark thoughts, Bianca had allowed Lord Harrington to lower her from the carriage and lead her back through the gate to the garden.

Astonishingly, she felt no distress at facing her father and enduring his awaiting lecture. Her troubles seemed rather petty at the moment.

Walking at her side, the large nobleman at last reached out to grasp her arm and pulled her to confront his searching gaze.

"You are very quiet," he murmured. "I suppose that I have offended you past all bearing?"

Bianca hesitated. Certainly no other gentleman of her acquaintance would ever have dared to take her to such a place. Nor to have challenged her smug assurance.

Oddly, however, she felt more grateful than offended.

While Stephen had readily taken her to any number of bawdy entertainments that had made her feel daring and oh-so-bold, they had been no more than titillating diversions.

They had revealed nothing of the stark, shocking world beyond her protected existence.

It was rather refreshing to be treated as if she possessed the sense and ability to deal with such hard truths, even if they were bound to give her nightmares.

"No. Indeed, you were right," she conceded with a rueful smile. "I did not realize . . ."

"What?"

"The misery of those poor people."

"Ah." He regarded her with open curiosity. "And now that you do?"

That was the rub, of course. It was one thing to realize something needed to be done. And quite another to know how to do it.

"I shall . . . well, I am not entirely certain, but I shall do something."

A slow, rather mysterious smile curved his lips. "I do not doubt for a moment that you will."

Her eyes narrowed in suspicion. "Now you are just patronizing me. You think me a spoiled henwit."

He gave a shake of his head, his hand lifting to gently cup her cheek.

"No, I think you a dangerously determined young lady who could very well alter the world if she wished to do so."

Bianca's heart missed a rather important beat.

For as long as she could remember, she had been acclaimed for her beauty, her charming manners, and, occasionally, her wit.

But never, ever had anyone admired her staunch will.

Indeed, it was more often than not branded a curse.

"Lord Harrington," she breathed.

"Yes?"

"That is really one of the nicest things that anyone has ever said to me."

His brows lifted as that familiar twinkle returned to his eyes.

"I comprehend why you have no desire to wed any of your suitors if I managed to best them in compliments. I have been told I have the charm of a blundering ox."

Suddenly aware of the warmth of his fingers as they stroked her cheek, Bianca found herself struggling to breathe.

Did the dratted man have no notion of his effect on poor females?

"I did not proclaim you to have charm," she countered.

As if not content with simply stealing her breath, the nobleman took a step closer, his legs tangling with her skirt.

"But you do think me charming, do you not?"

What she thought was that he was delectable.

And the desire to press against that solid, wholly male form was so hideously fierce, she nearly groaned aloud.

Shocked and more than a bit dismayed by her unladylike reaction, she forced herself to take a deep breath.

"Sir," she at last managed to protest.

As if sensing the heat simmering through her, the hazel eyes darkened as his fingers skimmed to the tender curve of her neck.

"Edward," he husked. "My name is Edward."

"Edward." The name tumbled far too easily from her lips.

Never allowing his gaze to stray from her own, the gentleman untangled the ribbons of her bonnet and tossed it aside. Then, cupping her chin, he tilted her head upward.

"Have you noticed that we always seem to end up alone in one garden or another?" he murmured.

Not entirely a bad thing, Bianca had to admit.

Despite a faint pang of guilt, she could not deny that she very much enjoyed being touched by this gentleman.

It was not the sweet longing that she had shared with Stephen, she hastily assured herself.

Instead, it was a sharper and infinitely more urgent awareness. As if she had suddenly discovered she was starving when she had not even known she was hungry.

He made her tingle. And shiver. And long to discover more of such sensations.

A dangerous, potent force.

Knowing she should step away, Bianca instead lifted her hands to place them on his solid chest.

"Perhaps not quite so surprising considering you seem to frequently lurk in gardens," she pointed out.

Beneath her hands she felt his heart give a sudden jerk, and a smile of satisfaction curved her lips.

Obviously he was no more indifferent to her than she was to him.

It seemed only fair.

"Well, I am a farmer," he retorted, his voice huskier than usual as his attention drifted down to her lips. "It is hardly surprising that I would prefer the comfort of nature to cramped, overcrowded rooms. Besides which, I am discovering that there are the most fascinating treasures to be discovered among the roses."

Her lips parted. She was not quite certain why until his head swooped downward and he captured her mouth in the kiss she had wanted from the moment he had appeared in the garden.

Oh yes.

This was it.

Just exactly what she had wanted.

Her lashes fluttered downward as his lips moved over her own with a demanding tenderness. He did not taste or even smell as Stephen did. There was no brandy on his breath and no expensive cologne upon his skin. Instead his lips held a hint of peppermint and his skin the clean scent of soap.

A combination she found strangely erotic.

Sparks flashed and smoldered behind her closed lids as his tongue stroked over her lower lip and then shockingly dipped into her mouth.

Her breath caught at the strange intimacy. A part of her realized she should protest. This seemed far more dangerous than a mere kiss. But a much larger part of her was far too intrigued by the wicked pleasure to call a halt.

His tongue brushed her own, and she gave a faint moan. Yes. Oh yes. Her stomach clenched and her fingers clutched at his coat as she went onto the tips of her toes.

A magical heat raced through her, warming places she did not know could be warmed.

His arms encircled her, pulling her relentlessly to the hardness of his body. Instinctively her hands lifted to tangle in the satin softness of his hair.

"What have you done to me, muirnin?" he rasped, his lips brushing soft, urgent kisses over her upturned countenance. "Have you cast some spell of enchantment?"

Bianca was quite certain that she was the one under a spell.

Absolutely nothing else could explain her fierce reaction to this gentleman.

After all, the daughter of a duke did not share such intimacies with a man in the midst of a sun-drenched garden.

Not, at least, if there were any danger of being caught.

Reluctantly regaining at least a portion of her fogged senses, Bianca wrenched her eyes open.

"Edward . . ."

Finding a delicate spot just below her ear, the nobleman devoted himself to sending chills of pleasure down her spine.

"Mmmm?"

Her eyes nearly rolled back in her head. Holy heaven.

"You . . . you really should not be kissing me in such a fashion," she breathed.

His soft chuckle tickled her ear. "You prefer I kiss you in some other fashion?"

Oh no. This way was utterly, wonderfully perfect.

"You should not be kissing me at all."

"I am offending you?" He pulled back to regard her with darkened hazel eyes. "Or perhaps you find me repulsive?"

She blinked in shock. "Of course not."

A smile curved his lips. "Good."

"No." She sucked in a deep breath, suddenly aware of just how near the looming townhouse was and how fortunate they had been not to have been seen by a passing servant. Or worse . . . her father. "It's not good."

"It's bad?"

Her hands lowered to his shoulders. She should step away completely, but it seemed wise to wait until her knees were not threatening to give way.

"This is not at all proper. And if anyone were to come upon us . . ."

"You would be compromised into wedding me," he completed.

"Exactly."

He seemed to consider a long moment, his gaze remaining steadily upon her flushed features. Then, just as she expected him to firmly come back to his senses, he allowed his hands to sweep down the curve of her back.

"Do you know, Lady Bianca, I could think of worse fates."

CHAPTER SIX

The next morning found Bianca banished to her chambers for the day.

Not that she truly minded.

Being in exile meant she would not be forced to endure yet another tedious lecture from her father on having disappeared for near four hours the day before, nor to make an appearance for the predictable crowd of hopefuls that filled the downstairs parlor.

And best of all, her cousin Alexander had arrived shortly after luncheon to dab upon the portrait he had been working on for the past year.

A slender, golden-haired gentleman with hazel eyes, delicate features, and polished charm, he was a favorite among both sexes of society. A privileged position he took full advantage of. Alexander had never encountered a lady he could not seduce nor a gentleman he could not fleece.

He was a plague and a pestilence, but Bianca adored him, and the torture of being forced to sit for his ridiculous attempt at painting her portrait was readily offset by his sly sense of humor.

At least upon most days.

Seated upon the window seat with her head turned to a

most uncomfortable angle, Bianca began to sense there was more to her cousin's unexpected arrival than a mere desire to chat.

A suspicion that was at last confirmed as he halted his aimless dabbing to regard her with a mysterious smile.

"I must tell you, my sweet, there are the most delicious rumors whispering their way about town."

Bianca forced herself not to react to the smooth words. Gossip had swirled about her since she had left the cradle. The only means to endure the relentless besiegement was to pretend utter and complete indifference.

"That is hardly earth-shattering." Her tone was one of sublime boredom. Practice had made it perfect. "Rumors are always whispering their way about town. Last week alone I heard that Lady Stolbert had taken the Russian ambassador as her lover, Lord Colefield's son had run off to Gretna Green with an actress, and the mad King had been miraculously cured and was about to return to the throne. None of which, however, proved to possess the least amount of truth."

"These rumors concern you."

"Ah, then they must be true."

Alexander chuckled. "Are you not even remotely interested in what people are saying?"

"Not particularly, but I sense that you intend to tell me anyway."

He dabbed a bit more. "What is the purpose of listening to gossip if you cannot pass it along?"

She rolled her eyes heavenward. No one could be more provoking than her cousin.

Well, perhaps her father.

And that conceited Miss Hennings who was forever lording it over the other debutantes that the Prince had once proclaimed her the Toast of the Season. The conceited tart.

"Oh, for goodness' sakes, Alexander, just tell me."

"They are saying you have been seen in the company of the Peasant Earl."

"And?" she prompted.

"And everyone is rabid with speculation as to why you would allow your name to be connected with the encroacher."

It was precisely what she had been expecting, and yet Bianca discovered herself tensing.

But why?

It had nothing to do with any ridiculous gossip.

No, that was not entirely true.

She might not care what others said of her. She was accustomed to the spiteful chatter. But she discovered she cared very much if Edward was harmed by such malicious talk.

For all his peculiar ways, he was an honorable man who deserved better than the nasty games played among the *ton*.

"Could it not be that I simply enjoy his company?" she demanded.

"It could be, but that would be far too tedious to please the scandalmongers. Or me," Alexander drawled. "I know you too well, Bianca. If you are encouraging the lumbering ox, it is because he possesses something you desire."

Her dark brows snapped together in a swift display of temper. She was uncertain if she were more angered by his insinuation that she was using Edward for her own devious purpose or the fact he had called him a lumbering ox.

Both of them were enough to make her consider throttling her beloved relative.

"What the devil is that supposed to mean?"

Alexander gave a click of his tongue as he tossed down his paintbrush. "Halt that frowning at once. My muse demands an exotic angel, not a petulant child."

She rose to her feet in a rustle of silk. "Your muse is going to have a blackened eye if you do not explain that insulting comment."

"My sweet, there is nothing insulting in the truth."

"Lord Harrington possesses nothing I desire."

"Not even the means to punish your father for refusing Lord Aldron's suit?" A sardonic smile curved his lips as a sudden heat flooded her cheeks. "Ah. The blush tells all."

The blush was understandable.

It was the sharp pang of regret clutching at her heart that was unexpected.

She had apologized, and Edward had accepted. That should have been the end of the matter.

Still, it gnawed at her to know her behavior had been as trite and shallow as that of those she readily condemned.

"I will admit that I . . . approached Lord Harrington out of annoyance," she reluctantly confessed. Then her chin abruptly tilted. "But I did not lie when I said I enjoy his companionship. He is unlike any other gentleman I have met."

Alexander studied her for a long moment, a mysterious smile playing about his lips.

"No, I should rather think not. He is, after all, a man tumbled into his title and not a born aristocrat. His bloodline is hardly pure."

Throttling became a more distinct possibility.

"Which I must admit has proven to be a vast improvement over most so-called gentlemen," she snapped before she could halt the revealing words.

A golden brow arched. "You are charmed by his rustic manners and strapping form? You are not alone, you know. More than one lady has been noted slipping him covert glances even as they condemn him for his lack of proper blood. Still, I must admit that I am rather shocked, my sweet."

Strapping form? Oh yes, it was strapping. And hard. And warm. And perfectly proportioned to hold a woman close.

And the thought of other women sneaking peeks made her jaw clench in the oddest manner.

The heat in her cheeks deepened as she attempted to thrust such disturbing thoughts from her mind.

"It is not that. Or at least not entirely," she amended with grudging honesty. "Do you know, he took me to an alms-house yesterday?"

The unflappable Alexander appeared momentarily stunned. "Whatever for?"

Bianca briefly recalled her afternoon spent in the company of Edward. Certainly there had been nothing romantic about the encounter. Well, except for that searing kiss that had nearly set the garden on fire.

Still, while it had been most unconventional, it had kept her tossing and turning most of the night.

"Because he believes I could alter the world if I chose," she said softly.

"Well, well." Alexander gave a low whistle. "It seems there is rather more to the farmer than I first suspected. He shall bear watching."

She felt an odd chill inch down her spine. "What?"

"Nothing." Still smiling, Alexander reached for his brush. "If you will return to your position, my sweet, we shall continue with this most important masterpiece."

Edward was disturbed.

And as always when something was upon his mind, he forced himself to take the necessary time to consider what precisely was troubling him and what steps must be taken to correct his unease.

He was not a man of impulse or hasty action.

Nor was he a man to simply hide his head and hope that by ignoring a problem it would somehow vanish.

He would ponder, weigh his options, and then act. Slowly and methodically.

Two days after his afternoon in the company of Lady Bianca, he was still in the pondering stage.

The woman . . . disturbed him. And worse, he did not understand why.

It was not just that she was beautiful. Or that he lusted after her. He was a normal man with the normal urges.

Perhaps this lust was a tad more forceful. Rather like the difference between a flickering candle and a raging fire. But still the sort of thing a man could comprehend.

If that were all, he would indulge in a bit of a flirtation, hope for a few kisses, and turn his more basic urges to a woman interested in sharing an intimate tryst.

Problem solved.

But the simmering lust could only explain a portion of why she continued to haunt his thoughts. Or why it was only with a stern effort that he avoided skulking about her garden on the off chance he might catch sight of her.

Or worse, considering the best means by which he might bring that radiant smile to her lips.

She was becoming a fever in his blood, and despite his lack of experience with the fairer sex he realized that it could not be a good thing.

A bout of unrequited love was not upon his list of experiences he wished to enjoy during his stay in London.

Calling for his mount, Edward set a brisk pace to Hyde Park. At such an early hour he would have ample room for a good gallop and hopefully the peace necessary to sort through his tangled thoughts and come to some sort of solution to his troubles.

A fine notion, he told himself as he cantered across the wide swath of open field. Unfortunately, as he circled about for another run, his gaze landed upon a disturbingly familiar female form trotting directly toward him.

Lady Bianca.

His breath lodged in his throat as he brought his restless stallion to an abrupt halt. By the fires of hell, she was a sight to behold.

Seated upon a dove gray mare, she was attired in a ruby velvet habit with black trim that hugged her body with loving tenacity. The vibrant color was a perfect foil for her ivory skin and glossy raven curls and obviously designed to attract and hold the attention of every male in the park.

Well, his attention was firmly held, he acknowledged with a sharp flare of excitement.

Held, riveted, and arrested.

Damn the evil modiste who had invented such a thing.

Realizing he was gaping at her like a witless moonling, Edward forced his mount forward. Perhaps it would be wiser to ride on with no more than a nod of acknowledgment. At least until he had decided whether he desired to pursue his strange feelings or not.

Wiser but impossible, he discovered. He was as helplessly drawn to her as a moth toward a lethal flame.

Halting at her side, Edward offered a bow from his saddle, painfully conscious of his tousled hair and the plain buff breeches and coat that Biddles had threatened to have burned.

O vanity, obviously thy name was not only woman.

"Lady Bianca," he murmured, relieved his voice did not reveal his inner disturbance.

A ready smile curved her lips. "Lord Harrington."

"Edward," he corrected softly.

"Edward."

His name had never sounded quite so wonderful.

Fool. Fool. Fool.

"You are up and about at an uncommonly early hour."

She wrinkled her nose in a charming manner. "Having been consigned to my chambers yesterday, I felt the need for some fresh air. Besides, I have never been one to lie abed."

He stiffened. "You were consigned to your rooms? Because of me?"

He instantly regretted his impulsive words as her eyes flashed with annoyance. If he had learned nothing else it was that Lady Bianca fiercely desired to be in control of her own destiny.

"Because of me. It was my decision to sneak away. You did not force me to go with you."

"I should hope not." He deliberately lightened his tone. "I have no particular talent for forcing women to do anything. Quite the opposite, in fact. A woman need only flash me a smile and I am clay in her hands. A sad case, indeed."

"Fah."

Edward blinked in disbelief. "Fah?"

"I do not believe you for a moment. I have no doubt you have left a string of broken hearts behind you in Kent."

His laugh echoed through the nearly empty park. Good God, did the woman imagine him some sort of rake?

The mere notion was ludicrous.

"You are far from the mark, muirnin. I have never been a gentleman of leisure. Being a farmer entails a great deal of work."

"But you have always loved it?"

He paused before deciding her interest was genuine. "I will admit there were times when I found it confining when I was younger."

"Ah." Her smile flashed once again. "You wished to be a dashing pirate or perhaps marching off to battle as a soldier?"

"I fear not. My dreams have always been boringly practical."

"Then what did you find confining?" she demanded, not seeming to realize that the restless movement of her mount had brought her close enough for his senses to be filled with the heat and scent of her.

He, on the other hand, was painfully aware of her proximity.

As well as the fact they were very much alone.

Oh lord, concentrate, Edward, he told himself.

And not on the soft swell of her breast or the ease in which he could pluck her from her horse and have her straddled across his stirring groin.

"My father was a good man. Loyal and devoted to his family and tenants, but he believed that the old ways were the best ways." He gave an unconscious grimace. "He refused to even countenance my notions of implementing the latest farming practices."

"But you did?"

"I have always been fascinated with the various innovations." He gave a lift of his shoulder. "I studied journals and even traveled to estates where they were experimenting with field rotations and fertilizers. It was obvious that we could make our lands far more productive for ourselves and our tenants."

"You made a study of farming?"

He smiled wryly at her startled tone. Very few shared his enthusiasm for such a tedious subject.

Absurd, really.

If he were obsessed with gambling and lewd women, he would be all the rage in London.

"I have already shared my opinion on investing money in any venture that has not been properly researched. Besides, my future, as well as that of those who depend upon me, rests on how successful I am as a farmer. Especially now that I am an earl. I have a great deal of land to keep profitable."

"I suppose that is true." An impish humor touched the dark eyes. "You know, I have always thought that you put seeds in the ground and prayed for the appropriate weather. I did not realize it could be so complicated."

His heart skipped a beat at her luminous beauty in the early morning sunlight.

Oh, damn. He was in trouble.

Big, big trouble.

"That is a mistake made by far too many," he managed to husk, shifting uncomfortably in his saddle. He was hard and aching in the midst of a public park. And before breakfast.

Yes, definitely trouble.

"Including your father?" she broke into his desperate thoughts.

Edward cleared his throat. "His mistake was in believing that any sort of change must be bad." He paused. "And I think it was difficult for him to accept that I was becoming a man with my own notion of how things should be done."

Her delicate features abruptly hardened. Clearly he had touched a raw nerve.

"Oh yes. Fathers have little wish to acknowledge that their children might become intelligent adults with the ability to think for themselves." There was no mistaking the edge of bitterness in her tone. "Especially if that child has the poor sense to be born a female. Why bother to allow us a brain when we are to be handed over to a husband to be treated as a witless idiot?"

Edward gave a lift of his brows. He sensed that he and his entire gender had just been insulted.

"I must beg to disagree."

"What?"

"Not all husbands would treat their wife as a witless idiot," he corrected in firm tones. "I assure you that my mother would have drowned my father in the nearest well had he attempted such a horrendous crime."

There was a silent beat, as if Bianca were contemplating the notion of a tidily placed well.

Hopefully for her father, not him.

"Your mother sounds a fascinating woman," she at last murmured.

Edward smiled even as a sharp pang of loss shot through his heart. He had been only sixteen when his mother had died of consumption. Even after all this time, he missed the woman who had taught him to search for the goodness in others, to trust in his beliefs, and never lose the ability to laugh at himself.

"She was," he agreed. "Intelligent, spirited, and yet filled with such kindness that there was not a soul who did not adore her."

"And that is the sort of woman you seek for your wife?"

Edward was momentarily speechless.

It was not so much from her perfectly mundane question.

Women seemed to find it an essential task to badger an unwed man about wives and such.

But before this precise moment, the mention of a wife had always roused nothing more than a vague, misty notion of the woman he might one day wed.

A goddess, of course. But one without face or form.

Now suddenly that goddess had a very distinct face. One with delicate features and flashing black eyes.

He stiffened, not at all certain if he should be delighted or horrified by the startling image.

Horrified seemed the more logical choice.

"I think those are attributes any man would desire in his wife," he forced himself to retort.

Her eyes widened in disbelief. "You must be jesting."

His lips twisted. "Not deliberately, although I have discovered that people quite often find my notions a source of amusement."

She regarded him with suspicion. "It is only that most gentlemen desire a wife who is dutiful and well trained, not intelligent, and certainly not spirited."

Dutiful? Well trained?

He gave a sudden laugh.

"Good God, you sound as if I am choosing a hound, not a wife."

"For some gentlemen there is little difference."

"Then they are fools." He met her gaze squarely. "I have no patience for shy, retiring misses or those who do not have the ability to think for themselves. I wish for a capable partner who can assist me in my plans for the future, not a pretty bauble to hang on my arm."

She gave a slow shake of her head, still far from convinced that he was sincere.

"You have only been in society a short time. No doubt you will soon discover the delight of a demure maiden who is anxious to pander to your whims."

He battled the urge to reach out and grasp her. Whether to shake her or kiss her senseless was open to debate.

Either was unacceptable.

"Only a weak man need fear a strong woman. I may have many faults, but being weak is not one of them." He said the words even as he knew that a part of him was lying. He was weak. At least when it came to this woman. She was a sweet temptation he possessed no defense against. "If you will excuse me, muirnin, I have a rather tedious appointment with my man of business. Good day."

CHAPTER SEVEN

The elegant gathering was much like any other.

Vast townhouse. Expensive food. Glittering guests. Endless flirtations.

The smell of money, power, and arrogance abundant in the air.

It was the power that had attracted Edward. According to Biddles, the most influential members of the House of Lords would be assembled at Hellion Caulfield's soiree. None would dare to miss the social event of the year.

A perfect opportunity to begin assessing those who ruled England from behind the throne and to learn which noblemen dared to embrace the future rather than clinging to the past.

With the organizational skill of a general going into battle, Edward set about cornering those gentlemen that Hellion kindly pointed out as his best choice to listen to his radical notions.

At the moment it was a gruff old viscount who had slipped into the library to indulge in a taste of Hellion's private stock of brandy.

The man was ill-tempered and inclined to speak whatever was upon his mind but rumored to possess a genuine concern for those less fortunate.

Gulping down the last of his brandy, the Viscount set aside the glass with a sharp bang.

"Well, I cannot deny that a few of your notions are too radical for my taste. To even think of tenants and chimney sweeps holding political power and noblemen lowering themselves to manufacturing . . . bah." A frown marred his ruddy countenance, but there was no missing the unmistakable glitter of shrewd interest in the pale eyes. "Still, you have a good, sensible head on your shoulders, and not even an old relic like me can deny that the future always demands change. If England is to maintain her power, she must be willing to accept that the old ways are not necessarily the best ways."

Edward was careful to hide his thrill of victory. Noblemen could be an odd breed. While they might grudgingly be forced to accept an interloper into their midst, they would most certainly balk at the notion he was thrusting his bourgeois nose into their business.

"It is my belief that only a strong industry and open trade will allow us to avoid the fate of France," he retorted with a suitably modest air. "Our people must have the opportunity to work and put food on the table for their families. A hungry lower class is a danger to us all."

The shrewd glitter was more pronounced, as if the old grouse was well aware that he was being slowly but relentlessly prodded down the road of reform.

"You have made your point."

"Then may I hope for your assistance in creating the sort of legislation that is needed?"

"We shall see, you persistent devil." The Viscount reached out to clap Edward on the shoulder. "Come to dinner on Friday and I will attempt to collect a handful of associates who might be willing to listen to your seditious drivel."

Edward offered a small bow. "I am honored, my lord."

"Recall I have not yet offered my support."

"Yes, of course."

The older man studied him for a grim moment and then without warning gave a short, rasping laugh.

"Ah, to be young and idealistic once again, Lord Harrington. How I miss the days."

Edward smiled wryly. "Actually I have been assured I am tediously practical and more inclined to plod than dash."

Walking toward the door, the Viscount paused to regard Edward with a steady gaze. "Do you know the difference between a radical and a revolutionary?"

"What is that, my lord?"

"The radical is like the shimmering fireworks at Vauxhall Gardens. A great deal of noise and pretty lights that delight and frighten the crowd before fading as swiftly as they appear." A faint smile touched the ruddy countenance. "A revolutionary is like a simple plow. Slow, steady, and yet capable of altering the landscape. The most dangerous sort of enemy."

With his parting shot delivered, the older man left behind a bemused Edward.

He certainly did not consider himself a revolutionary, but the words did warn him that not all noblemen were all fluff and nonsense.

At least a few possessed a well-honed knowledge of their power and precisely how to wield it.

He would be a fool to underestimate the treacherous path he was treading.

Satisfied he had at least made a start on his quest for change, Edward left the library and headed for the crowded salons.

A part of him longed to slip from the elegant townhouse so he could return home and begin making notes for his upcoming dinner. A larger part of him, however, knew quite well he was not about to leave.

Not when there was even the slightest possibility of Bianca making an appearance.

He was mad, of course.

Stark, raving mad.

But he had at last come to the conclusion there was nothing to be done. Bianca had utterly fascinated him, and he had little choice but to allow his heart to lead him at the moment.

A knowledge that was enough to wake him up sweating in the middle of the night.

Moving out of the room and down the hall, Edward was still brooding upon his odd fascination with the raven-haired minx as he entered the salon.

It was his distraction that allowed him to be suddenly waylaid by a tall, golden-haired dandy.

Edward instantly cursed his foolishness as the gentleman raised a quizzing glass to peer at him with an obnoxious sneer.

He had encountered such jackasses on numerous occasions since his arrival in London. The sort of arrogant pups who thought themselves second only to God. And a close second at that.

As a rule he did his best to avoid them. He desired no quarrels with worthless fribbles who presumed they were better than him just because of the amount of blue blood in their veins.

Even if he could rip them in two with his bare hands.

"Ah, my lord, what an exquisite stroke of fortune," the golden dandy drawled.

Edward folded his arms over his chest. "Have we been introduced?"

"Lord Aldron, at your service." A disdainful gaze raked over Edward's plain blue coat and breeches. "And you are the Peasant Earl."

"I prefer Harrington, if you do not mind."

"Yes, I can imagine you do."

Edward considered the perfect aristocratic nose. Ah, the pleasure of ensuring it was never so straight again.

He clenched his teeth instead. He was here to claim his inheritance, not to indulge in ballroom brawls.

A pity.

"Is there some way I can be of service?"

"You be of service to me?" A grating laugh rang through the air. "Hardly. However, I do believe I might be of service to you."

"Indeed?"

"A gentleman newly come to London is always in need of guidance." Dropping the quizzing glass, Aldron toyed with the lace at his cuff. "'Tis amazing the number of pitfalls that await the untutored."

A warning shivered over Edward's skin. He sensed that there was more to Aldron's sudden approach than a mere desire to torment the country oaf.

There was a hard glitter to the blue eyes that spoke of a more personal dislike.

"And you are offering to be that . . . guide?"

"Egads, no. I have no taste for tutoring the less fortunate." His gaze lifted to pin Edward with a challenging smirk. "However, I am prepared to introduce you to a few of my acquaintances. We were just about to gather for a few hands of cards. It would be a perfect opportunity for you to attempt to win their favor."

Good lord.

The trap was pathetically obvious. Get the clodpole bosky and fleece him blind.

The wise course of action would be to thank the man politely and walk away. Edward, however, found himself hesitating. He wanted to know more of this Lord Aldron and what grudge he might be nursing against him.

And if he were being utterly honest, he would have to admit a rather childish desire to turn the tables upon the puffed-up peacock.

Clodpole he might be, but the dandy would soon discover he was not easily fleeced.

"Very well, my lord, I thank you for your gracious offer."

Lord Aldron waved his hand toward the nearby card room with the smooth confidence of a gentleman who was insufferably certain of his superiority.

Edward allowed himself to be herded forward, the faintest smile curving his lips.

The party would no doubt be toasted as the event of the season.

Since their marriage, Hellion Caulfield and his eccentric wife had become the sort of mysterious recluses guaranteed to inspire a mad rush when they did condescend to open their doors.

And rush society did.

Bianca discovered herself in increasing danger of being squashed by the swirling crowd. And even breathing became a challenge.

Still, she found herself lingering.

She could not imagine why.

It was certainly not for the pleasure of being elbowed by desperate debutantes angling for the best spot to preen in all their glory.

Or having her slippers ruined by buffoons who had sipped too heavily of the rum and found her toes easier to trod upon than the dance floor.

Or to share the same gossip with the same friends she had seen only an hour before at the Marshfield soiree.

It was . . . She wrinkled her nose in disgust.

She might as well admit it to herself. She was waiting for Edward.

It had been near a week since she had last spoken with him in the park, and she could not deny a vague fear she had said something to drive him away.

Not that she expected him to flutter about her like one of those ridiculous fools anxious to gain her favor, she sternly assured herself.

It was quite simply that she missed his calm, sensible presence.

In a sea of frivolous stupidity, his solid presence was a welcome balm.

Furiously waving her fan in an attempt to relieve the smothering heat, Bianca flicked her gaze over the crowd. A futile task. She was far too short to see over most of the guests and far too much of a lady to bounce onto her toes like a child.

"If you are searching for your farmer, my sweet, I must inform you that he is otherwise occupied," a mocking voice whispered close to her ear.

Giving a small jerk of surprise, Bianca turned to discover Alexander leaning nonchalantly against the fluted column at her side.

"And what is that supposed to mean?" she demanded.

Appearing absurdly handsome in the flickering candlelight, the elegant gentleman offered a small smile.

"The last I saw of Lord Harrington, he was ensconced with Lord Aldron and his cronies in a rather cutthroat game of whist."

A sudden chill inched down her spine. "Edward was gambling? With Stephen?"

"A rather unnerving prospect, eh, sweet?"

"I did not realize Lord Harrington had any interest in cards."

"It did not appear he had much choice." Alexander gave an indifferent shrug. "Lord Aldron was rather insistent that Harrington join him. Without making a scene, there was little your farmer could do to avoid accepting the invitation."

"Stephen insisted?"

"Quite."

The chill became more pronounced. Although there was no reason that Stephen should not seek out an acquaintance with the newly titled earl, she found it difficult to accept that it was entirely out of the kindness of his heart.

For all his wonderful qualities, Lord Aldron did not lower himself to noticing those he considered beneath him.

"Why would Stephen do such a thing?" she demanded, absently toying with the locket at her throat.

Alexander smiled with sardonic amusement. "No doubt he intends to have a bit of fun with the rustic."

"What sort of . . . fun?"

"The usual." He waved a dismissive hand. "Plying him with brandy and urging him to make an ass of himself before the *ton*. And, of course, there is always the pleasure of fleecing him of a tidy sum." He flashed a wicked grin. "Blast, I wish I had thought of such entertainment myself. I can always use a bit of the ready."

The stirring unease suddenly flared into outright anger.

Blast gentlemen and their ridiculous games. No doubt most would think it fine sport to badger and tease the awkward farmer. Just another lark to ease their boredom.

Bianca, however, found nothing amusing in the notion of Edward being made a fool of.

Especially not when she sensed that Stephen had deliberately chosen Edward because of her.

"Of all the . . ." Her hand dropped to grasp her cousin's arm. "You must halt this at once."

"Me? Good God, why would I wish to interfere?" He stifled a yawn. "It will do the clod good to learn a lesson or two in the dangers of society, and if all he endures is a bit of embarrassment and the loss of a few quid . . . what is the harm?"

Narrowing her gaze, Bianca ruthlessly yanked at his sleeve, pulling him downward to hiss directly in his ear.

"Listen to me very carefully, Alexander. You are going to the card room and putting an end to this."

He stilled at the threat in her voice. "Or?"

"Or I shall tell all of society that those beautiful baubles you so generously bestow upon your mistresses are nothing more than paste."

She heard his sharply drawn breath. "Now, Bianca, be reasonable . . ."

Stepping back, she pointed toward the nearby card room, her expression grim.

"Go."

"Traitor," he muttered as he pushed from the column and began battling his way through the surging crowd.

Bianca trailed in his wake, discretely slipping down the short hall next to the card room.

Once out of sight of the guests, she anxiously smoothed her hands over her skirts as she waited for her cousin to re-appear.

Damn, Stephen, she silently cursed.

She understood his frustration. His need to seek vengeance for his disappointments.

She felt the same shimmering need within herself.

But she would not tolerate having Edward harmed.

Not when he was nothing more than an innocent victim caught in the fray.

She paced from one end of the hall to the other. Then paced again. How the deuce long did it take to collect a gentleman from a card table?

Just on the point of daring scandal and charging into the strictly male territory, Bianca caught sight of Alexander care-fully maneuvering a decidedly unsteady Edward through the door.

"Oh, dear God." Moving to the edge of the hall, Bianca waved an imperious hand. "Alexander, bring him this way."

There was a momentary pause before her cousin gave a faint shrug and obligingly turned to enter the hall.

"As you see, I have rescued your farmer as you demanded."

Edward merely smiled, his eyes unfocused.

"Follow me," she commanded, turning on her heel to lead

the two away from the salon. Bypassing several public rooms, Bianca at last entered a back drawing room that was secluded enough to ensure a measure of privacy. "Place him upon the sofa," she murmured, wincing when Alexander casually toppled the large Earl upon the cushions. "For goodness' sakes, be careful."

Straightening, Alexander impatiently smoothed his sadly rumpled coat.

"He is cast to the wind, not on the verge of death, Bianca. No doubt he would be happier if we were to toss him into the nearest carriage and have him hauled home."

Taking Alexander's hand, Bianca led him firmly back to the door.

"I will call for his carriage once he has managed to regain his senses," she whispered, her glance remaining upon the large Earl sprawled upon the sofa. With a lock of chestnut hair tumbled onto his brow and his eyes hooded by his long sweep of lashes, he appeared heartrendingly vulnerable. "I will not allow him to be the source of malicious amusement for the guests."

For some reason Alexander's brows lifted in surprise. "You intend to remain here with him?"

"Of course."

"My sweet, while most might claim I am the proverbial sinner about to toss the first stone, I would point out that it is hardly wise to remain closeted alone with a gentleman. Especially when anyone might stumble upon you."

Her chin tilted. "This is my fault."

"Your fault?"

Bianca heaved an impatient sigh. "Stephen would never have done such a thing if he had not been wounded from my father's refusal to wed me."

Alexander's lip curled. Like her father, he had never been particularly fond of Lord Aldron.

"I am not nearly so certain of that."

"What do you mean?"

"Aldron is always swift to prey upon the weak and defenseless."

Her brows snapped together. "Alexander, that is a horrid thing to say."

"It is true enough," he drawled. "Even if you refuse to acknowledge your Galahad might possess a few nasty flaws."

Bianca grimaced. It was entirely her fault that Stephen was feeling betrayed. She had blatantly encouraged his attentions. She had led him to believe that they would be wed.

Now he was suffering the embarrassment of having been found publicly lacking as a son-in-law to the Duke of Lockharte.

"He is not the only one with flaws," she muttered.

Alexander cast a glance toward the silent gentleman across the room.

"You are determined upon this course?"

"Yes, I will lock the door so that no one can stumble upon us until I have Edward sober enough to return to his carriage."

A mysterious smile abruptly touched his lips. "So be it."

"Alexander?"

"Yes?"

She regarded him with suspicion. "You are behaving very oddly. What is it?"

His smile widened. "Just pondering the notion you might very well have met your match. Take care, my sweet."

Flicking a negligent finger over her cheek, Alexander turned to leave the room, shutting the door firmly behind him. Still frowning, Bianca reached out to slide the bolt into position.

Really, her cousin could be most exasperating. Met her match? What the devil was that supposed to mean?

With a shake of her head, she turned and headed firmly toward the sofa and settled next to Edward so she could pull him gently into her arms.

Whatever Alexander was implying, she had no time to fret

over it now. She had a father determined to wed her to the first fortune he could latch on to.

An ex-fiancé who was clearly furious at having been thrust aside.

And a drunken earl who had to be kept from making an unwitting fool of himself.

That was quite enough.

Even for the daughter of a duke.

CHAPTER EIGHT

Although Edward had always dismissed his Aunt Esmeralda's prophecy of his ultimate march into the fires of the netherworld, he suddenly realized he might very well have taken a detour toward the proverbial path of hell.

It had not been an intentional detour, he reassured himself.

When Aldron the Pestilent had led him into the card room and settled him among the gathered gentlemen, it had seemed amusing to maintain his image of a bumbling buffoon. After all, the dashing blue bloods had been so painfully eager to ply him with drink and fleece him blind, he could hardly disappoint them.

And if he were not nearly so inebriated as they thought him to be, and if he was winning far more hands than he was losing . . . well, that was their bloody problem.

They deserved to be taught a lesson in manners.

But while Edward could convince himself that there was nothing wrong in deceiving Lord Aldron, and even the stranger who had come to haul him from the room, he could not pretend continuing the charade with Bianca made him anything other than a perfect cad.

My God, what sort of man would play a drunken sod simply so he could enjoy the feel of her arms about him?

His heart jolted as her fingers lifted to brush his hair from his forehead, her sweet breath brushing his cheek. Damn. He heaved a rueful sigh.

He was surely going straight to hell.

But for the moment, he could not make himself care.

"Edward."

His lips twitched at her soft whisper. "Mmmmm?"

"Do you have need of anything? Perhaps some coffee?"

He covertly shifted closer to her soft curves. Oh, he was a horrible, horrible wretch.

"No, I just wish to rest here a moment."

"Of course." There was a pause before she heaved a deep sigh. "Oh, Edward, I am very sorry."

She was sorry? "Whatever for?"

"I—" She abruptly halted, as if carefully considering her words. Odd, that. "For you having to endure what passes as amusement for those idiots. They should be heartily ashamed of themselves."

Edward briefly considered the near two hundred pounds he had managed to win before being physically hauled from the table. A smile curved his lips.

"I doubt shame is what they feel."

She sighed. "No, I fear not."

He shifted to study her pale visage. "Did you send in the rather large gentleman to rescue me from the den of iniquity?"

"The rather large gentleman is my cousin Alexander, Lord Calloway," she admitted, "and yes, I did request that he collect you."

"Why?"

"You are not yet accustomed to such entertainments. And . . ." Her voice trailed away.

"And?"

"And I believe those dolts wished to embarrass you."

"Ah." He held her dark gaze with his own. "You were concerned for me?"

She bit her bottom lip, as if reluctant to confess her feelings. "Yes."

"Why?"

"As I said, you are not yet used to such entertainments."

He reached up to grasp her hand. He would not allow her to evade him. Not when her answer was so strangely important.

"No, Bianca, those gentlemen no doubt fleece every greenhorn that arrives in London, none of whom I am certain you have gone to the trouble of rescuing." He brushed his lips softly over her fingers, relishing the taste of her skin. "Why were you concerned for me? Could it be that you care, just a little?"

Even in the shadows of the room, he could detect the faint blush that stole beneath her skin.

"Of course I care. I hope that I can count you as a friend."

Edward abruptly shifted and turned, managing to trap her in the corner of the sofa before she could guess his intent.

"Friend?"

She regarded him with a wary expression, no doubt sensing the tension humming through his body.

"Does that trouble you?"

"Yes."

"Oh."

Planting his hands on either side of her head, he allowed himself to drink in her exotic beauty.

"I would very much like to be your friend, Bianca, but that is never going to be enough," he confessed in thick tones.

Her lips parted. "What do you mean?"

"I mean this . . ."

Slowly, deliberately, he lowered his head. Every fiber of him longed to pounce and conquer. To take what he had ached to possess since he had caught a glimpse of her across the room. But he ruthlessly battled back his primitive instincts.

Stark, panting lust had its place, but this was not it.

Not with Bianca.

She was not just a beautiful woman that stirred his senses. She was the intriguing, maddening creature who was rapidly becoming an important part of his existence.

Allowing her ample opportunity to protest, Edward softly brushed his mouth over her own. It was no more than the merest touch, but it was enough to send a jolt of searing heat through his body.

Holy hell.

With a groan, he feathered kisses upon her mouth.

"I have wanted to do this for days," he muttered.

"Then why haven't you?" she whispered.

He shivered. She might be too innocent to realize the danger of the heat that smoldered between them, but he wasn't. With every kiss it became more and more difficult to restrain the need to ease his aching passion in the sweet heat of her body.

"If you knew what I was feeling, you would not encourage me," he muttered as he moved to explore her cheeks and the line of her jaw. She tasted of paradise. Sweet heaven. And he was quite certain he would never have enough of her.

She gave a small sigh of pleasure. "Is that what I'm doing?"

"God, I hope so."

Sweeping his tongue along the curve of her ear he returned to claim her lips in a demanding kiss.

Beneath him Bianca stirred, her hands lifting to grasp his shoulders even as her lips parted in welcome. Edward was swift to take advantage as he dipped his tongue into the moist heat of her mouth. Raw desire sparked between them, shimmering through his blood and hardening his muscles.

His breath caught in his throat as her tongue tangled with his own. Oh dear God, she was capable of making him forget everything but the need to know more of her.

His hands framed her countenance, his heart thudding against his chest.

Outside the room the music played and the guests enjoyed their foolish society games, but in the silence of the parlor nothing mattered but the feel of Bianca. This was right. Honest. And swiftly charging out of control.

"Muirnin, tell me to halt and I will," he husked as his fingers stroked down the length of her throat.

Her hands shifted to tangle in his hair. "I do not wish you to halt."

He pulled back to meet the hectic glitter in her dark eyes. "This is dangerous. More dangerous than you know."

With a smile that sent a shaft of need straight through him, the vixen firmly tugged his head downward.

"Then teach me," she whispered.

Bianca was innocent, not stupid.

She knew she was playing with fire.

Good heavens, she already felt singed.

But though the seemingly endless lectures she had received over the years on the subject of what was acceptable for a young lady of society had been drilled painfully into her head, her heart was not paying the least heed to them now.

Not when his kisses were making her head spin and his fingers were sending the most astonishing sensations racing through her body. Proper or not, she wanted to know more of the pleasure to be discovered in his strong arms.

Tugging his head down, Bianca heaved a soft sigh as his lips closed over her own. A heat that she felt to her very toes sizzled through her body. Everything tingled inside her. As if she were filled with the finest champagne.

She heard him give a low growl as his tongue swept between her lips, thrusting in a slow rhythm that was causing the most peculiar ache to clutch deep within her.

Instinctively she arched closer to the hardness of his body. She needed . . . something. Something more.

"Edward," she breathed as his lips shifted to burn a trail of kisses down the curve of her neck. "Please."

"I know, muirnin," he muttered, shifting until he was off the sofa and kneeling between her legs.

Bianca was briefly shocked by the intimate position until his clever fingers tugged at the ribbons of her bodice. With satisfying speed he had tugged down her gown and then her shift, lifting her straining breasts out of her corset with gentle care.

Oh . . . oh, yes. He obviously knew precisely what he was doing.

"My God," he breathed before he was leaning forward and tugging one hardened nipple into his mouth.

Bianca nearly swooned.

Who knew such pleasure existed?

Who could ever have suspected?

Her fingers clutched at his hair as she felt the stroke of his tongue and the rasp of his whiskers against her sensitive flesh.

"That feels so good," she whispered.

"You feel so good. So bloody good."

He shifted to attend to her neglected breast, teasing the hard bud with his teeth before closing his lips about it.

Bianca moaned as he leaned more heavily against her, his body pressed to the juncture of her legs. With every movement, he brushed against the vulnerable region, sending a jolt of breathtaking excitement racing straight to the pit of her stomach.

Her hands restlessly moved to stroke over his shoulders, delighting in the feel of his hard, rippling muscles beneath her fingers. He was so solid, so utterly male.

"Muirnin," he moaned, lifting his head to bury his lips in the curve of her neck. "I want to please you."

His breath whispered against her skin even as she felt the hem of her gown being tugged relentlessly upward. Bianca shivered as his fingers stroked over her silk stockings. Raw heat streaked through her blood.

"Yes . . . oh yes."

She nearly leaped off the sofa as his fingers at last reached the bare skin of her thighs. Dear God. She felt as if she were on fire. As if she were suddenly simmering with molten lava.

Claiming her lips in a devouring kiss, Edward continued his soft caresses. His fingers stroking higher and higher. And then without warning he discovered the moist heat between her legs.

Bianca would have cried out in shocked pleasure if his mouth had not covered her own. Nothing had ever felt so wondrous as the clever finger that gently slid into her damp heat.

She grasped at his arms, her fingers digging into his coat as she instinctively arched against his invading touch.

With a slow thrust he pressed his finger deeper, using his thumb to rub against her sensitive nub. Oh lord. There was a pressure building deep inside her as his finger slid in and out of her. A delicious, aching pressure that was threatening to shatter her.

"Edward . . . please," she husked.

She was not quite certain what she was pleading for, but thankfully Edward seemed to know precisely what she needed.

Trailing a string of searing kisses down her neck, he flicked his tongue along the line of her collarbone. The rhythm of his finger quickened as his tongue continued to swirl over her skin. And then, dipping his head, he latched his mouth onto the tip of her breast and suckled with sweet insistence.

Unaware she was even moving, Bianca wrapped her legs about Edward's waist, her entire body arching. She was hovering upon the crest of a most astonishing sensation. Just for a breathless minute the world seemed to stop. A perfect, crystallized moment.

Then, with a magical stroke of his fingers, she was vaulted

over the edge, and a cry of sheer delight was wrenched from her throat.

Blasted, blooming, bloody hell.

That had been . . . magnificent.

Still shaking from the force of her climax, Bianca was barely aware of Edward tenderly smoothing her dress back into order, or even joining her on the sofa to bundle her in his arms.

"Bianca?" he murmured softly.

Feeling oddly lethargic, Bianca allowed herself to rest against the hard planes of his chest.

"What?"

"Look at me."

With an effort she tilted her head upward. "Yes?"

In the shadows, his countenance appeared strangely harsh. "Are you well?"

"I am not yet certain," she murmured.

His arm abruptly tightened about her. "God, I am sorry. I did not mean to frighten you."

"Frighten me?" Bianca frowned in bewilderment. "I was not frightened. How could I be? That was the most thrilling thing I have ever experienced."

His features slowly softened, but a darkness lingered in the hazel eyes.

"I very much wished to please you, my love, but I should never have allowed matters to go so far." He heaved an unsteady sigh. "Perhaps the gossips are right. I am not at all suitable to be among proper society. Most certainly I am not suitable to be in the company of proper young innocents."

Bianca's frown deepened. She could not believe he would regret the moments they had just spent in each other's arms. Not when she had felt him tremble with the same aching passion that had . . .

Realization hit with the force of a bucket of cold water. It was not regret. It was guilt.

Pushing herself from his arms, Bianca glared into the handsome countenance.

"You are not suitable because you did not recall to treat me as if I am a witless idiot with no notion of how to use the lump in my head some call a brain?" she gritted. "God knows I cannot possibly know if I desire a gentleman's kisses or not."

"It is not that."

"Then what is it?"

He grimaced. "It is a gentleman's duty to protect a lady, not take advantage of her."

She met his male logic with a snort of disgust. It was just so predictable.

"Stop that at once."

He gave a lift of his brows. "I beg your pardon?"

"You did not force yourself upon me."

"Still . . ."

"No." She poked her finger into his wide chest. "What I do, the decisions I make, are mine, not yours. I will not have you taking that away from me."

He paused a long moment, considering her stark demand with his usual care. Unlike most men, Edward did not simply dismiss her as a frivolous creature without the ability to possess her own thoughts.

It was what she liked best about him.

Well, perhaps not *best*, she acknowledged with a blush.

"You are quite right, Lady Bianca." A grudging smile tugged at the corners of his mouth. "And now that I consider the matter, I am not at all sure that *I* was not the one to be seduced. Perhaps I should be demanding satisfaction."

Her annoyance faded beneath his teasing, and she offered him a flutter of her lashes.

"What sort of satisfaction were you considering?"

A flare of raw hunger darkened his eyes and sent a thrill of excitement racing through her blood.

"More than I should," he growled, reaching out to enfold

her in his arms. Lightly his lips brushed her temple. "I want you, Lady Bianca. I see you across the room and I can barely breathe."

A shiver of answering awareness trickled down her spine. "That sounds most uncomfortable."

"You cannot imagine. I am not a gentleman who is as a rule prey to such emotions." He pulled back to regard her with a tender smile. "Anyone will tell you I am practical, dull, and not at all the sentimental sort. Indeed, most who know me would laugh at the mere notion that I could possess the finer sensibilities." He lifted his hand to cup her cheek. "But when you are near, muirnin, I begin to believe I could learn to be as foolishly quixotic as the most absurd romantic."

Bianca's warm, fuzzy drowsiness was suddenly laced with a chill. There was something in his voice . . .

A soft yearning that sent a rash of warning prickling over her skin.

He had told her that he was not like other gentlemen. He was not shallow or frivolous or inclined to toy with a woman's affection. He did not attempt to seduce everything in skirts. Or even indulge in meaningless flirtations.

Instead he was frighteningly sincere. And quite incapable of hiding his emotions.

He would always wear his heart on his sleeve.

A heart he would readily allow to be broken by an uncaring female.

Bianca struggled to her feet, smoothing her skirts with an awkward motion.

"I have been gone far too long. We must return before we are missed."

Lifting himself from the sofa, Edward studied her with a somber gaze. He was far too astute not to have sensed her rapid retreat, but thankfully he did not press her for an explanation.

A good thing, considering she wasn't sure she possessed one.

"Very well." He reached up to tug a stray curl into place. "I think it best if I leave first and ensure that there is no one lurking about. If I do not return within a few minutes, you will know that it is safe to follow."

She swallowed a strange lump in her throat. "Yes."

"Bianca—"

"Edward, you really must go," she hastily interrupted.

His eyes darkened as if he were frustrated by her obstinate refusal to discuss whatever it was upon her mind. Heaving a faint sigh, he placed a gentle kiss on her brow and turned to walk toward the door.

Watching as his large form disappeared from the room, Bianca pressed her hands to her stomach.

The moments she had spent in Edward's arms had been magical. Earth-shattering. And something she could not convince herself to regret.

But while a part of her reveled in the pleasure Edward had taught her, another part could not deny that their relationship had irrevocably changed.

Just what that meant for the future, Bianca was uncertain.

But she did know she had better figure it out before she managed to wound Edward in a manner she never intended.

CHAPTER NINE

Despite the steady rain, Edward forced his feet to carry him through the mud and grime of Charing Cross Road.

A most unpleasant experience, and one that he was not quite certain why he was enduring.

It couldn't be for the lingering aroma of boiled eel and stale gin. Nor for the pleasure of being the target of every pick-pocket, beggar, and prostitute in the neighborhood.

Perhaps part of the blame could be laid at the feet of young Joseph. Edward had, after all, made a promise to do all he could to locate the lad's missing sweetheart. And he never gave his promises lightly.

But that did not explain why he had not simply given the task over to one of his numerous servants. Or why he had chosen to continue his search on a day fit only for waterfowl and lunatics.

Deftly avoiding the bucket of filth being tossed from an overhead window, Edward grimaced.

What was the point in attempting to fool himself? He was wandering through the wretched streets because he could not bear to spend another futile day attempting to thrust his way into Lady Bianca's presence.

Over the past week he had ridden miles through Hyde

Park, attended every tedious social event for which he had received an invitation, and even braved the ducal townhouse only to be turned away.

Again.

And all for nothing.

Bianca was nowhere to be found. At least, nowhere that he was in the position to find her.

It was bloody frustrating.

And more than a tad worrisome.

Halting as the door to a tailor shop was thrust open, Edward's broodings were interrupted by the glimpse of bright red curls and a round, freckled face.

He was so stunned at the sudden appearance of the very woman he was seeking that he did not so much as blink as she tossed the bucket of mop water directly upon his boots.

"Sally?" he muttered. "Good God, I cannot believe I have found you."

Lifting her head, the young maid gave a sudden squeak and dropped the heavy bucket. Thankfully not upon his toes.

"Sir." She swallowed heavily before abruptly performing an awkward curtsy. "I mean . . . my lord."

He waved an impatient hand. "Bah, do not start with that nonsense. Your father was my groom since I was in the cradle and has taken a willow switch to my backside more than once. I believe he would still be using that switch if he had not taken his pension."

Appearing pale and more than a bit distressed, Sally clutched at the apron that covered her threadbare gown.

"Whatever are you doing here?"

"Actually that was the question I was about to pose to you. We have all been very concerned for you, my dear."

"I left a note for Pa."

"A note that said nothing more than you were off to London and that you would write with your directions once you had settled," he pointed out gently, half afraid she might suddenly disappear into the gathering fog.

She bit her lip as a flush crawled beneath her pale skin. "Aye, well . . . I've been terrible busy."

Edward's gaze briefly took in her chapped and calloused hands before turning toward the open door, where he could see a recently mopped floor.

"So I see."

Her flush deepened. "'Tis good, honest work."

"Of course it is," he soothed, "but I do not believe you came to London to scrub floors, did you, Sally?"

There was a long pause as she struggled between pride and misery, and then without warning her eyes filled with tears.

"Nay. I thought I was to be an actress. Freddie promised that he would make me famous through all of England. It was all a clanker, of course. Once he got what he was wanting . . ." She sniffed and wiped her nose with her sleeve. "He was nothing more than a rotter."

Although Edward had never encountered the minor nobleman who had briefly visited the village near his estate, he had no difficulty in accepting that he was indeed a rotter.

Only the worse sort of cad would lure a naïve child from her home for the sole purpose of debauchery.

And if he ever tracked down the mysterious Freddie, he intended to lodge a lead ball in his arse. At close range.

"Once you discovered the truth of this Freddie, why did you not come home, my dear?"

A tear slid through the dust that coated her round countenance. "How can I? I have shamed myself."

"You were led astray by a cad," he corrected.

"Nay, I am ruined. 'Tis best that all believe me to be dead."

Edward reached out to grasp her work-roughened hand. "Nonsense. We all make mistakes and errors in judgment." His lips twisted as he recalled his ridiculous pursuit of the beautiful Bianca. "Some of us more than others. But whatever has happened, your father, and more particularly Joseph, are desperate to have you home."

She bit her lip, clearly wishing to believe his words of comfort and yet afraid to hope.

"How can they ever forgive me?"

"Quite easily." He gave her fingers a slight squeeze. "They love you."

Another tear slid down her face. And another. Then without warning she had tossed herself against his chest to sob in earnest.

"I've been such a fool."

Edward patted her back as he hastily flagged down a passing hack. He possessed blessed little experience in comforting distraught young maids. The sooner he could have Sally in the care of his housekeeper, the better.

"You have punished yourself long enough, Sally. It is time to return to your family."

"I would like that, but . . ." She stepped back to regard him with a troubled frown.

"What is it?"

She glanced toward the open door to the tailor shop. "Mr. Caster was kind enough to take me in when no one else would. I cannot just abandon him."

"Allow me to deal with Mr. Caster. I will ensure he is well-compensated for his kindness," he assured her as he led her to the waiting carriage and helped her to settle within the shadowed interior.

"You are . . . so very good, my lord."

Dismissing her gratitude with a wave of his hand, Edward pulled out a gilt-edged card and scribbled instructions upon the back of it.

"Here." He thrust the card into her fingers. "Take this with you and give it to my butler. He will ensure you are given a warm meal, and then one of my servents will see that you are safely returned to your father."

"Thank you, sir," she breathed. "Thank you."

"Your gratitude belongs to Joseph. He refused to give up hope that you would someday return to him," he said firmly.

The tears once again threatened. "I don't deserve him."

"I think that is a decision that should be left to him, my dear. Take care and be happy."

Stepping back, he closed the door and called out the address to the waiting driver. Then, as the hack rattled away, he turned to enter the shop.

Much to his surprise, it took longer than he had expected to satisfy the suspicious tailor that his intentions toward Sally were honorable. Somehow, the man had gotten it into his thick head that Edward was some sort of nefarious ruffian, and it was only with the promise that he would be allowed to visit Sally and ensure she was unharmed that Edward could leave the shop without having the magistrates called to haul him to Newgate.

With a shake of his head that anyone could think him a scurrilous cad, Edward returned to the damp streets and trudged his way toward the nearby almshouse. He had requested to review the quarterly accounts before offering his contribution, and now seemed as good a time as any to complete the rather tedious task.

Then it was back to his townhouse for a hot bath and another twelve rounds with his valet as he was groomed and wrangled into his evening wear for another tedious evening of what passed for entertainment in London.

Ah . . . the life of a dandy.

It was enough to make a sane man ram his head into the nearest wall.

Wallowing in his fine sense of self-pity, Edward paid no heed to the glossy black carriage directly halted before the almshouse. Not until a slender, painfully familiar female swept from the grimy building toward the waiting groom.

A terrifying jolt of happiness shot through him as he caught sight of the perfect ivory countenance and delectable curves.

Hell's teeth. Every part of his being longed to rush forward and sweep her into his arms. To carry her to his house and lock her away so that she could never again avoid him.

Despite claims that he was little better than a barbarian, Edward had never considered himself one.

Not until this moment.

With an effort, he squashed his primal urge to swoop and conquer and instead stepped directly into her path and performed a rigidly polite bow.

"Lady Bianca, what a delightful surprise."

Forced to halt or ram directly into his large form, the raven-haired beauty regarded him with a sudden flush.

"Oh . . . Edw . . . Lord Harrington."

His rare temper stirred and then flamed at her obvious discomfiture. Damn it all, only days ago this woman had writhed with pleasure in his arms. He still sported the bruises from where she had clutched at his arms and found her release.

Why the devil was she suddenly treating him as if he were something that should be swept into the gutter?

For once Edward did not ponder and consider before charging into action. Perhaps not so surprising. He was damp, chilled, and frustrated beyond all measure.

And this woman standing before him was entirely to blame.

With the speed that always caught others off guard, he reached out to grasp her arm and firmly pulled her toward the open carriage door.

"A word, Lady Bianca, if you do not mind."

"What . . ."

Edward had the contrary minx plucked from the street

and into the carriage before she could flay him with the sharp edge of her tongue. He even managed to slam shut the door before the outraged groom could lift a hand to help his mistress.

He was not quite swift enough, however, to avoid her unexpected kick to his knee as he settled in the seat opposite her.

"Ow." He glared at her as he tossed aside his dripping hat and pulled off his gloves. "If you must kick at me, you could choose a less painful location."

The dark eyes snapped with irritation. "I possess three brothers, Lord Harrington. You are fortunate I chose your knee at all."

Against his will he felt his lips twitch. "Vixen."

She gave a sniff as she settled back in the leather. "Do you mind telling me why you have thought fit to accost me on the street?"

"Because it was preferable to storming your father's fortress and no doubt ending up in some ducal dungeon," he retorted dryly.

A revealing heat touched her cheeks. "That is absurd."

"Is it?"

She shifted uneasily. "What are you doing here?"

It did not take a genius to realize she desired to avoid a confession of her reasons for treating him as if he carried the plague. Dammit all. He wanted to shake the truth out of her.

Of course, he would never do such a thing.

Gritting his teeth, Edward grudgingly accepted that for now patience was the better part of virtue.

Or some such nonsense.

"Searching for Joseph's young sweetheart."

"Did you find her?"

"As a matter of fact, I did. She was mopping the floor of a tailor's shop when I happened to stumble across her."

"Good heavens." She blinked in surprise. "Where is she now?"

He gave a lift of his shoulder. "Hopefully in the hands of my housekeeper, who will fuss over her until she can be returned to her home."

A portion of her wariness faded as a smile curved her lips. "But that is wonderful."

His breath caught in his throat at her smile. God, she was so beautiful.

"Yes, it is. Sally is young and inclined to be impulsive, but she will make Joseph a good wife." He folded his arms over his chest, regarding her with a brooding expression. "Now tell me what brings you to such a neighborhood."

She smoothed the pale green skirts, unaware of how the damp muslin was clinging to her body. Edward, on the other hand, was achingly conscious of every delectable curve.

"I did say that I would attempt to discover a means of helping these people," she muttered.

Edward gave a startled lift of his brows. "So you did. And what means have you decided upon?"

Her chin tilted, almost as if she expected him to deride her efforts.

"My father has been grousing that his land is lying fallow after so many tenants left to fight in the war. At the same moment there are endless soldiers filling the almshouses without employment. It occurred to me that two problems were actually one solution, so I requested my father's secretary to come here and begin interviewing those who might be suitable."

Barely aware he was moving, Edward had shifted to sit next to the astonishing woman, his hands cupping her face.

"I did say you could alter the world if you desired," he said softly.

Her eyes darkened with pleasure at his obvious admiration. "I am hardly altering the world."

"Every revolution has a beginning."

Just for a moment, their gazes locked and held. Then, as if

realizing the sheer intimacy of the shadowed carriage, she was abruptly pulling away from his touch.

"I should be returning home. My father will be expecting me for tea."

His early irritation returned. Once again she was anxious to flee his company.

And without one damnable explanation.

"'Tis early yet."

"Yes, but . . ."

He reached out to grasp her hands before she could elude him.

"Bianca, why have you been avoiding me?"

"Avoiding you?" She gave a futile tug of her fingers. "Why would you think such a thing?"

"Please do not play at being stupid, muirnin, it does not suit you," he growled.

Her eyes flashed with silent warning. "If you intend on being insulting, my lord, you can blasted well return to the rain."

He ignored her bristling. His patience was at an end. He wanted an answer. And he wanted it now.

"Tell me. Have I offended you? Frightened you? Disgusted you?"

She gave a small gasp at his blunt questions. "No, of course not."

"There is no 'of course' about it. Something has driven you away. Am I not at least deserving of an explanation?"

"Edward, please."

"Please what?" he demanded. "Pretend I am a proper gentleman and allow you to ignore and elude me without complaint? I am sorry, muirnin, but I cannot. I am not skilled to pretend an indifference I don't feel. Not with you."

Bending downward, he captured her lips in a fierce, possessive kiss. Blast it all, he had to know. He had to know that the memory of her eager response was not just a dream. That she truly had desired his touch.

There was a horrid moment when she remained motionless beneath his demanding kiss and his heart nearly failed. Then, with a choked sound deep in her throat, Bianca was arching forward and clutching at the lapels of his coat.

Sharp relief raced through him as he parted her lips with his tongue and delved into the welcome heat of her mouth. Oh . . . yes. She could deny anything but this. This was too powerful. Too potent.

This could not be denied.

Gathering her in his arms, he savored her warmth that surrounded him. He did not realize how cold he had been until her softness fit against him with sweet perfection. Now he felt as if he were drowning in her heat.

All sorts of things began to stir as he swept kisses over her upturned face. He forgot the fact that they were seated in a carriage. And that her small army of servants stood just beyond the closed curtains. He even forgot the reason he had hauled Bianca into the carriage in the first place.

Nothing mattered but the intoxicating feel of this woman in his arms.

"Bianca . . ."

Allowing his hands to trail down the curve of her back, he gently nuzzled the satin skin of her throat. Beneath his lips he could feel the thunder of her pulse, taste her honeysuckle. A shudder shook his body.

The rasp of her breath echoed through the carriage, but just as Edward was considering the best means of maneuvering her onto his lap, she suddenly stiffened and pressed her hands against his chest.

"No . . . we should not be doing this," she rasped.

"Why?" His brows snapped together. "Because I'm the Peasant Earl? Are you embarrassed to have others speak our names in the same breath?"

Her eyes widened as if in shock. "That is not it at all."

"Then what?"

She bit her lip as her lashes swept downward. At her side, Edward felt his muscles clench as if expecting a blow.

"It is not without reason that I have been called the Ice Princess," she at last confessed. "Although I have never intentionally intended to wound another, I have been accused of toying with the affection of my suitors. Some even claimed that I had led them to believe I would return their affection only to break their heart. I would not . . . I would not desire to hurt you."

It was not at all what Edward had been expecting, and he discovered himself battling a tangle of reactions.

On one hand, he couldn't deny a sense of relief that she was not so shallow as to fear being seen in his company. On the other hand, he could not ignore the less-than-subtle dismissal.

"Are you warning me that you could never learn to care for me?" he husked.

She caught her breath at his direct demand. "I do not yet know."

"Are you in love with another?"

His heart turned to ice as her gaze fell and she plucked at the silver locket hung about her neck. Oh no. Not that. He could bear anything but the thought that her affection already belonged to another.

That was something no man could battle.

"I . . . am pledged to no man," she at last conceded. "But that does not mean . . ."

The ice melted beneath a surge of relief. Thank God. Reaching out, he covered her chilled hands with his own.

"Bianca, do you recall telling me that your opinions and decisions are your own, and that I was not to take that away from you?"

Her gaze abruptly lifted. "Of course."

"Then surely I should be allowed to claim the same privilege," he demanded. "Unless you intend to shun me, why should I not choose to court you?"

She studied him for a long moment. "Is that what you are doing? Courting me?"

He arched a brow at her ridiculous question. "Well, you did claim we were to be wed. I think it best we spend at least some time in a traditional courtship before traveling down the aisle." His gaze briefly dipped to her lips, still reddened from his kisses. "Besides, you will have to make an honest man of me someday."

Her wariness did not ease. "Edward?"

With a rueful chuckle he leaned downward, resting his forehead against her own.

"How do I make it more obvious, muirnin? I will admit my courtship skills are sadly lacking, but I have chased you from one end of London to another. Not to mention done everything short of stealing your maidenhead. The only thing left is to kidnap you and hold you hostage."

"You wish to wed me?"

He swept his lips over her temple before pulling back to regard her with a somber expression.

"For the moment I only wish to know you better," he murmured. "I already know that I desire you and that I enjoy your company. I would like very much to know if it could become something more. Surely that is not so terribly nefarious?"

She slowly shook her head. "No."

"So you will no longer spend your days attempting to avoid me?"

An indefinable emotion flickered through the dark eyes. "Would it make any difference if I did attempt to avoid you? You seem to possess a rare talent for appearing wherever I might be."

Edward stiffened. Granted he had ridden through the park and attended a handful of parties in the hope of catching a glimpse of her. But dammit all, she made him sound like he stalked her through the streets like a damnable looby.

"If you wish to rid yourself of my presence, Lady Bianca, you need only say the word. I can assure you that I would never inflict myself upon a lady who has no desire for my company."

Annoyingly, a hint of humor touched her beautiful features at his stiff words.

Much less annoyingly, her hand lifted to gently stroke his cheek.

"I have no wish to rid myself of your presence, Edward," she said softly. "I find that I have missed your companionship."

She had missed him?

Edward's breath was snatched from his lungs as he help-lessly gazed into the flashing black eyes.

Oh God. He was in bad shape.

Very, very bad shape.

But for the moment, he didn't give a damn.

Not so long as she was smiling at him as if there were no other gentleman in the world for her.

CHAPTER TEN

There was nothing particularly notable about Lady Simmon's ball. Oh, perhaps the lobster in cream was better than usual and the illusion of a Grecian villa a nice change from the usual Roman ruins. But all in all it was just another ball amidst an entire season of balls.

Still, Bianca could not deny a tingle of excitement that inched down her spine and lodged in the pit of her stomach.

It was a growingly familiar sensation, and one that she was beginning to suspect was directly attributable to the large, handsome gentleman that was currently standing across the room regarding her with a brooding smile.

It made no sense.

He was no dashing rake to sweep a woman off her feet. Or even a practiced seducer who could flatter and woo a lady until her head was spinning.

So why did his mere glance manage to send her heart into a flutter?

It was all very strange.

"Ah, Bianca, here you are." As he stepped before her, Alexander's eyes abruptly widened in shock. "God almighty."

Bianca resisted the urge to lift her hands and cover the large amount of flesh her gown exposed. Had she not specifically requested her modiste to make the neckline a tad more . . . revealing?

Why she had made the request was not a question she had allowed herself to ponder.

"Good evening, Alexander."

The handsome features hardened with disapproval. "What the devil are you wearing?"

"It is commonly known as a ball gown." She smoothed the silver gauze skirt. "Perhaps if you have been residing in a cave you might consider them an astonishing creation."

"There are ball gowns and then there are ball gowns. Has your father happened to see you in this bare excuse for clothing?"

"He was the one who demanded that I shackle myself to a husband. A woman must bait the trap if she is to capture her prey."

Alexander gave a choked cough. "There is a difference between baiting a trap and creating a riot."

Bianca rolled her eyes heavenward. Anyone would think she was following the tradition of Lady Godiva and prancing about stark naked.

"My gown is no more shocking than any other."

"It is hardly your usual . . ." Alexander halted, his brows lifting as he turned to glance across the crowded room. "Ah."

"What?"

"I had forgotten you were hunting the rare country ox." He turned back to regard her with mocking amusement. "No doubt you need a bit stouter ammunition."

"Very clever," she drawled.

Leaning against the paneled wall, Alexander crossed his arms over his chest. For once he did not seem to note the languishing female glances being hurled in his direction.

"I must say that Harrington has managed to create quite a stir about town."

Bianca instinctively bristled. By God, she would not hear one more word on Edward's lack of blue blood.

Not when she of all people knew his worth.

"Not you too, Alexander," she snapped. "Lord Harrington happens to be a perfectly gracious gentleman who is far more deserving of respect than most of these supposed pinks of the *ton* fluttering about."

A knowing gleam entered her cousin's gaze. "Draw in your claws, kitten. I meant that your farmer has managed to rattle even the most indolent members of the House of Lords. There are those who are convinced he is determined to create another Reign of Terror right here in England."

Oh.

Well, that was an entirely different matter.

Bianca took great pride in Edward's fierce determination to battle for reform.

"He is rather passionate in his desire for change," she murmured, her attention shifting toward the gentleman currently being discussed.

Her gaze locked with the hazel eyes and a sharp flare of heat clutched at her as a hungry, almost predatory expression hardened his features. It had been near a week since they had been together in her carriage. Since then they had encountered one another at a variety of events and once in Hyde Park. But constantly surrounded by crowds, they had barely been allowed to do more than murmur pleasantries before social dictates had demanded they part.

She discovered herself increasingly frustrated.

She desired to have him to herself for a few moments. So they could speak. And perhaps kiss. And . . . well, there were all sorts of things possible.

If only they could be alone.

"A passion he seems to have inspired within you, my dear." Alexander broke into her brazen thoughts.

A sudden heat rushed to her cheeks. Good lord, could her cousin read her mind?

"I beg your pardon?"

"His passion for change. I hear you have taken on your own causes." He arched a deliberate brow, his lips twitching. "Whatever did you think I meant?"

All too familiar with Alexander's rotten sense of humor, Bianca offered him a pointed glare. Wretch.

"Is there not some poor, neglected wife anxious for your attentions?"

"Always, my dearest, always."

"Then do not let me keep you."

Readily straightening from the wall, Alexander reached out to lightly touch her shoulder.

"Bianca."

"Yes?"

His gaze swept her countenance in a searching manner. "Are you serious about this farmer?"

Bianca paused. Was she serious?

It was so difficult to know. She liked Edward. She cared for him. And she certainly craved his touch.

Perhaps more importantly, she had to admit that when he was not near she felt as if something vital was missing.

Still, she had always dreamed her future would be filled with . . . what? Daring adventures? Endless excitement?

At least something more than becoming a dutiful wife and retiring to a small country estate.

"I do not yet know. I like him very much. And . . ." Her voice trailed away as she realized what she had been about to admit.

Alexander chuckled. "You lust for him?"

"If you must be so crude, yes."

His hand shifted to tug on a raven curl that brushed her cheek. "You could do worse, you know. He seems like a good chap. Dependable. Loyal. Perhaps not quite so dashing as your beloved Stephen, but believe me when I tell you that rakes do not often make the best sort of husbands."

Absently, Bianca touched the silver locket about her neck.

Alexander was no doubt correct. He was, after all, a consummate rake who had devoted his life to breaking the hearts of women. Who better to warn her of the dangers of such treacherous animals?

But for once in her life she had no intention of blithely charging forward and hoping for the best.

Already she had managed to lure Stephen into humiliating himself before her father and society. Even if it had been unintentional.

She feared that another mistake would do far worse to Edward.

Sensing her cousin's growing curiosity, Bianca forced a stiff smile to her lips.

"You are being rather presumptuous, Alexander. There is no assurance that Lord Harrington will even offer for me."

"Oh, he will make an offer," Alexander drawled.

"Why, because I am the daughter of a duke?"

"Because he watches you the way a gentleman watches the woman he intends to bed or wed. If he wishes to survive the season, it had better be wed."

Her eyes widened. "Bed or wed?"

"Do not pretend innocence, my dear. Not even you can miss those heated glances."

She stole a glimpse toward the gentleman still staring at her with a fierce hunger. The tingling excitement returned.

"They are rather nicely heated," she murmured.

"Just so long as they lead to a trip up the aisle, my dearest." Her cousin lightly tapped her nose, but there was no mistaking the warning upon his handsome features. "I am off to brighten the evening of some fortunate lady. You . . . behave yourself."

Behave herself?

Hmmm . . .

Hiding a smile of anticipation, Bianca artfully weaved her way through the swelling crowd. More than once she was forced to halt and share pleasantries with her numerous acquaintances, but with dogged persistence she at last was able to slip through the French windows and onto the terrace.

From there she made a determined path to the large fountain shrouded in shadows.

She did not doubt that Edward would soon join her.

He did, after all, have a most delicious fascination with gardens.

Edward did not miss Bianca's retreat to the gardens.

How could he?

Despite his best efforts he had not managed to wrench his gaze from her the entire evening. Not even Biddles's whispered warning that he was wearing his heart firmly upon his sleeve had managed to bring him to his senses.

What did he care if he was not playing the game by the rules of society?

He was not cunning and sly as was Biddles. Or an experienced rake who possessed the skill to lure hapless females to his side.

He achieved his goals through relentless, straightforward means. That was the only method he understood.

Circling the edge of the dance floor, Edward ignored the narrowed gazes that followed in his wake. He had already resigned himself to the knowledge he would always be an oddity among society.

Ridiculous considering the foolish dolts that littered London.

Why, a gentleman who wore nothing but sickly green coats did not warrant a lift of the brows. And the Prince, who had grown so heavy and self-indulgent he could not even hoist himself into a saddle without a mechanical device, barely created a stir.

It seemed as long as your blood was blue enough, you could be as eccentric as you might wish.

Buffoons.

Giving a shake of his head, Edward stepped through the French doors and paused to suck in a deep breath of the fresh, rose-scented air. God, it felt so wonderful to be out of the cramped, smoky room.

Allowing himself only a moment to appreciate the moonlit peace, Edward forced his feet forward. Although Bianca had not appeared distressed as she had left the ballroom, he had to reassure himself that nothing had occurred to trouble her.

He would rip apart anyone foolish enough to insult or harm her in any way.

First, of course, he had to find her.

With a frown he glanced about the seemingly empty garden. "Bianca?"

"Good evening, Edward."

His frown only deepened as the soft voice floated through the air. "Where are you?"

"In the folly."

Edward hesitated a moment before moving the long distance to the back of the garden. He found the folly set in the darkest shadows and secluded enough to be easily overlooked.

He climbed the steps of the fanciful structure built to resemble a tiny cottage even as a voice in the back of his mind warned him that this was a bad idea.

A very bad idea.

Unfortunately, the distracting voice could not rival the urgent need to be close to Bianca.

It had been so damnably long since he had been allowed more than a distant greeting. So long since had been allowed to touch so much as her fingers.

He might be a man of great restraint, but he was no saint.

Halting at the doorway of the folly, he glanced into the shadowed interior to discover Bianca seated upon a cushioned chaise longue.

His breath tangled in his throat at the slight of her slender form draped in a shimmering swath of satin that revealed an indecent amount of flesh.

When she had sailed into the ballroom earlier that evening, he had nearly had a seizure. While he might fully appreciate the sight of her round, tantalizing bosom displayed in all its glory, he certainly did not enjoy the thought of every other rogue and scoundrel enjoying the view.

Only the knowledge he was hardly likely to earn the good will of the Duke of Lockharte had kept him from tossing the minx over his shoulder and hauling her from the crowd of ogling gentlemen.

Now that they were utterly alone, however, he was quite at liberty to fully appreciate the stunning beauty before him.

And appreciate he did. Fully.

At last the realization that he was already becoming hard and aching brought him sharply back to earth.

Hell's teeth, the woman should be locked in her chambers to preserve the sanity of gentlemen everywhere.

Clearing his throat, he gripped the edge of the open door. "Whatever are you doing in there?" he demanded.

Her slow smile did nothing to ease his stirring passions. "Why do you not come in and discover for yourself?"

His fingers nearly shattered the wood as he gritted his teeth. "Is everything well?"

"Perfectly well."

She did not appear to be troubled or distressed. Quite the opposite, in fact.

He should turn around and return to the ballroom.

Unfortunately, his feet were not currently attached to his brain.

"Then what are you doing out here?"

"Waiting for you."

His brows lifted. "You were so certain I would follow?"

"I could only hope you would." She tilted her head to one side as she patted the cushion next to her. "Are you not going to join me?"

Dear God, but she was a natural-born siren.

"I am not at all certain it is wise."

"Why?"

He gave a short, humorless laugh. "I have made little secret of the fact that I want you, Bianca. Desperately. Why do you think I have gone to such effort to meet you only when I knew we would be surrounded by others?"

"You also told me that you wished to become better acquainted. That is hardly possible in the midst of a crowded ballroom."

His entire body clenched at the husky invitation in her voice. How could any poor gentleman be expected to resist such temptation?

"Bianca . . . you are a very dangerous young woman."

"Will you join me?"

His sigh rasped through the night air. "I do not think I possess the power to resist."

Not taking his gaze from her delicate features, Edward moved forward, closing the door behind him before crossing to settle at her side.

At once the heated perfume of her skin reached out to wrap about him and he choked back a groan. That maddening scent had haunted far too many nights.

"It is a beautiful evening," she murmured.

"Beautiful. Astonishingly beautiful." His tone made it clear he was not discussing the weather. Reaching out, he brushed her cheek with light fingers. "My God, you take my breath away."

Her lashes fluttered as if caught off guard by his sudden boldness. "Edward."

Of its own accord his hand lowered, drifting down the curve of her neck before following the tantalizing dip of the bodice.

"This is an evil gown, muirnin."

He felt her breath catch even as she peered at him from beneath her tangle of lashes.

"Do you not like it?"

His hand trembled as he reached the curve of her breast. She was hot silk and honeysuckle. And he was rapidly hardening to the point of desperation.

"Dear God, if you knew how I ached for you . . ."

Without warning, she reached up to frame his face in his hands. "It can be no more than I ache for you."

Their gazes locked as the air shimmered with thick, potent awareness. Despite her innocence, there was no fear, no hesitation in the dark eyes. Only a smoldering need that was echoed deep within him.

He was lost.

A victim of his own searing desire.

"Dangerous, indeed," he muttered, lowering his head to capture the soft lips in a kiss of stark hunger.

Just for a moment she seemed to stiffen at his raw demand, but before he could even attempt to restrain his ardor, she was arching against him and returning his kiss with an enthusiasm that shook him to his very soul. He groaned, parting her lips so that he could plunder the moist cavern of her mouth.

This was what he dreamed of night after night. What he ached for even when he was devoting himself to his endless round of calls upon various Parliament members.

With an impatient motion he tugged upon the fragile silk of her bodice, astonished to discover she hadn't bothered with a shift or corset. His heart raced as the warm mounds of her breasts tumbled into his waiting hands.

Manna from heaven, he inwardly groaned, branding her

upturned countenance with fierce kisses before lowering his head to capture an already-straining nipple into his mouth.

He heard her moan of approval as his tongue brushed over the hardened peak. Yes, yes, yes. His blood rushed, his erection rising to press against the button of his breeches. This woman was a fever in his blood. An addiction he was not certain he could live without.

Over and over he teased the sensitive bud, circling and stroking with relentless care. He could devote the entire evening to discovering every curve, every soft inch of her delicious body.

Growingly restless, Bianca plunged her hands into his hair and urged him to perform the same service for her neglected breast. Edward eagerly complied. Turning his head, he suckled with growing insistence.

It had been so long. Too long since he had held her in his arms.

Tugging her closer, he allowed her to feel the full force of his arousal.

"I can taste you in my dreams," he breathed. "So sweet . . . so warm."

Her hands smoothed over his shoulders and down to his chest. Then, shockingly, she was tugging upon the buttons of his waistcoat and pulling his shirt from his breeches.

"I want to touch you."

Edward possessed a brief flare of sanity that warned him matters were spiraling way beyond his control, but as her fingers tentatively crawled beneath his shirt and over the rigid muscles of his stomach, sanity was tossed to the wind.

God almighty, who cared about something so tedious as good sense or wisdom or simple logic? At the moment, he was quite certain he would commit murder to keep her hands upon him.

"Yes. Oh God," he rasped as her fingers brushed over

his nipples. The sharp pleasure nearly jolted him off the cushions. "If you knew what you are doing to me . . ."

"Do you like that?" she whispered.

"Like it?" His voice was so thick it was barely recognizable. "I believe my body is making it fairly obvious just how much I like it."

Her head tilted back as he nuzzled his way up her throat. "You are so warm."

"I am burning." He nipped at the lobe of her ear. "If I do not have you soon, muirnin, I shall go out of my mind."

"Edward," she muttered, her magical fingers creating all sorts of chaos as they skimmed downward and hovered mind-numbingly close to his throbbing shaft. "Teach me how to please you."

Damn. Damn. Damn.

His hand curled about hers, pressing it against his erection. Readily she explored the hard length, the thin fabric of his breeches no barrier to her exquisite torture.

Edward gritted his teeth, a breath away from pressing her onto the cushions and spreading her legs.

He would give his title, his wealth, and everything he possessed be atop her and sheathed deep in her heat. Hell's teeth, he would give them up simply to have her clever fingers stroking him to heaven.

Thankfully—well, not quite thankfully considering the searing agony that wracked his body, but wisely—the bout of madness was brought to an end as a distant sound of laughter suddenly broke into the silence.

Sucking in a sharp breath, he struggled to regain some semblance of sanity.

He would not take the woman he intended to wed in a rushed, sordid coupling where anyone might stumble upon them. She deserved a night of slow, tender romance.

Once his ring was upon her finger, he would happily steal her away from any number of ballrooms.

And soirees, and picnics, and . . .

Barely even acknowledging the realization that he had so firmly determined to take Bianca as his bride, Edward pulled back to regard her with a tight expression.

"Bianca . . . this has gone far enough," he muttered, reluctantly pulling her hand from his aching arousal. Deep inside, his entire being howled in frustration. "Too far."

Her own breathing was labored as she fumbled to tug her bodice back into place.

"You sound angry. I thought you enjoyed my kisses."

He froze as he heard the faint edge of hurt in her voice. Cupping her face in his hands, he forced her to meet his narrowed gaze.

"For God's sake, Bianca, you know bloody well how desperately I enjoy your kisses. You felt the proof for yourself," he muttered. "But my restraint is not inexhaustible, and having you so near while knowing I cannot have you as I desire is swiftly driving me to the point of madness."

Her lashes lowered to cover her expressive eyes. "You wish to make love to me?"

"Yes, I wish to make love to you, muirnin. But I am no debaucher of innocents. I will not make you mine unless we are wed."

He felt the small shiver that raced through her slender form. Unfortunately, he had no notion if it was one of excitement or fear.

"Somehow we seem to keep coming back to that subject," she murmured.

Edward gave a soft chuckle. "For rather obvious reasons. When two people end up in each other's arms on every occasion they meet, they either wed, indulge in an affair, or learn to avoid one another."

Her gaze abruptly lifted. "An affair?"

His hands tightened upon her countenance. Damn but she was going to be the death of him.

"No. No affair. It is marriage or nothing."

Her eyes slowly narrowed. "That sounds remarkably like an ultimatum."

He heaved a sigh as his features softened. "It was not intended as such, but I cannot pretend that all I desire from you is a willing body." He paused, knowing he was bound to bumble this badly but unable to halt the words. "You are in my heart, muirnin. I want you at my side, as my lover and my friend. I want you to be my wife."

She froze, her eyes widening at his blunt confession. "Edward, I . . ."

Smiling wryly, he rose to his feet and arranged his rumpled clothing. "I did not mean to terrify you."

"It is not that," she whispered, her expression troubled. "It is just that I do not know what to say."

"Say nothing for now. Just promise me you will at least consider my offer." Softly he brushed his lips over her forehead. "I swear that I will do everything in my power to ensure your happiness."

Knowing he had pressed his luck as far as he dared, Edward forced himself to turn and leave the all-too-intimate folly. Another few moments and he would no doubt be on his knees pleading for her love.

A certain means of convincing her that he had lost his wits.

He grimaced as he headed back to the ballroom.

Oh lord, what the devil had he done?

CHAPTER ELEVEN

Pacing the darkened folly, Bianca pressed her hands to her fluttering stomach.

Married.

For better, for worse.

Till death do us part.

The words whirled through her mind with near-terrifying persistence.

Dear God.

It was enough to send her into a full-blown panic.

Ridiculous, perhaps.

She had received any number of requests for her hand over the years. Some elegant, some passionate, and some downright desperate. She had even briefly been engaged to Stephen, if only in private.

So why had none of those gentlemen's proposals made her heart lurch and her throat tighten to the point she could barely breathe?

Could it be that Edward's proposal touched her more deeply than the others? That it truly mattered whether or not he loved her?

Oh . . . lord.

She suddenly felt as if she had been tossed in the midst

of a stormy sea with no notion of which direction shore might be.

Sucking in a deep breath, she instinctively smoothed her rumpled gown before forcing herself to leave the folly. She would soon be missed, and the last thing she needed was her father charging about and creating a scene in search of her.

Unable to do anything about the flush still clinging to her cheeks or the frustrated ache that Edward always seemed to leave behind, Bianca stepped from the shadows and onto the graveled path.

Intent on keeping her skirts from the threatening rose-bushes, she failed to notice the tall form that was leaning negligently against the marble fountain until it moved to stand directly in her path.

"Well, well, if it is not the Ice Princess."

Jerking to a halt, she regarded the lean, almost pretty countenance of the gentleman she had once hoped to wed.

Oddly, the usual tingle of pleasure at the sight of him did not materialize. Her heart did not even miss a beat. Instead she found herself struggling to disguise a flare of impatience at his sudden appearance.

"Stephen." She covertly glanced down to ensure that her bodice had been properly restored to order. "Whatever are you doing out here?"

Elegantly attired in one of the numerous blue coats he demanded be specially dyed to match the color of his eyes, Lord Aldron allowed his gaze to roam over her with familiar ease.

"Precisely the question I was about to pose to you."

Bianca unfurled the fan that dangled about her waist. She possessed the most ridiculous urge to giggle at the thought of revealing she had been busily luring Lord Harrington to the secluded folly in the hopes he would have his way with her.

Not so long ago she had thought slipping out of her chambers to enjoy a naughty pantomime a dangerous lark.

"The ballroom is far too warm. I was in dire need of a breath of fresh air."

"You should take more care," he chided. "It is not safe for a beautiful young woman to be out here alone."

She gave a lift of her brows. Since when did Stephen ever preach caution?

"I can hardly be in danger a few steps from a crowded ballroom."

His lips curled in sudden disdain. "There are all sorts of disreputable chaps allowed into society these days. Some of whom should be back in the country mucking stalls."

Damn. Bianca heaved a sigh. She should have been expecting this confrontation.

It was only to be expected that Stephen would wish to punish her a bit. She had, after all, allowed him to court her for months believing she would be his wife.

And now her name was being linked to another . . .

"I suppose you are referring to Lord Harrington?"

"Peasant."

She bit her lip. "Stephen, I understand that you are angry and hurt, but you should not blame Lord Harrington. He had nothing to do with my father's refusal for us to wed."

He growled low in his throat. "It is disgusting, the manner in which he is sniffing about you as if he were a hound in heat. Someone needs to teach him a sharp lesson in how to treat his betters."

Bianca stiffened as a flare of pure fury raced through her. Stephen was fortunate she still felt a measure of guilt at having wounded him. Otherwise, she most certainly would have slapped his handsome face.

"We are hardly his betters," she pointed out stiffly. "He is an earl, after all."

"He is not fit to polish our boots."

She forced herself to count to ten. In English, French, and then Italian for good measure.

"You do not even know him, Stephen. He is a fine man."

"A fine man?" An ugly expression hardened his features. "My God. I had heard the rumors that you were encouraging Harrington's attentions, but I refused to believe them. You could not possibly be interested in that slow-witted dolt."

She tilted her chin. She had no intention of discussing her relationship with Edward with anyone. Not until she decided what the devil she was going to do with the aggravating man.

"I simply do not wish for an innocent bystander to be harmed for my sins. If you must be angry with someone, it should be me."

There was a short, tense silence. Then, without warning, his hands reached out to grasp her shoulders in a tight grip.

"Were you out here with him?"

"Stephen . . ."

His gaze raked over her flushed countenance and raven curls that had been dislodged during her delicious embrace with Edward.

"Did you allow him to kiss you?"

"Release me, Stephen."

"What a fool I was." His fingers tightened as he stepped far too close. "All those evenings we were alone together and I treated you as if you were a fragile child when you wished to be tumbled like a common tart."

Her brows snapped together. This was not at all the Stephen she had thought she knew. This Stephen was not her charming, carefree companion or indulgent admirer. This Stephen she did not desire to whisk her away from the confines of her life as the daughter of the Duke of Lockharte.

This Stephen she wanted to punch in the nose.

"That is enough. Release me at once."

"What is it, Bianca? Does the touch of a true gentleman offend you?" he sneered. "Do you prefer the groping of a country oaf?"

She struggled against his hold. "I prefer to be left alone."

"No. I deserve something for being led about by the nose for months only to be discarded like a bit of rubbish." His head began to lower with obvious intent. "You owe me, my sweet."

"Halt or I will scream."

His soft laugh held no humor. "I do not think so, my dear."

His lips landed upon her mouth with bruising determination, and for a moment Bianca was so stunned that she stood frozen in his arms. She had devoted endless hours to dreaming of being held in Stephen's arms. Of enjoying his kisses. Now she knew. Gads. She really did want to punch him in the nose.

Yanking her closer, Stephen attempted to thrust his tongue between her lips. She gave a violent shudder and wrenched herself from his grasp.

"That is enough," she rasped, unconsciously lifting her hand to wipe his taste from her mouth. Edward had only to touch her for her senses to go up in flames. Obviously it was a talent only he possessed. Somehow the knowledge only deepened the guilt she felt at having encouraged Stephen's pursuit. "I am sorry if you were hurt, Stephen, and I regret that I allowed you to believe we would wed. But it is in the past. I would hope we could still be friends."

As if sensing the pity stirring in her heart, Stephen abruptly spun on his heel to glare at the shadowed garden.

"Return to your farmer and his vulgar fortune, Lady Bianca. The two of you are clearly perfect for one another."

Bianca did not hesitate as she hurried up the path and onto the terrace.

She had so many tangled thoughts churning through her mind, she feared the top of her head might explode.

Stephen would have to be a worry for another day.

With a sense of relief, Edward at last escaped from the solemn cavern of the Parliament chamber and weaved his way through the clustered noblemen, many of whom regarded him with either outright hostility or wary approval.

None attempted to halt his passage, thank God.

The day had not been quite so nerve wrenching as his first Introduction. He grimaced as he recalled the rather ridiculous ordeal that had included offering his Letter of Patent and Writ of Summons, not to mention a great deal of bowing and scraping to the Cloth of Estate, to the Woolsack, and then down on his knees to have his Patent read aloud.

During every solemn moment he had expected to have someone call out he was a fraud. Even after he had taken his oath and signed the Test Roll, he had feared catastrophe.

Thankfully the roof had not collapsed, nor had lightning struck, which he took as a good sign.

Good enough to encourage his determination to bring forth what many considered his radical demand for change.

Today he had taken his first step, and he found himself not quite certain whether he should pat himself on the back for his courage or scurry back to Kent before he could be strung from the vaulted rafters.

Of course, first things first, he told himself wryly.

He would do nothing, not even be hung as a traitor, before he enjoyed a very large beefsteak and a glass of burgundy.

Stepping onto the busy street at last, he sucked in a deep breath of coal-tainted air and lifted a hand toward his waiting groom.

"Very passionate, old friend," a sardonic voice drawled close to his ear. "You quite moved me to tears."

With a smile, Edward turned to regard Biddles attired in a scarlet coat and pale yellow waistcoat. The combination was near blinding, and Edward's smile widened. Only Biddles would dare to mingle with the most powerful gentlemen in the world dressed as a court jester.

"I was hoping for persuasion rather than passion, and it is

your support I am depending upon," he informed his friend. "You may save your tears for poor Anna."

Biddles touched the end of his pointed nose with a hand-kerchief. "I fear that it may be more than mere persuasion that you have stirred in the hearts of many. I do believe Lord Jenkins was foaming at the mouth before you finished your eloquent demand that we all charge forward and rescue the downtrodden from the clutches of the evil feudal lords bent on their destruction."

Edward shrugged. "Someone must speak out for those in need."

"True, but you might wish to keep an eye out for a knife in the back." Biddles gave a covert nod of his head to a clutch of elderly noblemen glaring at him as they stomped toward their carriages. Thank God looks could not kill. "There are many among the older aristocrats who firmly believe that they possess a divine right to grind the lower orders into the muck."

Edward heaved a sigh. Did the old fools believe they could continue to repeat the mistakes from the past without consequence?

"It was precisely that attitude that led to the Revolution," he growled with impatience. "Do you suppose those older aristocrats would enjoy having their heads planted on a guillotine?"

Biddles gave a wave of his handkerchief. "Those in power never share it willingly."

"Providing education and the opportunity to earn a living is hardly handing the throne to the peasants."

With a short laugh, his friend clapped him on his shoulder. "Egads, you really have been in the country too long."

No doubt Biddles was right, but Edward felt no need to apologize for his humble beginnings.

Not to anyone.

"Will you join me for luncheon?"

The sly gentleman gave a small grimace. "A tempting offer. Unfortunately, Anna has developed the most peculiar craving for strawberries, not that common for a woman in her delicate condition, and I have been commanded to scour London for all that can be found."

Edward chuckled in delight. "A grave task. I wish you well."

"Laugh if you wish, old friend. Your day will come."

His chest abruptly tightened as the image of delicate features and dark eyes rose to mind.

Hell's teeth, it was painful just to think of Bianca.

"I hope so, Biddles, I most fervently hope so."

The pale eyes narrowed in warning. "Edward—"

"Be on your way." Edward sternly interrupted the undoubted lecture. "I am quite old enough to make my own mistakes."

Biddles glanced over Edward's shoulder, his expression suddenly shifting to one of sly amusement. "Obviously. Take care, my friend. It is not only decrepit Tories who wish to stick a knife in your back."

With his mysterious warning delivered, Biddles turned to mince down the street, leaving Edward to watch his departure with a small smile.

Obviously impending fatherhood had plunged Biddles the short distance to utter madness.

"Lord Harrington?"

Swift, delicious shivers raced through Edward. This was the last place he expected to hear the soft female voice, and he struggled to control his instinctive reaction.

Willing his treacherous body to behave itself, Edward slowly turned. In a blink his attempts of restraint were shot to hell.

Attired in a pale rose gown and chip bonnet, Bianca should have appeared young and utterly innocent. Instead, the dark, tilted eyes and lush mouth gave the impression of a sultry vixen ripe for seduction.

The very air seemed to sizzle with heat.

"Lady Bianca." He was forced to halt and clear his throat. "What brings you here?"

"My father mentioned that you would be speaking today."

Edward stiffened. "You were in the gallery?"

"Yes. You were very . . ."

"Passionate? Radical? Unhinged?" he helpfully offered, thanking the heavens above he had not known she was near. No doubt he would have ended up babbling like an imbecile.

Well . . . even more of an imbecile.

"Eloquent," she corrected firmly.

"You were not terrified that I am about to tumble the government of England?"

With a smile that warmed him to his very toes, she stepped close enough to lightly touch his arm.

"I would hope by now that you would realize that I share your desire to help others."

He did, of course. Her beauty came as much from within as without.

"Yes." Sensing the sudden hush that had descended around them, Edward covered her hand with his own. It was bad enough he had to be gawked at as if he possessed horns and a tail. He would not have Bianca endure the rude stares and whispers. "May I drive you home?"

She considered his offer a long moment before giving a faint nod of her head.

"If it will not be out of your way."

His lips twitched. China would not be out of his way if this woman was involved.

"Not at all."

She glanced toward his open carriage. "You have your groom with you?"

"He was quite insistent I could not appear without him," Edward assured her. "Obviously, once a gentleman is landed with a title he loses all ability to control something so dangerous as a team of horses without assistance."

A twinkle of amusement shimmered in the wickedly tempting black eyes.

"Then I shall send my maid on a few errands. If you will wait a moment?"

His hand lifted of its own accord to lightly stroke her cheek.

"I will wait," he husked, unable to disguise the thread of longing in his voice. "I will wait as long as it might take. That I have promised you."

"Edward . . ." A flustered heat touched her countenance, but thankfully she did not bolt as he half expected. "I shall return."

Refusing to allow himself to stand on the walk and gape at her like he was a smitten looby, Edward slowly strolled toward his waiting carriage.

He desperately wanted to believe that her appearance this morning indicated her interest in him. After all, a morning spent listening to political debates was not the usual entertainment for young ladies.

Unfortunately, he was too pragmatic to leap to conclusions.

With a minimum of fuss, Bianca had sent her maid upon her way and Edward had lifted her onto the leather seat beside him. He left the reins to his groom, preferring to concentrate upon his companion rather than dazzling her with his skill with the ribbons.

Not that his cleverness was readily rewarded, he silently admitted. Bianca appeared far more intent on studying the coal-blackened buildings they rattled past than in paying him heed.

Hardly flattering.

"You are very quiet," he at last broke the silence.

Her hands clenched in her lap before she slowly turned to regard him with a searching gaze.

"Why do you wish to wed me?"

Edward gave a choked cough. He hadn't been prepared for that.

"I could name a dozen reasons. All of them perfectly sensible." He reached out to grasp her hands in a tight grip. "But in truth there is only one reason that matters. I have fallen in love with you, muirnin."

Her lashes fluttered, but her gaze remained steady. "How can you be certain you love me?"

"Well, it is either love or utter madness. Let us hope for love."

"But what if you are mistaken?" she insisted. "What if you wed me and discover that I am not the wife you desire?"

Edward considered his words carefully. He did not comprehend this woman's odd fear that she would somehow prove to be a disappointment to him. Surely most women in her position would be concerned with his suitability?

"Bianca, there will never be a day that I do not desire you at my side or a night I will not want you in my bed," he said gently. "The only question is whether or not you can someday learn to love me as I love you."

"I do care for you, Edward," she murmured softly.

It was not quite the overwhelming declaration that Edward had been hoping for, but he was swift to disguise his disappointment behind a teasing grin.

He was nothing if not patient.

"And you are moved by eloquent speeches."

Seemingly relieved by his light tone, a smile touched her lips. "Of course."

He scooted close enough to feel the heat of her leg burn through his breeches. *Mmmm . . .*

"And you desire me to the point of insanity," he husked.

Her eyes darkened with satisfying awareness. "There is that."

His hands shifted to tug off his gloves and then her own.

Then, trailing his fingers over her sensitive palms, he paused at the pulse beating wildly in her wrist.

She could hide everything but this. She desired him.

It was a beginning.

"What more could a woman possibly wish for?" he demanded.

Not about to be outdone, the daring minx leaned close enough for her breast to brush against his arm. Edward instantly forgot to breathe.

"I suppose you could compose lovely odes to the beauty of my eyes or slay a dragon or two," she suggested.

Edward swallowed. Lost in the darkness of her eyes and feeling her pressed close to his side, he would happily have slain an entire herd of dragons.

"Only two?"

"It would be a beginning."

His fingers drifted up the curve of her arms. "I can think of a far more enjoyable means of convincing you of my love."

She deliberately lowered her gaze to his mouth. "Enjoyable for whom?"

All too easily the image of this woman spread beneath him, with her legs locked about his hips, rose to mind.

It was a fantasy that was becoming more difficult to ignore.

"For the both of us, I hope."

He felt her small shiver as she regarded him with a sultry gaze. "You said we were not to . . . do this anymore."

"I was a fool," he growled, his hands tightening upon her arms. "My God, Bianca, tell me you will wed me and put me out of my misery."

Her smile was wicked. "I believe I shall need a bit more of that convincing before I commit myself."

His body hardened with a speed that made him groan. Hell's teeth, the *Marquis de Sade* had nothing on this woman.

"You truly are determined to drive me batty." He forced

himself to take a calming breath. Whatever his body might demand, he could not take his future wife in an open carriage in the midst of London. "May I speak with your father?"

She abruptly stiffened, and a shaft of fear struck through Edward's heart. Dammit all, she was not going to deny him now. Not when he was so close.

"Allow me to speak with him first," she muttered, an odd expression upon her beautiful features. "I do not wish for any unpleasant surprises."

"Surprises?"

She gave a sharp shake of her head. "It is nothing. I just believe it best if I speak with Father before you approach him."

Edward did not question her more closely. What did he care? She had agreed to his proposal. Nothing else mattered.

Nothing at all.

"Very well." Hoping he was not smiling like a demented fool, he lifted her fingers to his lips. "Do you attend the Dellington soiree this evening?"

She offered a small grimace. "I fear not. My mother has taken a chill, and Father has a political dinner that he cannot avoid. Without a chaperon I must remain at home."

"A pity."

"Yes." There was a moment's pause before that slow, take-no-prisoners smile returned to her lips. Edward knew he was in deep trouble before she spoke a word. "I shall have to keep myself occupied somehow. A difficult task. I detest needlework, and I was the despair of my pianoforte teacher."

"Were you?" he husked.

"Utterly hopeless." Her smile never wavered. "It seems there is nothing to be done but take a very long, very private stroll through the garden."

Oh lord.

CHAPTER TWELVE

It was a decidedly subdued Bianca who sat down to luncheon with her father. Perhaps stunned was a more accurate word.

Good lord, she had agreed to Edward's proposal.

And even more astonishing, it had seemed perfectly natural.

Almost as if some part of her believed she knew precisely what she was doing.

Frightening.

"Do you suspect that Mrs. Blackwell has poisoned the soufflé, my dear?"

With a tiny jerk, Bianca lifted her head to regard her father seated across from her.

As always he was attired in a pristine style with his cravat perfectly tied and his silver hair brushed toward his handsome countenance.

He looked precisely what he was. A powerful aristocrat who commanded a small empire.

With an effort, she struggled to thrust aside her tangled broodings. Only a fool would engage in battle with the Duke of Lockharte with her mind elsewhere.

It may have taken two and twenty years, but she had at last learned her lesson.

"I beg your pardon?"

Settling back in his seat, the Duke regarded her with a hooded gaze.

"You have been frowning and picking at your food for the past half hour. I thought perhaps you suspected the staff was attempting to do you in."

Bianca grimaced as she pushed the plate aside. "I am not hungry."

"Good lord." A silver brow arched. "If you have lost your appetite, that can only mean that something is troubling you. Do you wish to tell me what it is?"

The moment had arrived, and Bianca inwardly squared her shoulders. On this occasion her father would not best her.

Not this time.

"Lord Harrington wishes to offer for my hand," she stated bluntly.

"Does he?"

Bianca did not trust her father's mild tone. It always meant he was one step ahead of her. Damn him.

"You do not seem particularly surprised."

His lips twisted with a humorless smile. "I am not an utter fool, Bianca. I am well aware you have done everything in your power to toss yourself in the path of the Peasant Earl."

Her brows snapped together. "I have asked you not to call him by that horrid name."

"And I have asked you to stay far away from the encroacher. Neither of us seems capable of following simple requests."

She pushed herself from the table and rose to her feet. "I would if your requests made the least amount of sense. You have no right to insult Edward. You do not know him as I do."

Far from impressed, the Duke leaned back in his chair. "The words sound astonishingly familiar. Were you not just making the same plea for your dearest Lord Aldron?"

Bianca flinched as she recalled the distasteful confrontation from the night before.

"I suppose I deserve that," she admitted softly. "You were right. I did not know Stephen as I thought I did."

There was a tense pause as her father rose to his feet and moved to stand at her side. A dangerous glitter hardened his eyes.

"Is there something I should know, my dear? Something that might call for a dawn appointment?"

"No." She reached out to grasp his arm, horrified at the mere thought of her father risking his life in such an absurd manner. "You will do nothing so ridiculous."

There was another pause before he gave a lift of his shoulder. "Perhaps you are right. Aldron is not worth rising for at such an ungodly hour. Such a worthless scoundrel will meet his end eventually."

"Edward is not at all like him," she burst out abruptly.

"How can you be so certain?"

There were a dozen reasons she was certain. Edward's steady nature. His determination to care for others. His patience. His unwavering loyalty.

Still, she was honest enough to admit that she had been easily dazzled by Stephen.

What if she were allowing herself to be blinded once again?

"That is the question, is it not?" she demanded wryly, her sigh echoing through the room. "How did you know you wished to wed Mother?"

There was a startled pause before her father cleared his throat. "It was never my decision. Our parents arranged the marriage while we were both still in the cradle. It was the wish of the King. Not an unusual circumstance at that time."

Bianca abruptly frowned. "You were forced to wed?"

He shrugged. "It was my duty, yes, but it is one that I have never regretted. Although it might not have been a love match, we have managed to be quite happy together. Indeed our relationship has been far more enduring than most."

She did not doubt the truth of his words. Her parents were not the sort to display their affection in public; they were a breath from royalty, after all, and it simply was not done. But she never doubted their unwavering dedication to one another.

"You do not believe in love?"

"I believe that most people mistake attraction for love. Such a shallow relationship is bound to wither and die. True love grows out of respect and friendship and mutual affection." He searched her countenance with a curious expression. "Do you believe yourself to be in love with the man?"

She heaved a frustrated sigh. It was easy to believe herself in love. Certainly there was a tingle of happiness whenever he was near. And the mere thought of having him disappear from her life was enough to make her heart halt in panic.

But she had thought herself in love with Stephen, had she not? A mistake that could very well have led to disaster.

No.

The word echoed through her mind without warning and without hesitation.

Edward was nothing, nothing like Stephen. There was nothing shallow or self-serving about him.

More importantly, he genuinely loved her.

Her. Bianca. Not Lady Bianca, the daughter of the Duke of Lockharte, not the toast of the season. Not the elusive Ice Princess. Her.

"Yes, I do love him," she admitted, an unwitting smile curving her lips.

Her father regarded her closely. "As you loved Stephen?"

"My feelings are not at all the same." Her smile slowly widened. "With Stephen I tried to convince myself I was in love simply because I wanted the freedom and excitement he offered. With Edward I have done everything possible not to fall in love. He is not at all what I thought I desired in a husband. But in spite of myself I cannot halt my feelings. He may not be dashing or adventurous or desperate to make a splash among society, but he possesses the most amazing ability to make me happy just by being near."

Her father reached out to grasp her chin in a firm grip. "Bianca . . ."

Her gaze narrowed. "If you are about to lecture me upon the unworthiness of Lord Harrington, Father, you might as well save your breath. He is no rake and no fortune hunter. He is not even impressed with the knowledge I happen to be the daughter of a duke."

"There will always be those who consider him an encroacher, not to mention the fact he has made dangerous enemies among the Parliament. As his wife, you will suffer any number of slights and insults."

Bianca did not so much as bat an eye. Good lord, that was her very last concern.

Pulling from his grip, she planted her hands on her hips. "Slights and insults such as being shunned by Lady Michaels because you called her husband a lack-witted buffoon?" she demanded sweetly. "Or being refused entry into the Ladies Horticultural Society because Aunt Lottie became foxed and claimed the ladies were all French spies and were using the meetings as a means to pass their nefarious information? Or—"

"Enough," the Duke growled.

"Perhaps it is Edward who should consider whether he wishes to be tarnished with my standing among society," she pointed out.

His lips gave a reluctant twitch, but there was no mistaking the warning in his eyes.

"This is no frivolous game, my dear. Once you are wed, there can be no altering your choice."

She waited for the surge of panic that should have raced

through her at his foreboding words. This was the most important decision she would ever make in her life.

Strangely, however, she felt nothing more than a warm glow of satisfaction that lodged deep in her heart. A glow that she was quite certain was directly connected to Lord Harrington.

"I am well aware of what I am doing, Father." She stepped forward, sticking her finger directly into his face. "I will have Edward as my husband. And if you attempt to stand in my way, I shall prove just how much your daughter I am."

An unreadable smile settled on his lips. "So be it, my dear."

The night was perfect.

Warm, with just the faintest hint of a perfumed breeze. A star-spattered sky. A full moon that carpeted the garden in a shimmer of silver. And in the distance the call of a nightingale.

A night for seduction.

Or at least it would be a night for seduction if only Bianca were not all alone in the secluded grotto at the back of the garden.

Tugging at the belt of her sheer satin wrapper, she paced the marble floor.

In any other young and very innocent woman, her pacing might have been an indication of nerves. Or indecision. Or even fear.

Bianca, however, was nothing more than impatient.

Blast the aggravating man. He had deliberately stirred her passions to a fever pitch. With every touch, every kiss, he had taught her the needs of her body she had never understood until he had entered her life.

Now she could not even think of him without her heart pounding and her body clenching with awareness. Or sleep through the night without tossing and turning as she battled the empty ache deep within her.

She was coiled so tightly she feared she might abruptly shatter, and it was all Lord bloody Harrington's fault.

So where the devil was he?

Spinning on her heel, Bianca barely squashed her instinctive scream as she caught sight of the tall, very male form blocking the entrance. Good lord, how could such a large man move with such silence?

"Edward." She pressed a hand to her racing heart. A racing that was not entirely due to her brief fright. "At last. I had begun to fear you would never put in an appearance."

Standing against the door jamb, Edward allowed his gaze to slowly roam over her slender form barely hidden by the sheer robe. Bianca shivered at the tension that abruptly sizzled in the air.

Even at a distance she could feel the desire that hummed through his body.

"I told myself I would not," he said, his voice low and husky.

She moved forward, instinctively drawn to his side.

"Why?"

In the moonlight his features were shadowed in mystery, but she did not miss the hectic glitter in the hazel eyes. A smile touched her lips. He was not nearly so in control of his emotions as he desired her to believe.

"If I am to be asking your father for your hand on the morrow, it did not seem at all proper to be seducing you in his garden tonight."

She stepped close enough for his heat to cloak about her.

"What changed your mind?"

His hand lifted to stroke over the raven curls that tumbled well past her shoulders.

"I was at Lady Dellington's doorstep when my very noble intentions were tossed into the gutter." His hand shifted to stroke her sensitive nape. "Right or wrong, there was not a force great enough to keep me from this garden tonight."

Bianca nearly purred at the delicious sensations feathering down her spine. She was melting. And he had not even kissed her yet.

Who could have dreamed a man's touch could create such magic?

"Thank God," she breathed as she reached up to rest her hands on his broad chest. "Just think of the scandal should I have been forced to arrive at Lady Dellington's and lure you away from the dance floor before all those guests."

Beneath her fingers she could feel the abrupt leap of his heart. Her smile widened. It was a decidedly heady thrill to realize she could affect him with the same power he wielded over her.

"And how would you have lured me, muirnin?" he murmured.

Emboldened by his ready response and her own absolute commitment to this man, Bianca allowed her hands to wander over his rigid muscles. There were no barriers to stand between them. Nothing to halt them from exploring the passion that held both of them in its grip.

Regarding him from beneath lowered lashes, she trailed her hands down his arms and tugged at the dove gray gloves that perfectly matched his jacket.

"I suppose I might have started by ridding you of these," she replied, pulling off the gloves and tossing them aside. Then, watching his jaw tighten and nostrils flare, she daringly turned her attention to the ivory buttons of his jacket. Her movements were not nearly so graceful or seductive as she might have wished. Hardly surprising considering her heart was pounding and her fingers shaking. Still, she managed to wrangle free the buttons, and at last she was smoothing the jacket from his body. Their gazes met and tangled as she dropped it onto the floor. "And that."

An arm lashed tightly about her waist as the other reached behind them to firmly shut the door.

"A suitable beginning," he rasped.

"Thank you."

His head lowered until she could feel his breath against her temple.

"And now?"

Tiny sparks seemed to flow through her blood as she moved to untangle his cravat.

"Mmm . . . still too many layers," she whispered.

His breath hissed through his teeth as his cravat joined his jacket on the floor. With jerky motions he moved to roughly drag his linen shirt over his head.

Bianca's breath lodged in her throat as the moonlight danced over his bare chest. Unlike society gentlemen, Edward was a man accustomed to hard labor. It was obvious in the smooth bulk of his muscles and bronzed cast of his skin. A virile, earthy male who had been sculpted to sheer perfection.

Her hands lifted to touch the faint spattering of hair that covered his chest. Her stomach clenched with excitement at the fascinating contrast to the heated silk of his skin. She had not expected to find such beauty in the male form. Intrigued, she brushed over the flat nipples that hardened in swift reaction.

"Dear God, Bianca," he moaned, his hands reaching up to cover her own.

She glanced up to meet his heated gaze. "Am I being too brazen?"

"Never," he breathed. "I would never have you withhold anything from me. Especially not your passion."

"Then teach me," she demanded softly. "Teach me how to love you."

A shudder shook his body as he held her gaze and slowly guided her hands downward.

"You cannot know the nights I have dreamed of this moment, muirnin," he rasped. "In my thoughts I have been your lover since the moment we kissed."

"I do hope that I pleased you in your dreams," she teased.

"Almost more than I could bear," he breathed. "But it was nothing compared to reality."

She had to force herself to recall to breathe as her hands reached to the waistband of his breeches. With a minimum of fuss, Edward managed the hooks, and then her fingers were wrapping about the hardness of his manhood.

It was larger than she had expected. Shockingly large. And hot to the touch.

More than a bit curious, she traced her fingers over the rounded tip and then down the shaft to the soft sack below. It seemed impossible to believe that such a thing could fit within her, but she was wise enough to realize that men and women had been managing to make love since the beginning of time. There was bound to be some means to make it work.

"Holy hell," Edward moaned, his fingers closing over her own as he taught her to pleasure his straining erection.

"This feels good?"

"So bloody good that the night promises to be over before it has even begun," he groaned, firmly taking her hand and placing it upon his chest.

On the point of protesting, Bianca was pleasantly distracted as his head lowered and he captured her lips in a fierce, demanding kiss.

White-hot heat seared through her as she wrapped her arms about his neck. She trembled as his hands slid down her spine to settle upon her hips. His heat and scent filled her mind until there was no thought but of his kiss, his touch.

Gently his tongue reached out to part her lips and slip within her mouth. Bianca eagerly opened to his caress, hesitantly touching his tongue with her own.

Edward growled deep in his throat as his hands ran a restless path up the curve of her waist and tugged loose the satin belt. Then, pushing aside the wrapper, he at last cupped the heavy fullness of her breasts. Bianca nearly sank to her knees.

Blessed heaven, yes. Her eyes slid shut as she savored the feel of his fingers teasing her nipples into tender peaks. Sharp-edged pleasure shot through her body, lodging in the pit of her stomach. She pressed against his hard form, greedy for more.

"Edward."

His lips nuzzled her cheek as his thumbs continued to caress her aching nipples.

"I want you, Bianca," he whispered. "I need to be in you."

The stark words sent a shiver of longing down her spine.

"I am yours, Edward."

"Mine." He pulled back to regard her with a heated gaze. "Yes . . . mine at last."

Her heart did a startled flip as he reached down to scoop her off her feet and moved into the shadows of the grotto. Bianca had never felt so small or so fragile as she did in his strong arms, and she turned her head to nuzzle the bare skin of his chest.

This was what it meant to be a woman, she hazily acknowledged. A woman who at last understood the power of love and desire.

Clutching his shoulders, she tensed as Edward slowly lowered her onto the pillows of the wide sofa. She lifted her oddly heavy lashes to watch as he hastily reached down to jerk off his boots and then wrestled with the remainder of his clothing. There was none of his usual elegance, but somehow his obvious impatience only increased the excitement that raced through her body.

He was so . . . beautiful.

A magnificent combination of hard muscles and sinew that would make any female shiver in anticipation. Even a female who possessed only the vaguest notion of what was about to occur.

Expecting Edward to join her on the sofa, Bianca was caught off guard when he kneeled beside her, his hands gently smoothing the wrapper from her body.

*Take A Trip Into A Timeless World
of Passion and Adventure with
Kensington Choice Historical Romances!*
—**Absolutely FREE!**

Enjoy the passion and adventure
of another time with Kensington
Choice Historical Romances.
They are the finest novels of
their kind, written by today's
best-selling romance authors.
Each Kensington Choice
Historical Romance transports
you to distant lands in a bygone
age. Experience the adventure
and share the delight as proud
men and spirited women
discover the wonder and
passion of true love.

Get 4 FREE Books!

We created our convenient Home Subscription Service so you'll be sure to have the hottest new romances delivered each month right to your doorstep—usually before they are available in book stores. Just to show you how convenient the Zebra Home Subscription Service is, we would like to send you 4 FREE Kensington Choice Historical Romances. The books are worth up to $24.96, but you only pay $1.99 for shipping and handling. There's no obligation to buy additional books—ever!

 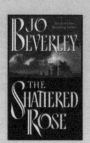  

Save Up To 30% With Home Delivery!

Accept your FREE books and each month we'll deliver 4 brand new titles as soon as they are published. They'll be yours to examine FREE for 10 days. Then if you decide to keep the books, you'll pay the preferred subscriber's price (up to 30% off the cover price!), plus shipping and handling. Remember, you are under no obligation to buy any of these books at any time! If you are not delighted with them, simply return them and owe nothing. But if you enjoy Kensington Choice Historical Romances as much as we think you will, pay the special preferred subscriber rate and save over $8.00 off the cover price!

We have 4 FREE BOOKS for you as your introduction to
KENSINGTON CHOICE!
To get your FREE BOOKS, worth up to $24.96, mail
the card below or call TOLL-FREE 1-800-770-1963.
Visit our website at www.kensingtonbooks.com.

Get 4 FREE Kensington Choice Historical Romances!

💗*YES!* Please send me my 4 FREE KENSINGTON CHOICE HISTORICAL ROMANCES (without obligation to purchase other books). I only pay $1.99 for shipping and handling. Unless you hear from me after I receive my 4 FREE BOOKS, you may send me 4 new novels—as soon as they are published—to preview each month FREE for 10 days. If I am not satisfied, I may return them and owe nothing. Otherwise, I will pay the money-saving preferred subscriber's price (over $8.00 off the cover price), plus shipping and handling. I may return any shipment within 10 days and owe nothing, and I may cancel any time I wish. In any case, the 4 FREE books will be mine to keep.

NAME _____

ADDRESS _____ APT. _____

CITY _____ STATE _____ ZIP _____

TELEPHONE (_____) _____

E-MAIL (OPTIONAL) _____

SIGNATURE _____

(If under 18, parent or guardian must sign)

Offer limited to one per household and not to current subscribers. Terms, offer and prices subject to change. Orders subject to acceptance by Kensington Choice Book Club. Offer Valid in the U.S. only.

KN066A

ll..l..lll....lll.l.l.l.l.l.l.l...lll.l..l...ll.l..lll...l

KENSINGTON CHOICE
Zebra Home Subscription Service, Inc.
P.O. Box 5214
Clifton NJ 07015-5214

"Bianca, you need to be very sure this is what you desire," he warned in unsteady tones. "I could not bear for you to have regrets."

The cool silk slithered from her heated skin, leaving her attired in nothing more than her silver locket and satin slippers. She shuddered at the flare of longing. How could he even speak of regrets? She was burning from within, and if he did not soon put her out of her misery, she was quite convinced she would commit murder.

Reaching up, she cupped his beloved face in her hands. "Edward, this is what I want. More than anything in the world." Her gaze narrowed. "Now can we get on with it before I expire of frustration?"

A slow, wicked smile curved his lips as he leaned forward to hover just above her waiting mouth.

"We cannot have that, muirnin. I have plans for our future that demand you be very much alive."

"Then rescue me," she pleaded.

"With pleasure, my lady." Skimming his mouth over her parted lips, Edward pulled back to watch as his fingers drifted down the slope of her shoulder and under the curve of her breast. His eyes darkened as she trembled in reaction. "You are so beautiful," he whispered. "So perfect."

Her breath was jerked from her body as he lightly circled her straining nipples in a teasing motion.

"Oh . . . good lord . . ."

With a low growl, Edward lowered his head to capture the tip of her breast in his mouth. Bianca smothered a cry of pleasure as she arched upward. Over and over his tongue tormented the hardened nub as she reached up to dig her fingers into his upper arms. No matter how many nights she might have dreamed of being made love to by this man, nothing could have prepared her for the blaze of sensations that shimmered through her.

Closing his lips over the straining nipple, he lightly caught the tip with his teeth, using his tongue with erotic skill.

Bianca clenched her teeth, unable to even think as delicious waves of delight speared through her.

She was pliant clay being molded by the hands of a most tender artist.

Suckling with growing insistence, Edward trailed his fingers down the quivering muscles of her stomach, his touch turning her blood to molten lava and tightening the knot of need that burned between her thighs.

With exquisite care he explored every inch of her satin skin, circling her belly button and drifting over her thighs before slowly moving upward.

Bianca squeezed her eyes shut. He was tormenting her beyond bearing, but while she writhed beneath his touch the pleading words remained locked in her throat. As desperate as she was to reach that shattering conclusion, another part of her longed to prolong the delight.

This was precisely as she had dreamed it would be, she silently moaned. A blaze of sensations that seared her to her very soul.

Lifting her hands to thrust them in the softness of his hair, Bianca directed his attention to her neglected breast. He readily tugged the nipple between his lips as his fingers stroked as light as a butterfly wing along the line of her cleft.

Bianca nearly leaped off the pillows. Lordy . . .

"Please, Edward," she rasped.

His head lifted and their gazes collided. In the shadows his features were hard with a raw desire that he did not bother to disguise.

"I want to watch you, muirnin," he murmured in the hushed silence.

Uncertain what he meant, Bianca opened her lips to demand an explanation only to have the words come out as a groan when his fingers dipped into the damp heat between her legs.

Her hips lifted as she gripped his shoulders. She was spinning away from the world, and the only thing left was the feel of his expert caresses.

Slowly his finger sank into her, his clever thumb brushing over the precise point of her pleasure.

"Yes," she moaned.

"Like this, muirnin?" he demanded as he began a slow, steady rhythm that clenched her muscles to a near-unbearable tightness.

Every stroke sent a flame of need surging through her, and Bianca found her breath coming in short gasps.

"Oh, yes."

"No, look at me, Bianca," he commanded as her lashes began to drift downward. "I want to see into your eyes."

With an effort, she met his smoldering gaze, her hands grasping the pillows as she gritted her teeth. A powerful force was building deep within her, and she feared she would soon be spiraling beyond control.

Keeping the same steady pace, Edward slipped a second finger into her heat, stretching her with gentle care. Bianca dug her teeth into her lower lip until she nearly brought blood.

The sweet release beckoned just beyond her reach. So close. Her hips lifted in a silent plea, but Edward refused to quicken his movements.

"Edward . . . please . . ."

"What do you need, Bianca?" he husked, his body stiff with his own restrained desire. "Tell me."

"You," she panted. "I need you."

"Bianca." He sucked in a harsh breath.

For a moment he seemed to pause, and her entire body froze. No. Not now. He could not deny her when they were so close.

"Now, Edward. I need you now."

He closed his eyes as if in pain. Bianca tensed, and then with a groan that was wrenched from deep in his throat Edward was moving to cover her body with his own.

She sighed in pure pleasure as his solid weight pressed her into the pillows. His hair-roughened skin rasped against her own to create a rash of excitement, his warm scent filling her head.

It felt so utterly right as he cradled his hips between her legs, his chest rubbing her aching nipples. As if he somehow completed her.

Allowing her hands to run down the width of his back, Bianca tested the hard muscles that rippled beneath her touch. He was sheer male.

And he was all hers.

She smiled as the love she felt for this man poured through her entire being.

This was why his touch ignited the fire within her. Why only his kisses created the frenzy of need that held her in its grip.

It was more than his raw masculine perfection. More than his skillful touch.

It was the knowledge deep in her heart that he was the man meant to share her life for all eternity.

Her hands reached the smooth curve of his buttocks, and Bianca felt him shudder as she cupped him with restless desire.

His hooded gaze swept over her countenance as he leaned upon his elbows.

"Tell me this is real, muirnin," he demanded. "Tell me this is not just a dream."

She reached up to frame his face in her hands. "This is no dream, my love."

"My love," he echoed, the tender yearning in his voice nearly bringing tears to her eyes. "Am I your love?"

"For all eternity," she swore.

A shiver wracked his body as he lowered his head and lightly brushed his lips over her flushed features.

"You hold my heart in your hands," he murmured against her temple. "There is no going back for either of us."

His breath whispered over her skin as he shifted between her legs and the head of his shaft pressed against her entrance.

There was a flutter of alarm as she felt herself being stretched far beyond what she had imagined.

"Edward?" she breathed.

His lips moved to nibble at the edge of her mouth. "All will be well, Bianca. Trust in me."

And she did.

She trusted that he would always take care of her. Always do what was best for the both of them.

Closing her eyes, she forced herself to relax, concentrating on the sensation of his erection relentlessly shifting deeper into her damp heat. Beneath her fingers his muscles trembled from the effort of leashing his powerful need, and she sensed when he paused at the barrier of her innocence.

"Bianca, I think it would be best if this was done swiftly," he rasped, his damp forehead pressed to her own.

She swallowed heavily, shaking from a combination of edgy unease and frustrated desire.

"Yes."

The word had barely tumbled from her lips when his hips flexed and with one smooth thrust he was buried to the very core of her.

Her tiny yelp was more one of surprise than pain, and as he pressed his lips to the curve of her throat, her aching passion was swiftly flamed back to life.

"That is . . . amazing," she murmured.

He gave a sound somewhere between a chuckle and a groan.

"We have only just begun," he promised, trailing his mouth over her skin to at last kiss her with a devouring hunger.

Instinctively Bianca lifted her hips as he began to rock softly against her. With each thrust his tongue stroked into her mouth, the matching rhythm building the tension that was centered low in her stomach.

Her fingers flexed as a moan was lodged in her throat. The sheer intimacy of having him sheathed in her body was astonishing. Never had she felt so connected to another. As if they had entwined into one soul.

His breath rasped in the shadowed silence as he pulled nearly out of her body and plunged back within. Her legs shifted to wrap about him, unwittingly opening herself to his quickening pace.

"Hell's teeth, you feel so good." he muttered against her lips. "So tight. So hot."

She was hot. She was on fire, burning from the inside out.

She stirred restlessly beneath him. His every movement was rubbing against her cleft, increasing her pleasure to a near-unbearable peak.

"I cannot . . . ," she moaned.

"Stay with me, muirnin," he commanded, his head lowering to take her breast in his mouth.

Using his teeth and tongue, he tormented her tight nipple, the wave of sensations soaring her ever upward.

Her breath evaporated as she hovered on a golden edge. Her body was clenched so tightly she was certain she would shatter apart. And then with a final, branding surge he toppled her over the edge into a whirlwind of pulsing bliss.

Her soft scream mingled with his low groan of completion as he slumped atop her, both of them lost in sublime release.

Time passed, a moment or an eternity, before Edward shifted to his side and pulled her into his arms. With a sigh Bianca rested her head on his chest, a sense of wonderment clouding her mind.

"I wish I had the words to tell you what you mean to me,

Bianca," he whispered as he nuzzled her ear. "I never thought to feel what I feel for you."

Bianca smiled, brushing his skin with her lips. He did not need the words. His every touch spoke of his love.

"I do hope that means you intend to wed me, my lord," she teased. "I fear I have become quite addicted to your kisses."

His arms tightened until she feared she would not be able to breathe.

"Nothing will keep you from being my bride, muirnin. Not even God Himself."

The oddest tingle of warning inched down her spine at his fierce words.

Ridiculous, perhaps. But she suddenly wished that he had not dared fate with such reckless disregard.

There was nothing more certain to call down misfortune.

CHAPTER THIRTEEN

Early in the afternoon, Hellion's Den was nearly silent. Only the sound of scurrying servants preparing for the night ahead broke the silence.

Seated at one of the numerous tables scattered about the room, Edward regarded the thin, rat-faced gentleman settled across from him. A wry smile touched Edward's lips.

After a sleepless night, his companion's scarlet coat and pink waistcoat were near painful to endure, but it was the fiercely twitching nose that held his attention.

He had not expected Biddles to be overjoyed with his announcement that he was to offer for Lady Bianca. In fact, he was quite prepared for a tedious lecture.

Not that he was particularly concerned, he conceded with a smile that refused to be dismissed. No one would be allowed to dim the giddy happiness that held him in its grip.

Leaning back in his chair, he folded his arms over his chest.

"You might as well have your say, old friend," he encouraged. "I fear you will burst if you do not get it out of your system."

"I would prefer to shake some sense into you," Biddles

groused, taking a long draw from his flask. "Unfortunately, you are far too large a lummox for it to do any good."

Edward gave a lift of his brows. "Lummox?"

"Slow-witted, paper sapskull who does not have the sense to avoid the most obvious trap ever laid for a man," Biddles clarified without apology.

"I suppose you are referring to Lady Bianca?"

Biddles leaned forward, his pale eyes glittering. "The woman is a blatant opportunist."

"Opportunist?" He gave a short laugh. "You are wide of the mark there, old friend. There is little to be gained by wedding me. Indeed, I do not doubt most will believe she has married quite beneath herself."

Biddles narrowed his gaze. "You are no longer a penniless farmer, Edward. You are an earl with enough wealth to attract the most fastidious schemer."

"Are you branding Lady Bianca a rank fortune hunter?"

"She told you herself she must wed for wealth."

Edward's warm glow did not falter, but there was no denying that the smooth thrust slid home. Biddles spoke nothing but the truth. Bianca *was* in need of a fortune. And a gentleman willing to haul her family from beneath the hatches.

Perhaps foolishly he had nearly forgotten.

Could it be that she had decided he was less repulsive than the suitors being thrust down her throat by her father? Had she decided that being the wife of a simple farmer was somehow preferable to being a pawn for a gentleman in search of power?

His chest tightened before he was fiercely thrusting away the disturbing thought.

No.

He would not doubt her.

He had held her in his arms, felt her passion and heard her cry out his name as she reached her climax. Not even the most proficient actress could respond with such fervor to his touch.

"I admire her loyalty to her family," he retorted firmly.

Biddles clicked his tongue in annoyance. "And it does not bother you that she considers you no more than a means to an end?"

"I believe she has come to care for me."

"She would, of course, wish you to believe that," Biddles pointed out. "She is hardly likely to reveal her true feelings so long as she needs you to wed her."

Edward clenched his jaw with a stubborn refusal to be swayed. Damn and blast, why could his friend not simply be pleased for him?

God knew he had never been so happy.

"You are very cynical, Biddles."

"I am practical," his friend corrected, his expression somber. "I have been among society far too long not to have seen any number of friends brought to their knees by a devious female. I would not have that happen to you."

Edward forced his stiff muscles to relax. He did not doubt that Biddles was truly concerned for him. Or that he believed he was doing what was best.

He could not be angry for possessing a friend who desired only to protect him.

His warm smile returned to his lips. "I appreciate your concern, but it is not necessary. Bianca is the only woman I wish to be my wife. I will have no other."

There was a long pause as Biddles studied his determined expression. Then, with a heavy sigh, he leaned back in his seat.

"There seems to be nothing left for me to do but wish you well," he admitted in resigned tones.

"Actually, there is one more thing."

"What is that?"

"I wish you to stand at my side when I say my vows."

The pale eyes widened as a pleased smile curved the gentleman's lips.

"I can think of no greater honor, my friend."

"Thank you." Rising to his feet, Edward sucked in a deep breath. One hurdle crossed. Unfortunately there was one still in his path. "And now . . . to confront the Duke. I do not suppose you have any suggestions?"

Biddles arched a brow as his smile turned sly. "You might wish to guard your . . . ummm . . . precious jewels. At some point you shall no doubt be in need of an heir."

Edward winced in spite of himself. "As always, you are the greatest of comfort."

"I do my best."

"You are an evil man," Edward complained.

Biddles produced a lacy handkerchief to dab at his nose. "Do you know, I seem to hear that with alarming frequency."

The elegant gentleman's club on St. James Street possessed all the comfort of a country home. Across the white and black marble hall the curved staircase led directly to the great subscription room where the younger blood attempted their luck at quintze and hazard.

It was all but empty in the early afternoon hours, and Edward did not pause as he moved toward a back, book-lined room where the Duke of Lockharte was well known to enjoy his weekly luncheon in privacy.

He was not disappointed as he stepped over the threshold and regarded the large, silver-haired gentleman settled in a distant corner.

Edward took a moment to gather his nerve before slowly crossing the carpet to stand beside the table that held the scraps of a beefsteak and a decanter of burgundy.

He waited with growing impatience for the nobleman to at last raise his head from the newspaper he had been scanning to stab him with a steely gaze.

"Yes?"

He offered a low bow. "Your Grace. May I join you?"

A shrewd glint entered the blue eyes. "I sense I could not halt you even should I desire."

"I do have a matter of some urgency I wish to discuss with you," Edward conceded.

The elder man waved a hand toward a nearby chair. "Oh, halt your hovering and have a seat." Waiting until Edward had settled himself in the leather chair, he reached forward to pour two glasses from the decanter. "Burgundy?"

Edward readily took the proffered spirit, grateful that it had not been tossed in his face or poured over his head.

"Thank you."

The Duke took a deep sip of the burgundy, pausing as he tested the richness upon his tongue before at last swallowing.

"Ah. Not quite so fine as mine, but passable. How do you find the Harrington cellars?"

Edward blinked at the abrupt question. He had expected . . . what?

Disdain? Anger? Aloof indifference?

Certainly not the near-pleasant tone that was somehow more unnerving than any angry outburst.

"To be honest I have yet to inspect them," he reluctantly confessed.

"You are not a connoisseur?"

Wondering if he were about to be cast as an irredeemable philistine, Edward gave a shake of his head.

"I fear not."

The mild expression did not alter. Thank the Lord.

"What are your interests?"

Edward paused before heaving an inward sigh. Obviously if he was not to be damned for one sin, it would be for another.

"Farming."

"Farming?" the Duke growled.

Edward gave a shrug of his shoulder. "I am intrigued with the latest technology and inventions that have been produced in the past few years. I have already implemented many of them at my own estates and discovered them to be an invaluable investment. I hope to establish similar changes throughout the Harrington estates."

"A laudable cause." The blue eyes narrowed. "There are those who consider you a radical."

Wondering if the wily aristocrat were deliberately attempting to rattle him, Edward forced himself to take a deep breath and consider his answer.

Hasty words only led to tragedy.

"A wise man recently told me that there was a distinct difference between a radical and a revolutionary," he at last said in low tones.

A silver brow arched. "You think yourself a revolutionary?"

"I think that power carries a sacred duty to help those who are in no position to help themselves." He briefly glanced about the room that carried with it the smell of old leather and older wealth. "My title is more than houses and farms and priceless collections. It is servants and tenants and families who depend upon me to do what is right for them."

The Duke of Lockharte absorbed his words in silence before a shocking smile curved his lips.

"I can almost believe you are sincere, Harrington. Most rare in such a young man."

Edward tossed back the contents of the glass before setting it aside. It was all going well. Far too well. He sensed he was being skillfully led into a neat trap.

The devious old coot.

Deciding to take the bull by the horn, he lifted his chin and met the piercing blue eyes.

"You know why I am here, Your Grace?"

The gentleman set aside his own glass before settling

more comfortably in his chair. A master chessman preparing for battle.

"Bianca spoke with me yesterday."

"I am aware that my bloodlines are not all that you would wish and that society might never fully accept me." He spoke the words before the Duke could toss them into his face. "But I do not believe any man would ever love your daughter more than I."

"Love is not all that I seek for my daughter. It is more important that she discover a husband who will treat her with the care she deserves."

"I will do everything in my power to ensure her happiness. I can make no greater promise than that."

They stared at one another. Man to man. Not threatening but silently measuring.

"She is stubborn and inclined to believe that she always knows best." The Duke broke the silence. "She will not be a comfortable wife."

Comfortable? Edward choked back the urge to laugh. Bianca would no doubt lead him a merry dance that would ensure his days never had a moment's peace.

"I have never sought the easy path."

"No, I do not suppose you have," the older man murmured in agreement.

Edward slowly leaned forward. "May we depend upon your blessing?"

"You have no need of it. Bianca is of age and seemingly quite determined to become your wife."

Sensing he was being tested, Edward gave a shake of his head. "No. If I have learned anything of Bianca, it is that she cares for you very much. She would be deeply saddened if you were to oppose our match. I would not have her begin our life together in such a manner."

His brows rose in surprise. "You would walk away from her?"

"Never, but I would do whatever necessary to win your approval."

"Hmmm." The lined countenance was impossible to read. "She has told you that she has no dowry?"

"I have no need for a dowry."

"And if I seek funds to stave off the vultures?"

Edward did not hesitate. "You are soon to be my family. I will do whatever is needed to assist."

Without warning, the silver head tilted back as the Duke chuckled with unexpected humor.

"A rare man, indeed."

Edward frowned, not certain whether to be relieved or terrified. "If you wish to contact my man of business . . ."

"You may keep your fortune, son," he interrupted brusquely. "Although I may not be as flushed in the pocket as you, I am more than comfortable."

The frown deepened. This time in shock.

"You are not in need of funds?"

"No."

"But . . ." Edward pondered a long moment. "You lied to your daughter?"

There was not the least hint of guilt upon the arrogant features. "I protected her from crass fortune hunters. Not an easy task, I must tell you. There are those gentlemen who will stoop to any means to turn a female's head."

"Still—"

"Enough," the nobleman barked. "I did what was necessary. And now you will reap the benefits."

With an effort, Edward bit back his instinctive distaste for such blatant manipulation of his beloved. He was a straightforward man who found such devious means abhorrent.

Now, however, did not seem the most suitable moment to point out his objections.

"I have your agreement?" he demanded instead.

An odd smile abruptly softened the stark features as the

Duke leaned forward to pour them both a measure of the rich burgundy.

"More than my agreement. You have my utmost admiration. I have chosen very well."

Edward stilled, wondering if the man had misspoken.

"You have chosen?"

"A toast." The Duke ignored the soft question as he raised his glass. "To Edward and Bianca, may they be blessed with love and friendship throughout the years."

A sharp flare of satisfaction settled in Edward's heart, dismissing the momentary curiosity. He had done it. Against all odds he had managed to capture the woman of his dreams.

And now nothing stood in their way.

Nothing.

Touching his glass to his companion's, he resisted the urge to shout out his joy.

"To love."

Intent on their private conversation, neither noticed the golden-haired gentleman hidden by the large potted palm. Nor the ugly smile that twisted his lips as he raised his own glass in a silent toast.

Well, well, well. Lady Bianca was precisely what he had thought her to be.

A wealthy young lady with a father who wielded enough power to ease all his troubles.

It seemed the future for Lord Aldron was not nearly so dark as he had begun to fear.

CHAPTER FOURTEEN

Bianca tugged upon the silver locket until the chain threatened to break.

Men were without a doubt the most aggravating of creatures.

Both her father and Edward must know she would be upon pins and needles to learn what had happened during their interview. For God's sake, it was her future they were discussing.

But while she had refused to step so much as a foot outside the townhouse, and had even delayed leaving for the Braxton's musicale until she was more than fashionably late, she had not heard a word from either gentleman.

She was going to choke the both of them, she decided as she gave the necklace another jerk.

Or take off her slipper and beat them over the head with it.

Anything that might jiggle loose a bit of sense in their thick skulls.

Glancing impatiently over her shoulder at the empty doorway, Bianca heaved a sigh of relief as the aria screeched to a halt and the guests were allowed a brief respite from the painful schedule of entertainment.

She was out of her seat before her mother could lecture her

upon proper decorum and on her way to the hallway, where she hoped Edward, or even her father, might be lurking.

She was just stepping through the entryway when a uniformed footman approached her and, with a small bow, handed her a folded note.

Her heart gave a leap of excitement as she smoothed the paper and read the short missive.

I await you in the conservatory. Do not keep me waiting, my dearest love.

Edward.

It could be no one else.

Tucking the note into her glove, she did not hesitate as she hurried down the staircase and headed toward the back of the townhouse. Thankfully, her mother was well aware of her dislike for such tedious musicales and would presume she was hiding in the withdrawing room until it was safe to leave.

She could disappear without causing a murmur.

A tingle of anticipation feathered down her spine as she searched the maze of hallways until at last she discovered the one that led to the conservatory.

Dear lord, she was utterly shameless, she acknowledged with a small smile. She had spent hours in Edward's arms quenching her passion last eve. He had taught her there were any number of means to pleasure one another.

Surely any other maiden would be at least a tad embarrassed by her brazen behavior?

But not her.

The mere thought of the man who was to become her husband was enough to make her ache for his touch.

Pressing open the glass door, Bianca stepped into the shadowed heat of the small conservatory. At once she was shrouded in the exotic scent of rare orchids. She instinctively wrinkled her nose.

She did not care for such a heavy, cloying scent.

Glancing about, she stepped farther down the paved path, her eyes slowly adjusting to the darkness.

"Hello?" she called softly. "Is anyone here?"

"Yes," a male voice answered from the back depths.

Puzzled by Edward's odd behavior, Bianca moved between the banks of lush plants, halting as she reached a marble fountain.

"Are you hiding?" she demanded.

"I have been hiding." A slender, elegantly attired form abruptly stepped into a shaft of moonlight. "Until now."

Bianca stiffened in surprise. "Stephen?"

He offered a half bow. "At your service."

"Whatever are you doing here?"

A practiced smile curved the lips that were just a trifle too thin.

"Awaiting you, of course. What else would I be doing?"

Realization struck with sudden force. Blast. She had been expecting a few glorious stolen moments with Edward. Now she would have to endure yet another strained confrontation with this gentleman.

She would rather listen to a dozen dreadful arias.

"You sent me the note."

"Who else?" Slowly strolling forward, Stephen narrowed his eyes. "Do not tell me you were expecting your farmer?"

"Why did you wish to meet with me?"

His smile briefly faltered at her impatient tone, but with a skill that had led to more than one broken female heart, he was once more revealing his perfect white teeth.

"To begin with, I intend to confess that I have been a fool and a coward," he murmured in golden tones. He reached out to grasp her hands in a tight grip.

"What?"

She found herself being tugged relentlessly closer. So close that the heavy odor of his cologne mixed unpleasantly with the thick perfume in the air.

It was a striking contrast to Edward's clean, crisp scent.

With a rather dramatic motion, Stephen forced her hand to splay against his chest, his expression assuming one of deepest sorrow.

"My dearest, when your father refused my offer of marriage I was out of my wits with suffering. To even think of my life without you was unbearable." He paused as if attempting to judge the affect of his words upon her. "And . . . there was, of course, the decided blow to my pride. Your father made it quite clear that I was beneath his contempt."

Bianca could not halt her small wince. Her feelings for this gentleman might have died a swift death, but she could not deny he had been treated badly by her family.

"I am sorry, Stephen."

"I am the one who is sorry," he startled her by insisting. "I behaved as a spoiled child rather than a gentleman who loves you desperately. I should never have walked away. What do I care of your fortune? Or even your father's approval? Nothing matters but our love. Possessing your heart is far more important than possessing a fortune."

A silence descended as she regarded him with a growing wariness.

She had expected his anger. Even accepted that she deserved some small measure of punishment. But never had she supposed he would still harbor the notion that they would wed.

She hid a sharp shudder. It was unthinkable.

"Stephen—"

"We will somehow survive, that I promise you, my love." He determinedly overrode her soft protest. "Perhaps it will not be as luxurious as you are accustomed to, but I shall do everything in my power to ensure you never lack for comfort."

Her wariness deepened. Something was not right. Stephen

was very much a gentleman of London. An expensive gentleman who would as soon slit his throat as to live in shabby gentility.

"Stephen, you are not thinking clearly," she said in careful tones.

"No, at last I am thinking clearly," he insisted, his eyes glittering with a hectic fire. "I know that you love me. I know you want to be my wife. You certainly have claimed it often enough. Or have you forgotten the impassioned letters you wrote to me? I still have them."

She inwardly cringed at the recollection of those letters. At the time it had seemed something a young woman in love should do. Only now did she realize it was merely an attempt to prove to herself that her emotions were genuine.

How else could she justify using him as a mere means to escape her golden prison?

"I did care, Stephen," she hedged, too embarrassed to admit the truth.

His eyes narrowed. "You still care."

"The situation has changed."

"Because you feel obligated to wed a fortune? Do not fret." He lifted her stiff fingers to his lips. "We shall no doubt be as poor as church mice, but we shall be together. Nothing else matters."

Her eyes widened. As poor as church mice?

All right. Now she knew something was wrong.

Clearly Stephen was either playing some cruel game or he was cast to the wind.

"Please, you must listen to me," she commanded, wanting nothing so much as to be out of the conservatory.

The blue eyes seemed to harden before his arms abruptly lashed about her and hauled her against his slender form.

"After I have kissed you," he muttered, pressing his lips to her unwilling mouth. "God, I have missed you so much."

A surge of panic raced through her as she battled herself from his clinging hold and wiped her hand over her lips.

"No."

Reaching out he grasped her arm before she could flee. "What is it, my love?"

"Whatever there was between us is over." With a futile effort she attempted to tug her arm free of his harsh grip. "You must know it is."

"Because of your dowry? I have told you that it does not matter."

Her expression hardened with annoyance. "I am promised to another."

"The Peasant Earl?"

She stiffened in shock. "How did you know?"

"Does it matter?" His lips curled into an ugly sneer. "My God, do you think that I could bear for you to sacrifice yourself to that awkward oaf just for my comfort? Never. You deserve a man who is worthy of you. A man who comes from your world, not from the stables."

She instinctively halted her struggle to glare at the countenance that was not nearly so handsome as she had once thought it to be.

"Edward is a wonderful man."

A sharp, humorless laugh echoed through the conservatory. The sound sent a chill down her spine. Suddenly she was aware of just how isolated they were from the other guests.

"No doubt you have tried to convince yourself of that. After all, he is disgustingly wealthy. But we both know he will never fit into society. He will be a never anything but an embarrassment to you and your family."

"That is not true—"

"Of course it is." He broke into her furious words. "Not that it matters. You will be my wife. You belong to me."

Belong to him?

She barely resisted the urge to slap his smug face. Gads,

how could she have ever thought this man to be worth a moment of her time?

Under that smooth charm he was a loathsome toad.

"You are very confident in yourself," she accused in frigid tones.

He shrugged. "I am confident in you. You have made it very obvious you still love me."

"What are you talking about?"

"The locket, my sweet." His fingers loosened their grip on her arm to touch the silver necklace. "If you no longer loved me, why would you still wear my portrait above your heart?"

"That is ridiculous. I—" A sharp sound directly behind her had Bianca spinning about to watch as a large, familiar form retreated from the conservatory. Her heart halted at the realization that Edward must have overheard at least a portion of the conversation. And that judging from the stiffness of his back, he was not best pleased to discover her alone with another man. Damn and blast. "Edward. Edward, where are you going?"

He had to have heard her anxious call, but his steps never slowed, and even as she stepped forward to halt him, the sound of the glass door being slammed shut reverberated through the room.

Her stomach clenched in dread.

No. Oh . . . no.

Edward stormed from the townhouse without a glance toward the various guests who sought to gain his attention. In truth, he did not even notice their presence. Nor the presence of the handful of servants who were forced to scurry from his path or be plowed over.

There was nothing but the red haze of fury that filled his entire being.

God . . . the rumormongers were right.

He was the worst sort of gapseed.

A sap-skulled, naïve dolt who should never have been allowed to step foot in society.

The evening had started so well.

After his interview with the Duke of Lockharte, he had devoted the afternoon to his tailor. After all, a gentleman about to wed Lady Bianca would be in need of the most elegant of wardrobes. He would do nothing to shame her, even if it meant attiring himself as a bloody dandy.

Then there had been a quick meeting with his man of business to ensure the paperwork for his upcoming nuptials would be set into motion as swiftly as possible before rushing home to dress for the musicale.

It was only because he had been running late that he had seen Bianca hurrying toward the back of the house in the first place. He had been curious but not unduly alarmed as he had followed in her wake. He had even paused at a mirror to ensure his damnable cravat had not wilted and that his hair was not mussed.

Just like a preening coxcomb, he had acknowledged with a hint of disgust at his vanity.

Of course, the delay had meant he had been late in entering the conservatory. So late that Bianca had thought herself alone with her beloved Lord Aldron and at liberty to indulge in a passionate, star-crossed-lover scene. One that was quite worthy of Shakespeare.

And had revealed the truth of the woman he had very nearly made his countess.

The red haze deepened to crimson as he swept down the steps and searched the line of carriages until he found his own. Irritably waving the startled groom aside, he yanked open the door and climbed within.

"Take me home," he growled.

"At once, sir."

Closing the door, Edward leaned against the leather squabs and clenched his fists in his lap.

He had never been so furious in his entire life. And yet at the same moment, there was a horrible part of him that longed for nothing more than to return to the conservatory and toss Bianca over his shoulder so he could carry her off and never let her go.

By God . . . he truly was a dolt.

"Edward."

Without warning, the door to the carriage was wrenched open and Bianca was clambering into the darkness with him.

Shock at her audacity held him momentarily speechless, but as she shut the door and firmly settled in the seat opposite him, he at last found his tongue.

"Get out of the carriage, Bianca," he gritted.

Her chin tilted to a determined angle. "No, not until you tell me what is the matter."

Against his will, he discovered his gaze roaming hungrily over her slender form. Even in the shadows he noticed that she appeared oddly ruffled, with her features flushed and her raven curls tumbling from the tidy knot atop her head.

Perhaps not so surprising, an evil voice whispered in the back of his mind. She did just come from the arms of another man.

A relentless pain clutched at his heart.

"Do not play the innocent, Lady Bianca. I am in no humor for it."

She bit her lip as if startled by his harsh tone. "You are angry?"

He gave a short, humorless laugh. "How did you think I would feel to discover you in the arms of your love?"

"He is not my love."

Her fierce words only fueled his anger. Of course she would deny her feelings for the other man. At the moment she was still terrified at the thought of his fortune slipping from her fingers.

"What a fool I have been." He gave a disgusted sound deep

in his throat. "Biddles warned me, but I refused to listen to his warnings."

A frown touched her forehead. "Edward, if you were listening, then you must have heard me tell Stephen that I no longer care for him."

"Because you were in need of a fortune. Something he could not give to you." His jaw knotted. Common sense warned him to bundle her out of the carriage and leave without a backward glance. What was the point in hashing through her deceit? But common sense had little sway over a broken heart and wounded pride. Suddenly he needed to know the truth. "Why did you lie to me?"

She blinked at his abrupt question. "I never lied."

"You swore to me that your heart was your own."

"It is, or it was until I gave it to you," she protested, even managing to conjure a shimmer of tears in the magnificent midnight eyes. Hell's teeth, she should be walking the boards.

"The truth, Bianca. Did you have a relationship with Lord Aldron?"

She paused, and for a moment Edward thought she would attempt a futile lie. Then, with a restless shrug, she gave in to the inevitable.

"For a short time."

"And you intended to wed him?"

"I . . . yes."

Edward flinched. Ridiculously, her grudging confirmation of what he already knew sent another flare of pain searing through his heart.

As if he had foolishly hoped there had been some terrible misunderstanding.

Sapskull.

"And you did not think it worthy of telling me?" he growled.

"It was in the past. My father had already refused his proposal."

Edward froze as the truth slammed into him. Damn the Duke of Lockharte. He had played the both of them for fools.

"My God," he breathed. "That was why your father played his devious game. He knew you were in love with a fortune hunter."

Bianca regarded him in puzzlement. "Game? What game?"

Tilting back his head, he gave a harsh laugh. "Congratulations, my dear, you are not quite so penniless as you supposed. I had it from the Duke that he has no need of my wealth. You have your dowry, and now you can have the man you want."

She lifted a hand to press it to her heart. The movement drew attention to the spill of her white breasts barely covered by the low cut of her bodice, and Edward was forced to shift uncomfortably on the seat.

Obviously his body had not yet received the message that this woman was a treacherous jade.

"My father lied to me?"

"It appears to run in the family."

She ignored his insult as her brows drew together. "Why would he do such a thing?"

"Obviously he thought it the only means to keep you from the man you desired as your husband."

"But—"

"Enough." Edward lifted a hand to rub at the knotted muscles of his neck. "Speak with your father if you wish to know what was in his convoluted mind. I wash my hands of the both of you."

She sucked in a sharp breath, as if he had actually struck her.

"This is absurd." She leaned forward, her features glowing with breathtaking beauty in the moonlight. "You know how I feel about you."

Edward eyed her with blatant suspicion. He had expected

her to flee to her former fiancé the moment she learned that she was no longer bound to search for a fortune.

It made no sense for her to continue playing her cruel charade.

Still, if he had discovered nothing else this night, it was that he could not trust this woman.

"I know what you desired me to believe."

"Last night—"

"What?" he rudely interrupted. "You gave me your body?"

She flinched at his bald words. "Yes."

"With another man's portrait about your neck." Before he even knew what he was doing, Edward leaned forward to tug the locket from about her throat. The cool silver seemed to burn his palm as he glared down at the delicate bit of jewelry. This, he realized, was the greatest source of his pain. Beyond the lies, beyond the knowledge he had been no more than a convenient means to a fortune, it was the cold-blooded manner in which she had pretended to love him while she clung to the portrait of another man. "I suppose you were imagining I was your precious Stephen when you took me into your body?"

"Never."

He tossed the locket into her lap. God, he could not stomach to touch it.

"Do you think he will forgive you for having sacrificed your innocence?" he demanded. "Ah, do not bother to answer. No doubt he will be willing to forgive any sin once he discovers your dowry remains intact."

She abruptly sank back in her seat, her expression one of wounded confusion.

"How can you be so horrible?" she whispered.

Just for a moment, Edward found himself nearly overwhelmed by a flood of guilt. She appeared so disarmingly hurt. As if she truly did possess a measure of feeling for him.

Then his gaze was caught by the flash of silver from the

locket upon her lap, and he sternly hardened his traitorous emotions.

Good lord, how many times did he need to have his heart stomped upon before he learned his lesson?

"How do you want me to be?" he rasped. "The simple, blundering farmer who does not have the wits to sense when he is being used? Sorry, but I fear that man has had his eyes opened. He will never be so naïve again."

Without warning, she reached down to grasp the necklace and tossed it onto the carriage floor.

"The locket meant nothing, Edward," she hissed. "For God's sake, I had forgotten that Stephen's portrait was even within it."

Edward abruptly turned his head to glare out the window. It was the very fact he so desperately wanted to believe her that made him realize he had endured enough.

He was furious, sick at heart, and well beyond coherent thought.

All he desired was a decanter of brandy and the comfort of his bed.

Tomorrow was time enough to sort through the mess he had managed to make of his life.

"Go, Bianca."

"Edward—"

"Go." He turned his head to stab her with a steely glance. "I have nothing left to say to you."

CHAPTER FIFTEEN

Having heard any number of scandalous rumors concerning London's most famous gambling hell, Bianca was rather startled to discover that Hellion's Den was a rather modest establishment with a subdued elegance that was not at all shocking.

Of course it was only midday, she had consoled herself. No doubt the half-dressed courtesans and drunken dandies seeking a duel did not arrive until at least after tea.

Stepping across the threshold, she swept between the numerous tables and headed directly for the nearby stairs. Hardly the behavior of a proper lady, but then she had already called upon Edward's townhouse without so much as a maid to lend her countenance.

If society desired to be scandalized over her brazen behavior, she did not give a fig.

Nothing mattered but that she somehow discover Edward's whereabouts.

Now.

Clearly rattled at the sight of an impatient lady of the *ton* marching through the gaming room, a young male servant hurried to block her path.

"Forgive me, but you cannot be here, miss," he stammered with a fierce blush.

Forced to halt, Bianca planted her hands upon her hips and conjured a haughty frown suitable for the daughter of a duke.

"It is Lady Bianca, not miss, and I am here to speak with Lord Bidwell. You will fetch him at once."

The lad's eyes bulged in terror, but much to his credit he managed to hold his ground.

"I fear that Lord Bidwell has not yet arrived. If you would be so good as to leave a message . . ."

Her eyes narrowed to dangerous slits. She had never been one to run roughshod over poor servants, but today she would allow no one to stand in her way.

She was a woman on a mission.

"I will not step foot from this spot until I have spoken with his lordship, so you might as well inform your employer that it will do no good to attempt to fob me off."

"Lady Bianca." The drawling voice drifted from the top of the stairs. "Is it not rather early in the day to be terrifying my servants?"

Bianca stiffened as she watched the slender, thin-faced gentleman mince his way down the stairs. Attired in a blinding yellow coat and green breeches, he lightly dabbed at his nose with a lacy handkerchief. However, it was his expression of mocking amusement that set her nerves on edge.

"Where is Edward?" she demanded in stark tones.

"Good morning to you as well," he chided with a lazy glance toward the nervous servant. "That will be all, Cookson." He waited for the lad to scurry away before returning his attention to her rigid expression. "May I offer you coffee?"

Her teeth clashed together in annoyance.

God almighty. She had just spent the worst night of her life as she had paced the floor and wrestled with the fear that she had lost Edward forever.

That had been followed by a frantic morning spent attempting to find her elusive fiancé.

She was in no humor to be patronized by a gentleman who

had obviously done everything in his power to turn Edward against her.

"No, I thank you."

A sardonic smile touched the thin lips. "Tea? Brandy? Arsenic?"

"All I want is Edward," she snapped with impatience.

"And you believe I have him tucked in my pocket?"

"I believe you know where he is."

With a flutter of his handkerchief, Lord Bidwell strolled to straighten the silver candlesticks upon a nearby table.

"It is possible; however, you cannot imagine I would betray his whereabouts to you. You are, after all, the reason he disappeared in the first place."

Bianca winced in spite of herself. She refused to accept that she was entirely to blame for Edward's unreasonable behavior. After all, he had been quite eager to believe the worst of her.

But there was no denying that she had not been utterly honest with him.

"I must speak with him."

The nobleman abruptly turned about, an unnerving glitter in his pale eyes.

"You were not yet finished torturing him? Perhaps you had another knife to thrust into his back?"

She ignored the sudden danger that shimmered in the air. She would not be intimidated. This was too important.

"I am well aware that you have never approved of me, Lord Bidwell." She confronted him directly.

If she expected him to reveal the least discomfort, she was doomed to disappointment. His smile merely widened.

"I possess impeccable taste."

"I also know that you have attempted to convince Edward that I am untrustworthy," she charged.

"Clearly I am brilliant as well."

The thought of choking the infuriating man briefly flashed

through her mind. The pleasure would no doubt make up for being hung for murder.

Unfortunately, she needed the man to discover the whereabouts of Edward.

Stepping forward, she stabbed a finger toward his pointed nose. "But you have been mistaken in me. I love Edward. And nothing and no one is going to keep me from becoming his wife."

He did not so much as flinch. "No doubt you said similar words to Lord Aldron and who knows how many other gullible fools."

Arggg . . . the man was truly loathsome.

"You have never done anything foolish in your life, my lord?" she demanded. "You have never allowed yourself to be dazzled by a pretty face or said words you wished unspoken? You have never kept secrets because you feared what might occur if they were revealed? You must be a remarkable man."

Shockingly, the slender man seemed to stiffen at her challenging words. Almost as if she had managed to touch a nerve. Then, with startling swiftness, his mocking expression dropped to reveal the shrewd intelligence he kept so well hidden.

"What is it you want, Lady Bianca?"

She took a moment to consider her words. She did not doubt she could cry and moan and plead until she swooned and not sway the man. It would only be by convincing him that she had no intention of hurting his friend further that she would learn what she needed to know.

"I want the opportunity to prove to Edward that I love him," she said with soft sincerity.

"And how do you intend to do that?"

Well, that was the question, of course.

How did a woman convince a man that she loved him?

That was a worry for later, she told herself sternly. For now all that mattered was finding Edward.

"I will do whatever is necessary."

"He is a stubborn man who feels he has been betrayed. He is not likely to make matters simple for you."

Her lips twisted. Lord Bidwell was not acquainted with her or he would never have made such an absurd statement.

"He could not possibly be as stubborn as I. Lord Harrington may not realize it yet, but sooner or later he will be my husband."

The pale gaze regarded her for a long moment before the slender gentleman at last heaved a resigned sigh.

"Edward returned to Kent this morning."

Her heart clenched with an awful dread.

So he truly had abandoned her.

Hardly the actions of a gentleman who hoped to sort out the troubles that brewed between them.

Could it be that Edward truly had washed his hands of her? Had he so convinced himself she had betrayed him that he would refuse to listen to reason?

"He has returned to his estate?"

Lord Bidwell gave a lift of his hands. "He claimed he had lost his taste for London."

She swallowed heavily. "Does he intend to return?"

"That I cannot say." He regarded her intently. "I did warn you that it would not be a simple matter."

She fiercely battled back the tears that threatened.

No.

She would not give in to despair.

Somehow she would force Edward to face the truth.

They belonged together no matter what the thick-skulled oaf might believe at the moment.

"Thank you, Lord Bidwell. I will trouble you no further." Turning on her heel, Bianca crossed carefully toward the door, sternly refusing to allow her shaking legs to betray her. Once upon the threshold, however, she turned to regard the brilliantly attired nobleman with a somber gaze.

"Are you a betting man, Lord Bidwell?"

A smile curved his lips. "My dear, I own a gambling hell."

"What odds would you give for my success?"

Without warning, he tilted back his head to laugh with genuine amusement.

"I would as soon wager that the sun will rise in the west as to wager against a female determined to haul a male to the nearest vicar."

Moving through the servants' quarters of his small estate, Edward stifled a sigh at the sound of muffled tears that echoed through the hall.

Although it had been near a week since his return to Kent, he had still not fully accustomed himself to shouldering the tedious day-to-day troubles that inevitably cropped up.

In London he had been the Earl of Harrington. No one would dare to trouble him with anything but the most crucial decisions. And in truth his household ran with such smooth efficiency that he had not dared to interfere.

Here he was just Edward Sinclair. A man considered more family than master.

Halting at the open door to the housekeeper's rooms, he regarded the large woman with steel gray hair who was currently mopping her face with a large handkerchief.

"Mrs. Green," he softly chided. "What is this nonsense?"

"Oh, sir." Turning her bulk toward the door, the housekeeper regarded him with a tragic expression. "I cannot possibly leave you in the lurch like this. Who will tend to you if I am gone?"

They were the same words he had heard over a dozen times since his unexpected return, and he bit back yet another sigh.

The older woman had been a mainstay at the estate for decades and was quite convinced they could not survive a day without her.

Or perhaps she merely wished to be assured that they could not survive without her, a tiny voice whispered in the back of his mind.

Thrusting aside his unworthy flare of impatience, Edward forced a small smile to his lips. He would not allow his ill humor to be taken out on his staff.

"We will all miss your services, my dear, and no doubt the house will be in shambles by the time you return, but we will manage to muddle through." He reached out to pat her shoulder. "You cannot possibly miss the wedding of your granddaughter."

She twisted the handkerchief in her hands, obviously torn between being with her family and the fear some calamity might descend while she was gone.

"I did promise Betsy I would be with her."

"And that is precisely what you shall do."

"But—"

"The carriage is waiting at the door, and you know how I dislike having my cattle left standing," he interrupted with a stern glance.

"It does not seem right." She gave a small sniff. "Who will see to you?"

He resisted the urge to glance down and see if he was still in short coats. The elder members of the staff never seemed to realize that he had actually left the nursery.

"Mrs. Chester will take care of the meals, and there are Maggie and Liza for the cleaning," he soothed. "Besides, it is not as if I intend to do any entertaining."

The round countenance abruptly hardened with disdain. "You may not intend to entertain, but you know the Vicar and his wife will be landing on your doorstep the moment they learn you have returned. Mrs. Allison must always be first to know the latest gossip."

Edward hid a smile at the woman's sour tone. There were few in the neighborhood who had not run afoul of Mrs. Allison's sharp tongue and habit of spreading about the most ridiculous tales.

"And when have I ever possessed the least amount of gossip to share?"

"Mark my words, without me here she will force her company upon you and will be quizzing you on everything from the Prince to the latest color of ribbons to every female who might have batted a lash in your direction. Not to mention devouring every biscuit in the house."

Edward froze at her unwitting words.

Every female who batted a lash in your direction . . .

Bianca.

Hell's teeth. It had been a week since he had last seen Bianca. A week during which he had done his best to struggle through his tangled emotions and decide what the future might hold for them.

A perfectly reasonable means of making the proper decision.

Unfortunately, not a moment passed when he was not battling the fierce need to rush back to London. He ached for her with a force that denied logic.

"I am perfectly capable of giving Mrs. Allison a short shift if necessary," he muttered, not surprised when the housekeeper regarded him with a searching gaze.

Although the staff had been careful not to probe into his abrupt return from London, they all were aware that something had occurred. It was in the manner they tiptoed about him, as if they feared he might suddenly combust.

"Capable, perhaps, but not willing," she murmured.

Taking her arm, he firmly led her toward the door. "You can trust in me."

"Well, I suppose it shall only be for a few days."

"Downstairs with you," he commanded.

Entering the hall, the housekeeper swiveled about to stab him with a stern frown.

"You are to eat every morsel that Margaret puts before you, and do not be wearing your good boots to the field. Oh, and if Mrs. Horwitt drops by one of her sponge cakes, you are to thank her and throw it directly in the rubbish. Her mind is not at all what it was, and there is no telling what might be in—"

"Good lord, enough." Edward chuckled as he waved his hand toward the front door. "Now shoo."

"It is good to have you home, sir." She reached up to pat his cheek as if he were no more than five. "We have all missed you."

His heart warmed at her obvious affection. However much his heart might urge him to return to London, it truly was good to be home.

"As I have missed you." He squeezed her fingers before gently stepping back. "Now go before we both embarrass ourselves and break out in maudlin tears."

Seemingly convinced that the roof would not tumble down the moment she stepped foot outside the door and that Edward was not secretly plotting to have her replaced, Mrs. Green at last turned and firmly headed down the hall.

Edward heaved a small breath of relief as he abandoned the servants' quarters and headed upstairs to his study.

There were endless stacks of bills and estate accounts awaiting his attention. Thus far he had accomplished little more than shuffling them from one pile to another. And of course his steward had left a list of various repairs he wished to begin as soon as Edward offered his approval.

Today he intended to complete one task.

The thought was forefront in his mind as he entered the small room that was nearly overwhelmed by the heavy walnut desk and shelves that were stuffed with every farming book, manual, and article he could collect. Unfortunately, his feet did not lead him toward the cluttered desk. Instead he discovered himself standing at the window as he blindly gazed at the fertile fields and rolling meadows.

It was a view that always filled his heart with quiet pride. It might not be the largest, most profitable estate in England. But it was his.

Today, however, he did not even notice the tidy cottages or recently cleared hedgerows. Instead his thoughts were once again wrenched back to London and the woman he had left behind.

Leaning against the thick wood of the window frame, Edward allowed time to slip past, barely noting when Mrs. Chester brought his tea tray and left it to grow cold on the study.

He was still standing there when he heard the footsteps entering the room and the unmistakable sound of someone clearing their throat.

A grimace twisted his features as he kept his back firmly turned. "Thank you for the tray, Mrs. Chester, but I am not hungry at the moment."

"You really should eat, you know," a soft female voice urged. "Your cook will be very disappointed to find her offering left untouched."

Edward briefly squeezed his eyes shut. Had he at last tumbled over the edge into madness?

Was he hearing voices now?

If he turned, would there be no one there?

His question was answered as a familiar, unmistakable heat swirled through his body.

His reaction was real enough. Which could only mean that Bianca was real as well.

Waiting until he was certain he had managed to hide his shock, Edward at last slowly turned to confront the woman standing in the center of the room.

His breath caught at the sight of her. He had not forgotten her beauty. What man in his right mind could?

The perfect features, her exotic midnight eyes and raven curls. The manner in which the crimson carriage gown clung to her slender curves.

God knew they had haunted his thoughts often enough.

But it was the jolt of sheer pleasure at the sight of her that he had underestimated.

Thank God his muscles had clenched so tight he was unable to rush across the worn carpet and haul her into his arms.

"Bianca." His voice came out shockingly flat. Strange considering his insides felt as if they had been tossed in a churn.

"Edward."

"What the devil are you doing here?"

Unease fluttered over her pale countenance before she determinedly squared her shoulders.

"Obviously I came to see you."

His shock began to recede, and a welcome dose of logic managed to wiggle its way through the fog. He had been so caught off guard by her arrival it had not occurred to him how it had been accomplished.

"Alone?"

"Yes."

"Good God." His brows snapped together. "Have you lost your wits? The Duke will have me hung from the rafters. Or worse . . . gelded."

She shrugged, not nearly as concerned with the danger to his manhood as she should be.

"My father and mother left yesterday for Surrey, where they await my brother's impending heir. As far as they are aware, I am currently with Aunt Winifred in London."

"And when they discover you are not?"

Moving toward the desk, she absently removed her chip bonnet and gloves and tossed them aside. His mouth went dry at the graceful sway of her hips. Among the shabby furnishings, she glowed like the finest jewel.

"I assure you my parents are far too preoccupied to take note of my absence, and my aunt is far too relieved not be forced to accompany me about town to question my sudden decision to join my parents." She turned back to eye him with a guarded expression. "No one will know I am here."

No one will know . . .

For a crazed moment, his body threatened open revolt.

The mere thought of having her alone and at his mercy stirred a primitive part of him that he had not even known he possessed.

Sucking in a deep breath, he grappled to retrieve his fading wits. Dammit. He did not even know why she was here.

Besides which, the last thing he needed was a bloodthirsty duke landing on his doorstep. Especially not one that might potentially be his father-in-law.

"This is madness. I cannot believe that even you would dare such a thing," he scolded.

"What did you expect me to do? You were the one to flee London."

His pride instantly rebelled at the implication of cowardice. "I did not flee."

"No?"

"I have responsibilities here that cannot be entirely ignored."

The dark gaze never wavered from his stiff expression. "You could not even bother to say good-bye?"

His lips twisted. "I was in something of a hurry."

"And you wanted to hurt me?" she demanded softly.

"Is that even possible?"

She seemed to wince at his harsh words. "More than I ever imagined. Why else would I be here?"

He sharply turned away. He had been so bitterly hurt on the last occasion they were together that he had been capable of smothering his instinctive urge to toss good sense to the wind and simply gather her in his arms and never let her go.

Now he had to struggle to maintain even the hint of aloof command.

God, to have her here.

In his home, where he had imagined her being a hundred times before.

The reality unnerved him to the very depths of his soul.

"I am no longer foolish enough to even hazard a guess at what is in your mind."

"Edward," she breathed softly, making his heart clench with fierce need.

Heat and temptation stabbed through his body as she stepped close enough behind him to touch his back. Hell's teeth. He had to get away long enough to collect his composure.

He could not possibly carry on a reasonable conversation while his body was thick and aching to possess her.

For the moment, retreat was the better part of valor.

"I must go."

"Edward . . ."

CHAPTER SIXTEEN

Bianca stood in the middle of the study and battled the flood of tears.

Dear God, what did he want from her?

Had she not dared her father's wrath, her reputation, and her very future to come here and prove her love to him?

Had she not offered her heart to him on a silver platter despite her own considerable pride?

Did he have to be so bloody well impossible?

For long moments she struggled to control her raw emotions. She wanted nothing more than to flee back to London and salvage what was left of her pride.

Or perhaps to search out Edward and thump his thick head.

In the end she did neither.

As her initial surge of embarrassment began to fade, her common sense slowly returned.

She had caught Edward off guard. And he was not a gentleman who handled surprises well.

He liked to ponder every situation with great care. And heaven knew he would not make a decision without considering it from every angle possible.

Impulsive he was not.

If she returned to London without at least giving him the opportunity to soften his feelings toward her, she might very well live with regrets the rest of her life.

Gathering up her bonnet and gloves, she forced her heavy feet to carry her back down to the lower floor. Once in the foyer, however, she was forced to pause in annoyance.

Damn and blast.

She was a young lady accustomed to having a small battalion of servants to see to her every need. When she traveled, her path was smoothed by expensive carriages and nights spent with acquaintances who made every effort to ensure her comfort.

Now, with the post chaise she had hired to bring her to Kent gone and her luggage piled upon the front step, she was stuck in the ignoble position of seeking out the housekeeper to assist her in traveling to the nearest village.

Once there she would hire rooms at the local inn. Assuming that they would be willing to allow a young lady without family or servant to remain beneath their roof.

Her features tightened as she turned on her heel and headed toward the back of the house. She reached the tidy kitchens without stumbling over a servant, and, stepping upon the flagstones that had been ruthlessly scrubbed, she took a moment to appreciate the scent of roasting beef and freshly baked bread. Oh . . . ambrosia.

Her mouth began to water. It had been hours since her light luncheon at the Posting Inn, and she abruptly realized just how hungry she was.

An apple tart would surely hold her over until she could find rooms for the night.

Following her nose, she had taken several steps toward a table laden with various treats when a slender, gray-haired woman bustled in from a side pantry.

They both halted in surprise, the older woman hastily

wiping her flour-dusted hands on her apron before giving an awkward bob.

"Oh, forgive me, miss, you gave me a right start. I'm not accustomed to having visitors in my kitchen."

Sighing at the loss of the apple tart, Bianca forced her most charming smile to her lips. Soon enough she intended to be mistress here. It was important that she win the respect and confidence of the staff.

"I am searching for the housekeeper."

A portion of the cook's unease faded. No doubt she had heard the rumors a young lady had come to visit her employer and was relieved that Bianca was not there to make demands for some lavish meal to be prepared in her honor.

"Mrs. Green? You just missed her."

"Has she gone to the village?"

"No, miss. Left to help her granddaughter git wed over in Oakview."

Bianca felt her smile falter. "Oh."

"Was you needing to speak with her?"

Damn and blast. The day seemed to be going from bad to worse.

"I did hope to catch her before she left," she muttered.

"Aye, well, she was in a right state over leaving the master in the lurch, but he insisted," the cook babbled, seemingly unaware of Bianca's dismay. "Never one to think of himself."

Bianca was not at all surprised by the woman's obvious loyalty. Edward had always spoken of his staff more as family than servants.

"No, Lord Harrington is a very kind gentleman."

Moving toward the wooden table, the cook began to efficiently chop a pile of carrots.

"Too kind for his own good most times. What he needs is a wife to look after him. There are several lovely maidens in the neighborhood. We all hope he will choose one before the summer is done."

Bianca suddenly stiffened. The mere thought of Edward married to another was enough to make her foam at the mouth.

Edward belonged to her. No one else.

"He will not be wedding any local maiden." Wincing as the cook abruptly glanced up at her harsh tone, she firmly forced the smile back to her lips. It was not this woman's fault that Edward was making her batty. "How long will . . . Mrs. Green be gone?"

"At least a fortnight."

Bianca bit her lip, considering whether to simply head to the stables and demand that a carriage be prepared. Surely she would not be forced to haul her bags to the nearest inn?

"I see."

The cook heaved a long-suffering sigh. "I hate to admit it, but she shall be sorely missed with the master home. Maggie is a fine girl, but she has her head in the clouds. Mr. Sinclair . . . begging pardon, Lord Harrington, has only to glance in her direction and she is dropping a plate or tripping over her feet."

Bianca possessed full sympathy for the poor maid. Edward had that affect on most women.

"He is rather a handsome gentleman."

A measure of pride settled upon the thin countenance. "The most handsome about."

"Yes."

Eyeing her with open curiosity, the cook tilted her head to one side. "Is there something I can be doing for you?"

Bianca glanced about the small kitchen. She should be on her way to the stables. Soon enough it would be dark, and she disliked the thought of entering the inn when the taproom would be filled with curious tenants and drunken travelers.

Far better to be safely tucked in a private chamber before the locals began to descend.

Somehow, however, she could not make her feet budge. Whether it was because of her reluctance to leave Edward or because of the cook's insinuation that a devious horde of local females was lurking about in the hopes of becoming Countess of Harrington was impossible to say.

What if she left and Edward commanded his servants to deny her entrance? She could be only a handful of miles away and never set eyes upon him.

Obviously the only means to ensure that Edward could not thrust her from his life was to remain firmly entrenched beneath his roof.

He could hardly avoid her then.

And she knew precisely how to accomplish her goal.

Squaring her shoulders, Bianca called upon her years of rigid training. If nothing else, a duke's daughter learned at an early age how to command others.

"Actually, there is." She deliberately glanced about the kitchen with an air of authority. "It is obvious that you are in need of assistance. I shall take over the duties of house-keeper until Mrs. Green can return."

The cook gave a startled cough, her widened gaze skimming over Bianca's gown that had no doubt cost more than the servant earned in a year.

"You, miss?"

"Well, it would be more a matter of supervising the house-hold," she conceded.

"But—"

"Do not fret, I shall see to everything. But first I must have my bags brought upstairs." She knew only boldness would win the day. If the cook had time to consider the strange turn of events, she might very well demand Edward's approval. "Could you send someone to fetch them from the front yard?"

The woman frowned. "You will be staying here?"

Bianca attempted to look surprised. "But of course."

"And Lord Harrington . . ."

"You many leave Lord Harrington to me. Now, if you will send a footman to fetch my bags, I will choose which bed-chamber I prefer."

On the point of turning away, Bianca was halted as the woman scurried forward, her expression troubled.

"Perhaps I should speak with the master first."

Bianca lifted her brows, her heart racing. She was taking an incredible risk. Who knew how Edward would react to her brazen daring? Still, she could not leave. Not while there was the smallest hope she could earn back his love.

"Well, if you feel you must do so, but we both know just how proud men can be. He will never admit to needing the help of a woman even if it means being utterly miserable for the next fortnight."

The cook paused. Bianca had struck her at her most vulnerable spot. She would do anything to ensure that her master was happy.

"You are friends with his lordship?"

Bianca allowed a secretive smile to curl her lips. The sort of smile that revealed just how intimately acquainted she was with Edward.

"The closest of friends."

A hint of redness touched the thin countenance. "Oh."

It was less than an hour later that Edward returned to the study to find Bianca.

He had not intended to be gone such a length of time. But after a brisk walk through the garden he was at last forced to take a quick dip in the freezing cold lake to gain control of his wayward passions.

Not that he was truly rid of them, he had conceded. At least not where Bianca was concerned. He would desire her until he drew his last breath.

But at least he might be able to have a reasonable conversation without constantly imagining her naked on his bed with him atop her.

Pulling his clothes back on, he had smoothed back his damp hair and hurried back to the house. As he entered the study, however, he halted in painful shock.

Bianca had disappeared.

Pure panic raced through his heart as he charged down the stairs and glanced at the front lawn. There was nothing to be seen. No carriage, no bags, no beautiful woman attired in crimson.

Where the devil had the woman gone?

Had she thought his abrupt departure was a rejection?

Could she believe that he had wanted her to leave before they could even discuss their troubles?

No. It was impossible.

But even as he assured himself that Bianca would never be so foolish, he was turning toward a side door that would lead to the stables.

By God, he would chase her down if necessary.

She was not leaving Kent until he discovered precisely what was in her heart.

Not even if he had to chain her to his bed.

That dangerous heat threatened to return at the delightful image of Bianca sprawled upon his bed, her white limbs spread on the sheets and her raven curls spilling over the pillows. . . .

No. First things first.

He had to capture his elusive fiancée before he could begin making his fantasies come true.

Nearly at the door, he was startled by the sound of rapid footsteps following in his wake. His heart gave a sudden leap as he turned, fully expecting to see the delectable woman who had become a vital part of his life.

He was doomed to disappointment as he recognized the

thin form of his cook. Biting back his frustration, he waited for the servant to join him.

"Sir, if I may have a moment," she said in flustered tones.

He held up his hand to halt the familiar complaints of the butcher's outlandish prices, the gardener's lack of skill with growing root vegetables, and the need to replace the ancient stove.

"Mrs. Chester. Have you seen Lady Bianca?"

She blinked at his abrupt tone, a red flush staining her cheeks. "Your . . . lady friend?"

Edward gave a lift of his brows at her strange manner. "Yes."

"Aye." The servant wrung her hands together. "She is in the blue room, I believe, sir. Maggie is unpacking her bags."

Sharp, biting relief flared through him.

She had not disappeared.

She was here.

Tidily within his grasp.

"The blue room?"

The painful color deepened. "I did think it odd she would be staying here. I mean, a lady like that, and you a bachelor. But she did insist that she would be taking over Mrs. Green's position and that you wouldn't be minding. I hope I did not do wrong, sir."

His housekeeper? The daughter of a duke?

A slow smile of anticipation curled his lips.

Deep in his heart he had known all along that Bianca would be his wife. No matter how wounded his pride might be. Or how difficult the task of overcoming her infatuation for Lord Aldron. Had his father not taught him that anything of value was worth fighting for? The moment he had seen Bianca standing in his home, he had known she was worth that fight.

No man could ever love her as he did, of that he was convinced.

And certainly no man would ever pledge to keep her as happy.

Still, a small part of plain Edward Sinclair remained within him.

Although he could offer Bianca a dozen estates and town-houses to suit her mood, this tiny farm would always hold a dear place in his heart. This was who he was.

Simple, uncomplicated, and tied closely to the earth.

In fairness to Bianca it would be perhaps best for her to see him as he truly was. Not the Earl of Harrington. Not a sophisticated gentleman of society. But Edward, gentleman farmer.

A few days together would surely allow her to determine if he were indeed a man she could love.

And, of course, it would no doubt be quite amusing to watch her play the role of housekeeper.

"Sir?" Mrs. Chester prompted, a concerned frown marring her brow. "Did I do wrong?"

Collecting his scattered thoughts, he reached out to pat the woman's bony shoulder. "Not at all. Thank you, Mrs. Chester."

She breathed a sigh of relief. "Aye, sir."

Indifferent to the knowledge that he was revealing just how anxious he was to be with his wife-to-be, Edward brushed past his servant and hurried up the carpeted stairs. The staff was bound to be abuzz with curiosity at having Bianca beneath his roof, but soon enough they would learn the truth.

And he did not doubt that they would soon come to love her as he did.

Bypassing his own chambers, Edward moved to those that had once belonged to his mother. Somehow it seemed fitting that Bianca would have chosen them.

Stepping over the threshold, he paused as he regarded Bianca standing beside the window that led to a small balcony.

The delicate blue and ivory of the room suited her to perfection, and his breath lodged in his throat.

He wanted her so desperately.

But only if she could be happy as his wife.

Perhaps sensing his presence, Bianca slowly turned and regarded him with a wary gaze.

"Edward. You startled me."

A smile touched his lips as he strolled toward the center of the room. "Imagine my own surprise. I did not realize I was in such desperate need of a housekeeper."

A delicate color touched her cheeks even as her chin tilted to that familiar stubborn angle.

"It is obvious you shall be in need of my services," she informed him in defiant tones. "A gentleman never fully realizes the effort that it takes to run an efficient household."

His smile widened. "And you do?"

"Of course. I have been trained all my life to be the mistress of a household."

"This is hardly a ducal palace," he pointed out with a wave about the room. No doubt her own bedchamber was as large as his entire home. "Your talents are bound to be wasted."

"I think I should be the judge of that."

He took another step closer, sharply aware of the large bed just a handful of steps away.

It was a fortunate thing the lake was just a short distance down the path, he ruefully acknowledged. He had a feeling that he was going to be using it with great frequency over the next few days.

"Actually, as the owner of this estate, I believe I should be the judge of that," he corrected gently.

She stiffened, almost as if expecting a blow. "Do you intend to have me thrown out of your house?"

His smile widened. Not even a French battalion would be capable of forcing him to allow her to leave this estate.

"After you traveled such a great distance to visit me? I am not quite so lacking in manners."

She searched his expression as she attempted to assure herself he was not playing some cruel jest.

"Then I shall be allowed to remain?" she at last demanded.

He hid his flare of amusement at her arrogant tones. She sounded far more commanding than pleading.

He caught and held the dark gaze. "Is that what you desire?"

She stepped forward. Close enough to surround him in her honeysuckle scent.

"All I desire is to be with you so that I can prove my love."

He was melting. She had not so much as touched him, and his entire body was aflame.

"How?" he rasped, his hands lifting to tenderly brush back the curls that lay against her cheeks. "By polishing silver and counting linen?"

Her own breathing became uneven as she stepped even closer. "By whatever means necessary."

"Whatever means?"

"Yes."

His hands slid downward, stroking the bare skin of her neck before slipping down her shoulders. He sucked in a deep breath. The feel of her warm and so utterly feminine beneath his fingers was sheer bliss.

"That is rather dangerously vague, muirnin." He gently tugged until she was pressed fully to his aching body. "What if the means I chose include carrying you to that bed?"

She did not hesitate as her arms lifted to wrap about his neck. "I would suggest that you close the door. The servants would be very shocked to discover their master in bed with the housekeeper."

His knees threatened to buckle as his arms wrapped about

her slender waist. It had only been a week, but it felt like an eternity since he had held her near.

"Dear God . . . I believe you truly have bewitched me," he muttered as he lowered his head to stroke his lips over her satin-soft cheeks.

Her taste filled his senses, and with a low moan he turned his head to claim her lips in a branding kiss. God, not a moment had passed that he had not hungered for her. Her touch, her smile, her mere presence.

She shivered as her lips readily parted, and Edward stroked his tongue into the damp heat of her mouth. Heavens, yes. Desire flared through his body with clawing insistence. He knew precisely how it felt to hold her naked in his arms. To slowly thrust himself into the tightness of her body.

It was paradise.

His hands tightened on her hips, pressing her against the hardness of his ready erection. With a restless moan, he nipped at her full bottom lip and scattered hungry kisses over her upturned countenance.

He wanted to devour her. To lay her on the bed and claim her as his own in the most primitive manner possible.

"Edward," she husked, tilting back her head as he trailed his lips down the vulnerable curve of her neck.

Just for a moment all shreds of sanity threatened to be overwhelmed by the wild blaze of passion that raced through his blood.

What did it matter why Bianca was here?

She was in his arms and perfectly willing. What more did he need?

Then, the more practical part of his nature, a part that had always been something of a bother, reared its ugly head, and his lips stilled upon her skin.

Hell's teeth.

She had been in his home little more than an hour and already he was ready to toss all to the wind for the pleasure of making love to this woman.

Stifling a moan, he reluctantly pulled back to regard her with brooding regret.

"This was not what I intended."

Her lashes slowly lifted to reveal eyes darkened with desire. "Why?"

Against his will, his gaze dropped to the fullness of her lips, reddened by his kisses.

It did nothing to ease the tension clutching at his body.

"We still have much to settle between us."

His words were perfectly reasonable, but with a sudden movement Bianca was thrusting herself away from his body, her expression one of annoyance.

"You doubt me? Even after I have come all this distance to be with you?"

He gave a slow shake of his head. "I am not entirely certain you know your own heart, Bianca."

Her eyes briefly closed, as if she were battling the urge to throttle him.

"You are truly the most stubborn of men."

"You are not the first to make such an observation. I prefer to think of myself as cautious."

Her frown revealed precisely what she thought of his cautious nature.

"You are fortunate there is no well nearby," she muttered.

Edward blinked before a wry smile touched his lips. "Is that a threat, muirnin?"

"Yes."

"Bianca . . ." His hand reached out to touch her, only to halt at the sound of Maggie bellowing from the bottom of the stairs.

"Sir, Mr. Black has arrived with the drapes you ordered from his shop."

Edward grimaced, knowing Bianca must be wondering if his household was one of savages.

He was quite certain that the Duke of Lockharte would insist upon the finest staff in all of England.

"I fear I must go. Maggie will continue to screech like a fishwife until I make an appearance."

Surprisingly, Bianca reached out to grasp his arm before he could make his retreat, her eyes narrowed.

"Actually, I believe this is my duty. If you will excuse me?"

She moved to sweep past him with a proud set of her shoulders. A smile curved his lips.

She looked every inch the daughter of a duke about to march into battle.

"A moment, Bianca," he murmured.

Turning, she gave a lift of her brow. "Yes?"

Before she could guess his intention, he was stealing a swift, delicious kiss.

"Take care with Mr. Black," he whispered against her lips. "He will attempt to rob me blind if you are not firm with him."

With a flustered motion, she stepped back and pressed her hands to her stomach.

"I am perfectly capable of dealing with merchants, my lord," she informed him, although her tones were not nearly so haughty as she no doubt intended.

"Good." He brushed a finger down the length of her arrogant nose. "I should hate to have my accounts thrown into disarray your first day as my housekeeper." With a bow, he moved to the door and stepped into the hall. He paused to glance over his shoulder with a wicked smile. "I have a new plow being delivered today that I wish to assess in the fields before I order more. I shall expect a hearty dinner to keep up my strength."

He was moving down the hall before she could reach anything convenient to toss at his head and whistling a merry jig he passed by the startled Maggie as she climbed the stairs.

He could not recall a day that had seemed brighter.

CHAPTER SEVENTEEN

The plow was all that Edward had hoped it would be. Sleek and compact rather than following the bulky lines of the past. With this a tenant would be able to till the fields at a much swifter pace and allow him to take on additional land.

A benefit to his people and himself.

Of course, he was always a cautious man, and, collecting his tools from the outbuilding, he set about disassembling the plow to ensure that the various parts were sturdy enough to endure years of labor.

He had nearly finished when a shadow fell over his bent form and he glanced up to discover Joseph regarding him with a hint of amusement on his round, ruddy countenance.

"Is everything . . . well, sir?" he asked as he squatted beside the plow.

Edward gave a lift of his brows. Despite their differences in station, the two had grown up side by side on the estate. As lads they had fished, hunted, and indulged in endless mischief together. Over the years their friendship had endured.

"It could not be better, Joseph, why do you ask?"

"I have not seen you smile since your return from

London," he said bluntly. "This afternoon you have done nothing but grin like a madman."

Edward's smile merely widened. Now he comprehended why the tenants had been glancing at him as if they feared he had become batty.

"Ah, well, there is nothing like a well-made machine to make a gentleman happy," he said with an assumed nonchalance.

Joseph's dark eyes twinkled with amusement. "Actually, there is one thing."

"And what is that?"

"A well-made woman." He tilted his head to one side, his expression one of curiosity. "The gossips have already spread the rumors that a beautiful woman has come to stay at the manor house."

Edward gave a low chuckle, his heart filling with warmth at the mere thought of Bianca.

"More beautiful than any other woman."

"I might have to disagree with that," his friend warned.

Abruptly recalling the return of Joseph's beloved, he reached out to lay his hand on his friend's shoulder.

"How is Sally?"

A hint of sadness touched the ruddy features before the placid smile returned.

"London changed her, and there's no denying that, but not all for the bad," he admitted. "She no longer frets to be free of the village or believes that a quiet, comfortable life is for those too dull to dream of better. She has even begun stitching her marriage gown."

Edward felt a genuine surge of happiness. Joseph had loved Sally since they had left the cradle. It seemed inconceivable that they would not be together.

"But that is wonderful."

"Yes."

There was a pause as Edward dropped his hand and

considered all that had occurred since he had left the estate for London.

"And you, Joseph?" he at last asked softly.

"Me?"

"How do you feel after knowing she left you for another?"

Joseph flinched, but he did not seem offended by the blunt question.

"I will not deny that it cut me deep."

"But you have forgiven her?"

He gave an awkward shrug. "It was never about forgiveness. I love her. That is all."

Edward stilled. So simple, and yet so eloquent. Joseph loved and that was enough.

"What of trust?" he could not help but probe.

"Love and trust must go together. Neither can survive without the other."

Edward gave a slow nod. "You are a wise man, Joseph," he murmured.

Joseph gave a short laugh as he rose to his feet and held out his hand to Edward.

"Wise enough to send you back to the manor and your beautiful guest before you manage to mangle this new plow beyond repair."

Placing his hand in Joseph's grip, he allowed himself to be yanked upright. Already his stomach was clenching with anticipation of being in the company of Bianca.

"I suppose I could be convinced."

Joseph gave his hand a shake before stepping back with a grin. "It is good to see you smile again."

"And you as well, old friend."

"You sent home my heart. I can do nothing but smile."

"She is a fortunate woman to have you."

"As fortunate as yours."

Edward turned to head back toward the house. He wanted

to be near Bianca. To assure himself that she was not just a figment of his imagination.

To convince himself that she was precisely where she belonged.

Entering the manor, he barely resisted the urge to seek out Bianca in all his dirt. Sanity thankfully returned and he forced himself to enter his chambers and have himself properly bathed and attired in dark breeches and a coat of blue superfine. He even chose a crisp length of linen to style in an elegant knot about his neck.

A splash of cologne and he was on his way to the dining room, where his place was set in isolated splendor upon the glossy walnut table.

A frown touched his brow as he noted the silver candelabra and large bowl of fresh flowers upon a sideboard. Obviously the sophisticated touch of Bianca, but where the devil was she?

He glanced up as Maggie entered the room bearing a tray heavy with platters of fresh trout in cream, steamed carrots, and potatoes with basil.

He took the tray from her hands to set it on the table, not surprised when she gave a startled squeak. The poor girl was always jumping or stammering when in his presence.

"Maggie, have you seen my guest?" he asked softly, so as not to send the maid into a panic.

"Oh . . . aye, sir."

"And?" he prompted.

"Sir?"

He firmly held on to his thinning patience. "Where might I find her?"

The girl flushed as she stumbled backward. "I . . . I believe she be in the conservatory, your lordship."

"Please set another plate at the table. I shall return in a moment."

"Yes. At once."

The maid bobbed a hasty curtsy before rushing back toward the kitchens. Edward did not bother to watch her retreat as he left the dining room and made a direct path to the conservatory his mother had constructed just off the garden.

He supposed he should not be surprised by Bianca's absence from his table, he acknowledged ruefully. She was determined to play the role of his housekeeper. At least when it suited her purpose.

The door had been left open, and with silent steps Edward moved through the banks of flowers to where Bianca stood arranging a large vase of tulips.

He halted as he was assaulted by the scent of flowers and sweet woman, the memory of the night spent in her father's grotto nearly sending him to his knees.

Dear lord, would there ever come a day when he could glance upon this woman and not feel as if his body were being flooded with pleasure? When he would not ache to carry her off to his bed and hold her in his arms?

A smile curved his lips.

No, such a day would never, ever come.

Moving forward again, he did not halt until he stepped directly behind her, rather surprised to discover she was humming beneath her breath.

"Very lovely, muirnin," he murmured. "I do hope those are for my bedchamber."

With a squeak that could have rivaled Maggie's, the slender woman spun about to regard him with flashing eyes.

"Good Lord, do you make a habit of frightening your staff in such a fashion?"

He brushed a wayward curl from her cheek. "It does tend to keep them on their toes."

"It is a wonder they have not all had heart failure."

He smiled without the least hint of apology as his finger stroked down the curve of her neck and halted just above the plunge of her neckline. For a breathless moment, he allowed himself to savor the feel of her rapidly pounding heart.

He did not believe for a moment that its frantic pace was due to fear.

"There is only one heart I care about."

Her breath caught, but before he could take proper advantage she was stepping backward to smooth her hands over her skirts.

"I assumed you would be enjoying your dinner. Was the food not to your satisfaction?"

He leaned against the table she had been working upon. "Mrs. Chester has prepared a meal fit for a king. Or at least for an earl and the daughter of a duke." He paused to stab her with a knowing gaze. "Which leads me to wonder why you are hiding among the flowers instead of sitting at my table where you belong."

Her thick lashes fluttered downward to shield her expressive eyes. "A housekeeper does not eat at the master's table."

"This housekeeper does," he informed her.

"Edward . . ."

"Will you come of your own accord or must I carry you?"

Her gaze jerked upward at his soft threat. "You would not dare."

Too hungry to bother with a protracted argument that he fully intended to win, Edward took matters into his own hands.

Or actually his arms.

With a smooth motion, he had moved forward to scoop her off her feet, not even noting when she smacked him on the chest for his blatant manhandling.

"Edward, put me down this moment," she commanded in imperious tones. Then, as they left the conservatory and entered the main house, her eyes widened in horror. "Edward . . . someone will see."

He smiled at her unease. For all her bold and adventurous nature, she was still a proper lady at heart.

"You will walk with me willingly?" he demanded as he halted upon the threshold.

"If it is the only means of halting this foolishness."

Slowly he lowered her to her feet, his expression revealing he would not hesitate to chase her down should she be foolish enough to bolt.

Preferring dignity to flight, she walked at his side with her nose tilted in the air. She did not even balk when he led her to the dining room and settled her in a chair next to his own.

"There, this is not so terrible, is it?" he murmured, reaching to take her plate and filling it with the bounty. "Allow me."

A reluctant amusement softened her features as he set the plate before her.

"Good heavens, I cannot possibly eat all this."

Taking his own share, he allowed his gaze to lower over her pretty rose gown. "You have grown thin."

She reached for her glass of wine. "I have always been slender."

"Bianca, I am not such an idiot as to believe you would offer your patronage to a seamstress who cannot fit you properly."

Her glass landed back on the table with a distinct thud. "I suppose you wish me to confess that I have been pining for you like a sickly mooncalf?"

"Never." He reached to grasp her hand and pressed his lips to her fingers. "The last thing I would ever wish is for you to be unhappy. That is why—"

He bit off his words before he could reveal his deepest vulnerabilities, not surprised when she regarded him with a puzzled frown.

"Why what?"

"Let us enjoy the meal." Nipping her fingers, he gently

laid them back onto the table. "We would not wish to wound Mrs. Chester's sensibilities by not appreciating her efforts."

Bianca wished to ponder the odd manner that Edward had so abruptly halted his words. She was certain that he had been on the point of revealing something important. Something that might give her a hint as to why he remained so elusive.

But lulled by the delicious food and Edward's charming stories of his childhood, she found herself simply enjoying the rare treat of being alone with the man who had captured her heart.

She was fascinated by the play of emotions over his handsome features as he spoke of his parents and their obvious love. His self-deprecating humor when he shared his youthful pranks. And most of all, his deep, unwavering devotion to the place he called home.

The dinner passed so swiftly she was caught off guard when Edward quit his chair and politely escorted her to a small library toward the back of the house.

Stepping across the threshold, she glanced about the room, her eyes widening at the endless shelves that were laden from floor to ceiling with leather-bound books.

"Good heavens," she breathed, moving to stroke her fingers over the rich leather.

Strolling over the faded carpet, Edward poured two glasses of brandy from the decanter on the desk before returning to her side and pressing one of the glasses into her fingers.

"My one indulgence has always been fine books. I have been collecting them since I was a child."

Bianca took a tentative sip of the amber spirit, pleased when she managed to swallow the liquid fire without coughing. It splashed into her stomach with a flare of warmth that she found oddly pleasant.

"You have much in common with my father," she murmured.

"He is a collector?"

She smiled with wry humor. "My mother has accused him of devoting more care to his musty manuscripts than to her. His library in Surrey is one of the largest private collections in all of England."

He leaned against the shelves, his eyes darkening as they drifted over her slender form.

"You are not attempting to seduce me with the lure of rare books, are you?"

Whispers of desire feathered down her spine. He was standing so close. Close enough she could almost feel his strong hands stroking over her bare skin. The taste of his lips. The heat of his body.

She shuddered. Heavens, but she ached for him.

"Is that how you desire to be seduced?" she demanded, her voice already husky with need.

"There is nothing quite so intoxicating as the scent of aging leather." His hand lifted to trail down the curve of her neck. Her breath rasped through the heavy air as he reached the pulse beating wildly at the base of her neck. "Unless of course it happens to be warm honeysuckle on ivory skin. Now, that is a temptation no man can resist."

Tension shimmered between them as their gazes locked and held. Bianca was hardly a lady of vast experience, but even she recognized that matters were slipping down a dangerous slope.

"I . . ." She was forced to halt and clear her throat. "Did your plow satisfy you?"

His brooding gaze lowered to watch his fingers trail along the cut of her bodice. Bianca bit her lower lip as a dark wave of pleasure surged through her body.

"In truth, I found it difficult to concentrate upon something so mundane as a plow," he husked. "I had other things upon my mind."

"What other things would those be?"

"Your unexpected arrival," he readily confessed, those damnable fingers wreaking havoc as they lingered upon the curve of her breast. "The realization of just how desperately I have missed you."

She froze in surprise. She had not expected his blunt revelation.

"Have you?" She frowned with uncertainty. "I thought . . ."

"What?"

"I thought you were determined never to forgive me."

Something that might have been regret rippled over his countenance. And then, without warning, his hand was shifting to gently cup her cheek.

"Bianca, I am not going to deny that I was wounded when I overheard your conversation with Lord Aldron. The thought you might have loved the man and lied to me . . ." His jaw tightened with remembered pain. "Well, it made me a bit crazed."

"Yes, I had noticed."

He smiled wryly. "Of course I have only to be in your presence to be a bit crazed. I barely recognize myself when you are near."

Bianca knew precisely what he meant. Since she had tossed herself into his arms, nothing had been the same.

"Will you listen to me now?" she demanded softly.

"There is no need. Your past is your past and not for me to judge." His gaze ran a restless path over her upturned countenance. "It is your future that interests me."

"I want to tell you of Stephen," she persisted, knowing that the horrid man would haunt them forever unless she could banish his memory.

He grimaced. "I am not certain I wish to hear."

"Please, Edward. It is important to me."

"Very well." With obvious reluctance he dropped his arms and moved back to the table to pour himself another shot of brandy. Only after he had emptied the glass did he turn back to regard her with a guarded expression. "What is it you wish to tell me?"

Bianca had waited for this moment for days.

She had plotted and schemed and risked her entire future for the opportunity to confront Edward and force him to believe that Lord Aldron meant nothing in her life.

But beneath his steady regard she found it oddly difficult to discover the words that would convince him of her sincerity.

"This is not so simple as I hoped."

His expression did not ease, but he seemed to take pity upon her. "Tell me how the two of you met."

She gave a lift of her hands. "It was not nearly so dramatic as our own meeting. Stephen attended a charity luncheon that I hosted, and he offered to escort me to a pantomime that was being held that evening."

"And you went with him alone?"

Looking back, she realized it had been foolish. She had trusted Stephen with no knowledge of his true character, preferring to be blinded by his smooth charm. It was a wonder he had not attempted to force her into marriage from the beginning.

Of course, at the time he no doubt assumed that he would have her in a more conventional manner. It was never wise to anger a duke unless absolutely necessary.

"I was weary of my father's determination to keep me sheltered from the world. I felt as if I were smothering, and Stephen offered hope of salvation." She winced at the rather pathetic explanation, although at the time her desperation had been very real.

"Salvation?"

"He offered me freedom. The opportunity to see the world that was denied to me."

He considered her words in somber silence. Bianca was deeply relieved he had not dismissed her rash behavior as that of a ridiculous child.

If he were to be her husband, she needed him to understand her hunger for a measure of independence.

"I suppose it would be thrilling for any young woman."

She smiled wryly. "It was a grand adventure."

"I see."

She did not miss the edge in his voice. His emotions were still raw when it came to Lord Aldron.

"I thought him daring and bold," she murmured as she slowly began to walk in his direction, "but now I realize it was nothing more than an illusion."

He watched her approach with darkened eyes. "What do you mean?"

"There is little daring in taking a lady to a naughty pantomime or horse races or even boxing matches. What is the risk beyond a bit of scandal? It was not a true adventure."

His large form stiffened as she halted directly before him. Close enough that her skirts brushed his legs.

"Then what is a true adventure?" he demanded in husky tones.

She met his gaze squarely. It may have taken a while. Goodness knew she was not always as bright as she should be. But at last she understood.

"Standing firm in your beliefs even at the risk of being shunned and disdained," she said softly. "Devoting your life to helping others because it is right, not to impress society."

His hands reached up to grasp her shoulders, his breath rasping in the still air.

"That sounds more like duty than adventure. Hardly the dreams of a young and beautiful woman."

"I might have agreed until I encountered a gentleman who revealed that I possessed the most amazing opportunity to alter the world. Now, that is an adventure that is far more lasting than a brief moment of enjoyment."

His fingers tightened. "Enough to last a lifetime?"

"An eternity."

His gaze searched her countenance. Searching perhaps for some reassurance.

"Bianca, did you love him?"

She grimaced as a pang of guilt shot through her heart. As furious as she might be with Stephen, she could not deny that she had treated him ill.

"I loved the thought of being rid of my father's constraints and being my own mistress. But as far as Stephen . . . I am shamed to admit that I was merely using him."

"How can you be so certain?"

She lifted her hands to lay them against his chest. Beneath her fingers, she could feel the rapid beat of his heart.

"Because when I realized that my father would never allow our marriage, I felt nothing but anger at having my will thwarted. But when you left London . . ." She gave a slow shake of her head. "There was nothing that could have kept me from following you. Not Stephen. Not my father. Not even the entire English army."

Something flashed deep in the hazel eyes, but his expression remained stoic.

"The life I offer is bound to be as confining as that with your father."

Bianca gave a lift of her brows. "You think to rule me?"

His lips twitched. "I am not that foolish, but I will never be capable of devoting myself to society and frivolous pleasure. My responsibilities are too great. How can you know that you will not become bored at my side?"

Her brows lifted even higher. "Because I have no intention of only being at your side."

He blinked at her brisk retort. "I beg your pardon?"

"You have taught me that I have much to offer, Edward. I intend to use my position and power to assist others in my own way. I wish a life with you, but I must also have the opportunity to discover what I can accomplish."

A slow, heart-fluttering smile curved his lips. "You have

no need to convince me, Lady Bianca. I am quite eager to witness all you can accomplish." With a touch as light as a breeze, his fingers skimmed down her back, coming to rest upon the slight swell of her hips. "And speaking of accomplishments . . ." He leaned forward to press his lips against the tender curve of her throat. "I might have one or two that might be of interest to you."

CHAPTER EIGHTEEN

Edward watched the soft color steal beneath Bianca's cheeks. Dear God, she was so beautiful she made his heart ache. But it was not just a physical beauty.

She was much more than raven curls and ivory skin and soft curves.

She possessed courage and intelligence and a passionate spirit that was nearly a tangible force.

And he wanted her as his wife with a desperation that could no longer be denied.

Slipping his hands about her hips, he tugged her firmly against his body. He was done with his uncertainty. Who could ever know what the future might hold? Or if the happiness of today would be guaranteed for tomorrow?

Bianca claimed that she desired to be his wife. She offered him her love.

He would be a fool to allow her to slip away.

Tasting of her satin skin, he allowed his hands to sweep up the back of her gown to dispense with the aggravating ribbons and hooks. He needed to feel her warmth. To have her held so close that she could not possibly escape.

Allowing his tongue to trail up her neck, he gently nipped

at her ear. She shivered in response, her fingers clutching at his lapels.

"Is this a part of your accomplishments, Lord Harrington?" she breathed.

He chuckled as he tugged open the back of her gown and savored the silken skin that was exposed. There was surely nothing more delectable.

"Actually, that is for you to decide, muirnin." He nuzzled her cheek as his body clenched with a burning need. "But I would request one thing of you."

"And what is that?"

"That you not rush to judgment." Pulling back he studied her flushed features, his fingers lowering to wrestle with the knots of her corset. Damnable thing. "There are a few skills where being a gentleman of slow and methodical habits tends to be an advantage."

A smile of pure feminine temptation curved her lips. With a boldness that made his heart leap, she tugged at his cravat and tossed it aside. Then without hesitation she set about ridding him of his jacket and waistcoat.

Edward felt his body swiftly harden at her brazen response. Hell's teeth, was there anything more erotic than a woman who knew exactly what she desired?

"Precisely how slow and methodical do you intend to be?" she demanded as she lifted his shirt over his head and allowed her hands to run a searing path over his chest.

Edward clenched his teeth as he resisted the urge to lower her to the floor and plunge into her damp heat. Like any man he enjoyed a swift, searing coupling upon occasion. Hot, sweaty sex had its place.

But not tonight. Not when he had dreamed of all the delicious things he intended to do with this woman.

Finishing his battle with the evil corset, he gave a sigh of relief as he tugged at her sleeves to pull aside the layers of clothing.

"Exquisitely slow and very, very methodical," he growled as his hands were allowed to skim over her warm, bare skin.

Her breath caught as he gently cupped her breasts, his thumb brushing over the hardened peaks.

"There is something to be said for haste," she husked.

"Upon occasion," he agreed, his head lowering. "This, however, is not one of them."

She moaned in approval at his lips covered her nipple, her fingers thrusting into his hair.

"What of the servants?"

Edward could barely think as he teased the puckered nub, lightly nipping it before laving it with his tongue. Bianca groaned her approval as her body molded to his own. The soft swell of her stomach pressed against his throbbing erection. Her bare skin sent a thousand prickles of delight racing through his heated blood.

Oh . . . God. He needed her.

Allowing his lips to smooth over the curve of her breast, he breathed deeply of her honeysuckle scent.

"I have few demands of my staff, but one I insist upon is that I am never interrupted when I am in my library," he managed to mutter. "I would never get my paperwork dealt with if I were being forever intruded upon."

She rubbed against his hardness, her hands moving in a restless path down his shoulders and over his chest.

"They will not believe you are doing paperwork at this hour."

He hissed sharply as her fingers brushed over the rigid muscles of his stomach and tantalizingly close to his straining manhood.

"Actually, this is the hour I usually deal with the more tedious details of the estate," he gritted.

A knowing expression touched her beautiful features. The vixen knew precisely how she was torturing him.

"Then I shall be banned from the library as well?" she

murmured as she lightly outlined the bulge in his pants. "A pity. I am rather fond of this room."

Edward was becoming increasingly more fond of the room. It had never occurred to him it was a perfect spot for seduction.

Not until this moment.

Determined to offer a bit of his own brand of torture, Edward traced the silhouette of her hips and down to her thighs. He waited for her legs to instinctively part before stroking slowly upward to discover she was already moist and ready for him.

"Actually I have been considering hiring a secretary," he assured her.

She bit off a moan as his finger slipped into her heat. "Have you?"

"It only makes sense." Pressing his finger deeper, he used his thumb to rub against her point of pleasure. "With my new-found responsibilities, I shall have great need of assistance."

Her head fell back as she panted with a building need. "An earl's work is never done."

He leaned forward to press his lips to her neck. "I was referring to my responsibilities as husband and father."

He felt her momentarily stiffen in shock. "Oh."

"There will be no more nights bothered with reports and petitions and endless correspondence from relatives whom I have never clapped eyes upon."

Lifting her heavy lashes, she regarded him with a glittering midnight gaze. "Whatever will you do with your time?"

"I—" His words were brought to a sharp halt as she fumbled with the buttons of his breeches and astonishingly curled her fingers about his erection. "Hell's teeth, muirnin," he choked in near-painful pleasure.

"I can think of one or two possibilities to keep you occupied," she promised, her fingers working magic as they explored his shaft.

Edward sank his teeth into his bottom lip. He wanted to make her halt the exquisite torment before he embarrassed himself. He wanted to plead for her to never stop.

He wanted . . .

He wanted her.

Every silken, satin inch of her.

"That feels so good," he groaned, incapable of halting his slow thrusts into her hand.

"This?" she murmured as she leaned forward to press her lips to his chest, biting and trailing her lips ever lower. "And this?"

Edward leaned heavily against the desk as she tugged his breeches downward, her lips traveling down his stomach and then at last covering the tip of his manhood.

Never had he been assaulted by such intense sensations. The blood thundered in his ears, and his entire body clenched with sharp, aching delight. If he died this moment he would not care. Nothing could ever compare to the feel of her tongue stroking him to madness.

"Bianca . . . ," he breathed.

She paid him no heed as she continued to taste of him, seemingly fascinated by his hard length. A cry was wrenched from his throat as she took him fully into her mouth. His fingers briefly clenched in her hair as he urged her to continue her ministrations. Then, as the pleasure threatened to overwhelm him, Edward gave a sharp shake of his head.

No. He would not seek his fulfillment until she had reached her own.

Shifting his hands to her shoulders, he firmly tugged her upward, and before she could protest he had swung her onto the desk and stepped between her legs.

"You, Lady Bianca, are going to be the death of me," he muttered.

She smiled with a hint of smugness. "You seemed to be enjoying yourself well enough."

"Shall I demonstrate how well?" he murmured before he lowered himself to his knees and pressed his lips to the inside of her thigh.

Her sigh whispered through the air as he kissed a path toward paradise.

Bianca should have been abed.

Heaven knew she had spent precious little time sleeping the night before. In fact, the dawn had been breaking when she had silently crawled from Edward's bed and returned to her chambers.

But oddly she discovered that a night spent in the arms of the man she loved had invigorated her in a manner she had never before experienced. Who needed sleep when her body was tingling with energy? And her feet so light she felt as if she might very well float away?

Taking a swift bath, she attired herself in a plain muslin gown and firmly tugged her wayward curls into a tidy knot. Once prepared for the day ahead, she went in search of the household maids.

Although Edward's estate was a tidy, well-run establishment, she had been raised by a mother who demanded nothing short of perfection within her home. Her discerning eye had caught a few flaws she intended to correct.

Beginning with the silver, which did not appear to have had a good polishing for several years.

Assuming an air of brisk efficiency, Bianca soon had the maids busy with their various tasks and the cook preparing a meal fit for a titled nobleman.

She had just set about inspecting the linen when a familiar flutter in the pit of her stomach warned her that Edward had entered the cramped closet. Spinning about, she discovered him leaning against the door, a rather bemused smile upon his lips.

"Good morning, muirnin."

Bianca took a moment to appreciate the sheer beauty he offered. Even casually attired he managed to make her heart leap with excitement. He was so fiercely handsome. So deliciously male.

And worse, there was a devilish glint in his eyes that warned her he was recalling her heated responses during the long, sensuous night.

A flush of heat raced through her as she slowly straightened and brushed her hands down her skirt. It was indecent, the way he had only to be near for her body to sizzle with longing.

"Good morning, Edward." She discovered to her relief that her voice at least sounded coherent. She had not babbled or drooled as she had feared. "Breakfast is awaiting you in the morning room."

Stepping further into the closet, he backed her against the wooden shelves. His hands landed on either side of her shoulders to effectively trap her. Then, with intimate care, he allowed his gaze to roam down the length of her body.

"Actually, I hoped to have something else awaiting me this morning. Why did you slip away?"

His husky voice shivered down her spine. He could not know just how difficult it had been to leave his side.

Only the fear that one of the servants might stumble over them had kept her from waking him to continue their pleasurable interlude.

"It would hardly do to have your housekeeper sleep late on her first day," she murmured.

His lips slowly curled as his gaze deliberately lingered on the bodice of her gown. "Who mentioned anything of sleep?"

Hearing the distant sounds of Maggie beating the carpets, Bianca sent him a chiding frown.

"Edward, behave yourself."

"Why?"

"Because you will not convince me that you have your staff trained not to enter the linen closet."

"We could return to the library." He lowered his head to brush his lips over her temple. "There is a very comfortable sofa we have yet to enjoy."

Her lower stomach clenched at the memory of the library and the delights they had discovered there. Who knew that a desk could prove such an interesting piece of furniture?

Still, she was not yet so comfortable with her intimate relationship with Edward that she could ignore the staff that buzzed about them.

"Surely you have duties awaiting your attention?" she demanded.

His tongue lightly touched her skin, as if savoring her taste. "Countless duties."

Breathing was becoming an effort. "Well?"

The distracting lips moved down her cheek to nibble at the corner of her mouth.

"I have decided I prefer being a gentleman of leisure. You, my lady, are clearly a bad influence."

"Me?" Her hands lifted of their own accord to rest against his chest. He seemed to surround her with his heat and scent, and it was proving devilishly difficult to keep her thoughts in order. The sensations swirling within her did nothing to help. "I should rather think you are the bad influence. After all, I was quite occupied until you intruded."

He chuckled softly. "Ah, yes, I noticed the maids scurrying about in a most frantic fashion. Have you been terrorizing them?"

She pulled back with a frown of annoyance. She might readily display her ill temper with her father and even Edward, but she would never bully a hapless servant.

"Certainly not. I possess great respect for servants and the work they perform."

His features melted to a tender expression. "I know you do,

muirnin. Which is only one of the many reasons I love you so desperately."

Desperately?

Oh . . . she liked the sound of that.

She liked it to the very depths of her soul.

Slowly she twined her arms about his neck, arching against his stirring body.

"What are the other reasons?"

He shuddered as he cupped her hips and pressed her firmly to his erection.

"I am attempting to reveal them to you if only you would cooperate."

She laughed as she regarded him from beneath lowered lashes. "I really am very busy."

His eyes smoldered with a passion that nearly set the air on fire. "Then you may consider yourself relieved of your post."

She blinked in surprise. "I beg your pardon?"

"I no longer desire you as my housekeeper."

Ridiculously, she found herself offended by his blunt dismissal. "That is not fair. I happen to be doing an excellent job."

He smiled at her sharp tone. "You are, but I have another post in mind for a lady of your undoubted talents."

"And what is that?"

"My wife."

Her heart came to a perfect halt. Wife. Until this moment she was not certain she truly understood the simple beauty of being a wife.

This man's wife.

It was enough to bring a flood of tears to her eyes.

Embarrassed by the surge of unexpected emotion, Bianca hastily forced a lighthearted smile to her lips. Poor Edward would think her daft if she began weeping whenever he mentioned the word "wife."

"I fear I have no references for such a post."

"No?" His lips twitched. "A pity, but I am willing to trust in my instincts on this occasion."

"Very generous of you, my lord." She toyed with the curls at his nape. "Are there many other applicants?"

Without warning his smile faded and he regarded her with an intensity that seemed almost tangible.

"Not one," he swore in husky tones. "There is only you, Lady Bianca. Only you."

She felt as if she were melting. Oh heavens, she loved this man. More than she thought it possible to love anyone.

Shifting onto the tips of her toes, Bianca allowed her lips to trail along the line of his jaw.

"About the library . . . ," she whispered.

"Oh yes," he muttered.

In a heartbeat, he had swept her off her feet and was hurrying toward the nearby stairs. Bianca laughed with heady delight as his head swooped down to crush her lips in a fierce, possessive kiss.

Suddenly the curious glances of the servants did not bother her a whit.

Bianca's earlier bout of vigor was decidedly absent as she lay wrapped in Edward's arms. In truth, she was quite certain she might never be capable of moving again.

Not that she minded, she acknowledged with a sated smile. She could think of no more pleasant means of devoting a morning.

And half the afternoon.

With her head pillowed on the broad chest, she absently ran her hands over hair-roughened skin.

"Breakfast is bound to be cold by now," she murmured in lazy tones.

Edward ran his fingers through her curls. He seemed fascinated by the tumbled mass.

"Mmmm . . . perhaps we shall rise in time for tea."

"It seems rather decadent to be lying here in the middle of the day."

"I did say you were a bad influence upon me. I have been thoroughly corrupted."

She tilted her head to meet his hooded gaze. "Do you mind?"

"Not as long as you make an honest man of me."

She studied him a long moment, her heart lodged in her throat. "You are certain, Edward?"

He smiled with a slow tenderness. "Yes, muirnin. I am very certain."

She blinked back those absurd tears that seemed to be always hovering. What the devil was the matter with her?

"You do realize the fuss and bother my parents will expect for my wedding?" She felt duty bound to warn him. She better than anyone knew her mother had been planning her wedding since the day she entered the world. "It is bound to be the worst sort of spectacle."

His smile never faltered. "As long as you are there, I do not care if they have dancing bears and monkeys leaping upon on the altar."

"Do not jest. My mother has a great fondness for peacocks, and she will no doubt have the grounds filled with the beasts. Not to mention the entire royal family."

"Egads, peacocks and the Prince?" He gave a dramatic shudder. "Perhaps we should consider eloping."

Bianca snuggled closer to his warm body. She could think of nothing better than simply being done with the business so she need never be taken from his side.

"I will not object if that is what you prefer."

He gave her curls a gentle tweak. "We could not possibly disappoint your mother. Besides which . . ."

Her brows lifted as his words trailed away. "Yes?"

The hazel eyes smoldered with a heat that touched her very

heart. "Besides which, I want the entire world to know beyond a shadow of a doubt you are mine."

She touched her lips to his chest. "And that you are mine."

"From the moment I saw you across that crowded room."

His head lowered, but before he could reach her lips there was a disturbance outside. With a shocking lack of embarrassment, he rose from the sofa and crossed to the window. Not that Bianca truly minded. She fully enjoyed the view of his hard, perfectly chiseled male form.

Of course, she preferred it when it was not quite so far away.

There was a moment of silence before Edward turned back to regard her with a small grimace.

"I fear our delightful solitude is about to come to an end, muirnin. We have a caller."

A faint flutter of fear raced through Bianca as she sat up and reached for her shift. Dear God, surely her father had not discovered her disappearance so swiftly?

"Who is it?"

"Biddles."

She breathed out a sigh of relief. "Good heavens, what would Lord Bidwell be doing here?"

He turned to flash a wry smile. "Whatever it might be, he will not be satisfied cooling his heels in the foyer. Whether we might wish it or not, he is about to stick that pointed nose directly into our business."

CHAPTER NINETEEN

Several hours later, Edward found himself strolling the gardens with his friend. Thus far they had discussed nothing more pressing than the latest news from Parliament and the usual gossip swirling about London.

Bianca had disappeared shortly after tea, no doubt sensing that the two men desired to be alone, but still Biddles had avoided revealing his reasons for traveling to Kent.

An avoidance that was beginning to stretch Edward's renowned patience.

As much as he enjoyed Lord Bidwell's companionship, he would far prefer to devote himself to Bianca. All too soon this stolen interlude would come to an end and she would be forced to return to her parents' home until the lavish wedding could be properly planned and conducted.

It might be months before he had her alone again.

Still, he could not be openly rude to the gentleman who had been his friend since they were both grubby lads. Sooner or later Biddles would confess his reasons for his unexpected arrival.

He could only hope it would be sooner.

Reaching the edge of the garden, Biddles came to an

abrupt halt, his nose wrinkling at the unmistakable scent of rich earth and manure.

Hiding his smile, Edward stepped beside his friend and arched a teasing brow.

"I assure you that the natives will not attack if you go beyond the grounds."

Flicking open his fan, Biddles wafted it vigorously beneath his pointed nose.

"It is not the natives that concern me, old friend. It is those horrid cows. They are always eyeing me as if they intend some nefarious business."

Edward could not halt his laugh. He had never encountered a gentleman more suited to London.

"They are no doubt in shock," he murmured, his gaze moving over the crimson coat and yellow breeches. "It is not often they encounter such a brilliant ensemble."

Biddles offered a sniff. "Of course they do not. There are few who possess my flare for fashion."

"Thank God."

"Careful, Harrington." A dangerous smile curved the nobleman's lips. "I recall a certain pair of pink stockings that nearly got you beat to death at school."

Edward shuddered at the unpleasant memory. A boarding school was no place for the weak or helpless. It was a brutal environment that tested the staunchest of nerve.

"They were a gift from my horrid Aunt Esmeralda. Since she was paying for the school, what could I do?" He gave a small shrug. "Besides, I held my own."

Biddles rolled his eyes heavenward. "Why should you not? Even then you were big as an ox."

"And you were a sly little ferret that always managed to slip out of trouble."

A decidedly smug expression settled on the narrow countenance. "When you are half the size of other lads, you must learn to protect yourself by means other than brawn. Thankfully, I discovered that information is a powerful weapon."

"You managed to hold the entire school hostage with your nasty little skill, from the head master to the lowest servant."

"Except for you." Abruptly turning, Biddles regarded him with a piercing gaze. "You were so damnably perfect that I could not discover even the smallest sin to hold over your head. Gads, I do not believe you even cheated upon an exam."

"Hardly perfect."

"You are one of the few honest men I have ever encountered."

Edward found himself oddly embarrassed beneath the steady gaze. Hell's teeth, he possessed all the faults and weaknesses of every other man.

Perhaps even a few additional ones if he were to search hard enough.

"Are you going to tell me why you have come to Kent?" he abruptly demanded, anxious to change the subject. And even more anxious to be alone with Bianca.

Biddles paused before he at last gave a lift of his shoulders. "I was concerned."

"For me?"

"Lady Bianca did not reveal my part in her arrival here?"

A frown touched Edward's brow. "No."

Biddles returned his attention to the distant meadows. "She came to me and demanded to know where you had disappeared to."

Edward could not deny that he was surprised. Oh, not by Bianca confronting Biddles. He had discovered his soon-to-be wife possessed a stubborn will that would allow nothing to stand in her path. But he was taken off guard that Biddles would allow himself to be bullied. He had faced Napoleon himself without batting a lash.

"And you told her?"

"Obviously."

"Why?" Edward probed, his curiosity thoroughly roused. "I thought you disapproved of my relationship with her."

"I did. But . . ."

"Yes?"

The pale gaze slashed back in his direction. "She managed to convince me that she loved you despite her reputation of being without a heart. Did I do wrong?"

"No." Reaching out, Edward placed his hand on his friend's shoulder. "In fact, I am in your debt."

"You have decided to forgive her?"

Edward gave a firm shake of his head. "There was nothing to forgive. I realize now that I was merely using Lord Aldron as a reason to push Bianca away."

Biddles shut his fan with a snap. "You do not love her?"

"God, I love her so much it makes me ache," Edward readily admitted.

"Then why would you push her away?"

"Because I did not truly believe she could be content as my wife." He sucked in a deep breath, his gaze instinctively turning toward the small manor house. "What do I have to offer such a woman? I am a plain, simple man who prefers being among my tenants to dashing about society. Even worse, I have managed to make an enemy of half the aristocrats with my radical notions. What if she finds herself shunned by her friends and family?"

Shockingly, Biddles tilted back his head to laugh at his dark mutterings.

"Good God, Edward, Lady Bianca is not only the daughter of a duke, but she possesses the stubborn determination of a mule. I do not doubt she will rule society no matter how radical your notions."

Edward could hardly argue with such obvious logic. Bianca was a force to be reckoned with. He knew that better than anyone.

"No doubt," he conceded with a reluctant smile. "Still, I am hardly the sort of dandy she has become accustomed to."

Biddles gave a dismissive wave of his hand. "You cannot believe a woman might prefer honor and integrity to shallow sophistication?"

Edward felt himself stiffen at the accusation. How could a gentleman such as Biddles possibly understand? He had been born and raised to consider his blood bluer than that of others. He would never doubt his own worth.

"I can only trust that she does," he said so softly that the breeze stole the words from his lips.

Still, Biddles must have at least sensed something of his inner doubt as he frowned in sudden concern.

"Edward—"

The sharp sound of pounding footsteps interrupted whatever Biddles had been about to say, and both gentlemen turned about to watch a young lad charge up the path toward them. "What the devil is that?" Biddles muttered in surprise.

"My lord." The lad waved his arms in a frantic manner. "You must come quick."

Edward stepped forward. "What is it?"

"The Foster cottage has caught fire."

"Good God." He glanced toward his companion. "I must go."

"I will join you," Biddles swiftly offered.

"No, I need you to stay here with Bianca. If the blaze becomes out of control, I want you to take her to the village. There should be rooms at the inn."

"But—"

"Please, Biddles." He grabbed his friend's arm, his expression fierce. "I need to know she is in no danger."

Biddles gave a nod of his head. "Very well."

Assured that Bianca would be safe, Edward set off at a swift run. Collecting the young boy, he commanded him to race to the church as quickly as possible to ring the bells.

Soon the entire neighborhood would be gathering to assist in putting out the fire.

Until then he had to ensure that the Fosters had reached safety.

Bianca regarded Lord Bidwell with a hand pressed to her heart. There was something upon the narrow countenance that sent a chill down her spine.

"A fire? Dear God, where is Edward?"

There was a short pause, almost as if the gentleman was debating whether or not to lie to her.

"He has gone to assist," he at last grudgingly admitted.

The chill became more pronounced, and without thought she turned to hurry from the parlor. "No. I will not allow it."

"Hold." Moving with a speed that caught Bianca off guard, the nobleman was standing directly in her path. "You must remain here."

Her hands clenched at her side as a wrenching pain clutched at her heart. Dammit all, why was this man pestering her? She did not have the time for this nonsense.

"When Edward is in danger? Do not be daft," she growled. "Now move aside."

Lord Bidwell held up a slender hand. "Lady Bianca, I cannot allow this. Edward specifically commanded me to ensure you remained far away from the fire."

She narrowed her gaze with seething impatience. "And what of Edward?"

"He will be quite safe. No doubt by the time he reaches the cottage, the tenants will have it well in hand."

"And if they do not?" she demanded, her vivid imagination already filled with ghastly images of her fiancé dashing to the flaming cottage. "You know Edward. He is so blasted noble he is bound to risk his bloody neck if he thinks it necessary."

"Edward will do nothing foolish," he retorted, his expression one of grim determination. "And neither will you. Not even if I have to tie you to a chair."

Bianca attempted to charge around the slender lord, not at all above an ugly brawl if that was what was needed to reach Edward. Unfortunately, the slender man was astonishingly strong, and even as she darted forward he had captured her in his arms with a grip that she could not break.

"Lord Bidwell, I insist that you release me," she gritted in rising fury.

"Not until I have your promise that you will obey Edward's command."

Knowing that she had no hope of physically overcoming her captor, Bianca accepted that deception was her only hope of escape. A knowledge that did not trouble her a whit.

Not when Edward might very well be in danger.

With practiced ease, she smoothed her expression to one of resigned petulance.

"Oh . . . very well," she muttered, stiffly waiting until he warily lowered his arms. "At least I must request that cook prepare some food for those assisting Edward. I trust that meets with your approval?"

His eyes narrowed with suspicion. "So long as you do not leave the manor."

She managed a tight smile. "Make yourself comfortable, Lord Bidwell. I shall return as soon as I have completed my task."

Without a backward glance, she swept out of the parlor and down the short hall to the stairs. She even turned to head toward the kitchen in the event the sly man was keeping an eye upon her. Only when she was out of sight did she hastily dodge into a side passage that led her to a small door.

Once out of the manor, she headed straight for the stables, calling for a horse the moment a groom appeared.

Edward was out there, and he needed her.

Whether he knew he needed her or not.

* * *

The flames had spread to the roof of the cottage as Edward approached. His heart sank as he realized the poor Fosters had no doubt lost everything.

Of course he would ensure the cottage was rebuilt, and the neighbors would collect clothing and food to assist them. But nothing could ever replace the small, personal items that made a house a home.

At least the tenants had already gathered to begin passing buckets of water from the well to the burning house, he acknowledged. It was imperative that the fire be put out before it could spread to the outbuildings or even another cottage.

The thought had barely flittered through his thoughts when his horrified gaze caught sight of the brawny, silver-haired woman battling her way through the gathering crowd, her cries of distress filling the air.

His swift pace became an all-out run as he recognized Mrs. Foster. The daft woman was obviously determined to return to the cottage despite the flames.

Thrusting aside those in his way, he frantically attempted to halt the woman before she reached the open door. For all his speed, however, the determined woman had made it over the threshold before he managed to get his hands upon her.

He choked upon the thick smoke as he wrestled her to a halt.

"Mrs. Foster, you must get out. The roof is about to collapse."

"Jacob came back for the silver," she moaned, her long face blackened with soot as she struggled against his hold. "He's all I have."

His heart gave a squeeze of fear as he frantically glanced about the narrow room. Through the gloom he spotted the elderly man lying beside the fireplace as if he had become overwhelmed by the smoke.

"Go, I will get Jacob," he shouted.

She dug in her heels, her expression frantic. "I won't leave without him."

"I said I would save him, now go."

With a sharp push, he had her out of the cottage. He paused only long enough to tie his handkerchief over his lower face before he inched his way toward the unconscious tenant.

The heat from the gathering flames was nearly unbearable, and the thick smoke threatened to choke him, but Edward pressed onward. He did not know if the man was alive or dead, but he was not about to leave him to burn.

Reaching the still form, Edward bent down to scoop the man into his arms. Then, with a loud grunt, he tossed him over his shoulder. It was an effort to rise to his feet, and he realized that he was weakening.

He had to get them out of the cottage before he was overcome by the smoke as well.

A blackness had descended within the room, and Edward was forced to trail his hand along the heated stone wall to keep from becoming disoriented. Sweat flooded down his countenance and he could feel his clothes sticking to his body as he struggled forward.

Even worse, his breathing was becoming so labored he knew it was only a matter of moments before he lost consciousness.

Willing himself to keep moving, he assured himself that he had to be near the door. Only a few more steps. One step after another, he coaxed his straining muscles.

And then, without warning, disaster struck.

Blinded by the smoke, he could not see the chair directly in his path. Not until he had already stumbled over it.

With a furious cry he tumbled to his side, attempting to protect Mr. Foster from the blow. A fine notion until he realized that he had left himself utterly unprotected and with a helpless sense of destiny felt his head smack against the flagstone floor.

There was a burst of pain and a flash of light.

Then there was nothing.

No one had ever accused Biddles of being naïve.

Sly, devious, and downright immoral. But never, ever naïve.

As soon as Lady Bianca left the room, he had slipped from the manor house to station himself outside the kitchen door. He did not believe her seeming resignation for a moment. She had been desperate to reach Edward's side, and she was not about to let anyone stand in her way.

Unfortunately, he managed to outwit even himself.

While he was waiting for her to make an appearance, she managed to sneak through a side door and was already at the stables when he spotted her scurrying form.

With a curse at his stupidity, Biddles was in swift pursuit.

Damn and blast. Edward would have his hide if anything happened to his fiancée.

He managed to reach the stables just as she charged out the doors upon a gray mare, and with a sharp command he had the harassed groom retrieving his own mount. Precious moments passed before he was at last in the saddle and demanding directions to the Foster cottage. Moments that allowed Lady Bianca to gain a considerable advantage.

Taking the nearest lane, Biddles bent low as he urged his horse to a gallop. He could already smell the acrid smoke that filled the air, and his heart sank as he realized that Bianca was bound to reach the cottage before he could catch her.

All he could do was hope that Edward was wisely standing aside and allowing his tenants to battle the blaze.

A hope that withered and died before it could even take root in his heart.

Like Bianca, he knew Edward far too well. He would never

be capable of standing aside. If danger was to be found, he would be right in the thick of it.

Forced to slow as he cut through a thick copse of trees, Biddles could begin to see the dark wisps of ashes in the air. The cottage was near, and he had yet to even catch sight of Bianca.

Seething with impatience, he urged his horse to a faster pace and at last crested the small hill to discover the burning cottage along with a crowd in the throes of obvious panic. He vaulted from the saddle, his only concern finding Edward and his stubborn fiancée.

He grabbed the arm of the nearest man and gave him a small shake to capture his attention.

"Where is Lord Harrington?" he demanded.

The broad man with a ruddy countenance and shock of black hair looked near to tears.

"Went inside to save poor old Foster." His voice broke as he forced out the raw words. "He hasn't come out again."

With a sense of doom, Biddles glanced toward the cottage to witness Bianca hurtling through the open door.

"God have mercy," he muttered as his fingers tightened upon the man's arm. Edward had been a fool to go in after the man. And Bianca an even bigger fool to go after Edward. So what did that make him? A fool's fool, obviously. Assuming an expression that had managed to intimidate even Prinny, he leaned toward his brawny captive. "I am going in there. I will need your help."

The broad face turned a sickly white. "But—"

"I do not have time to argue," Biddles growled, already tugging the reluctant savior forward. "Now come along."

The heat was nearly overwhelming as they approached the burning cottage, but Biddles did not allow his pace to falter. Despite the thick smoke, he could see the trailing end of Bianca's gown as she bent downward. Which could only mean that Edward was thankfully close to escape.

Stepping over the threshold, he bent beside the slender woman, realizing that she was pushing aside a chair that had caught fire and landed upon the unconscious Edward. She did not even notice his presence until he touched her shoulder.

With a gasp, she turned to regard him with a grim expression. "He is alive, but we must get him out of here," she commanded in tones that defied argument.

"You take one arm and I will take the other," he directed, grasping an arm as he turned his attention to the hovering man at his side. "You take Mr. Foster."

"Aye," the man agreed, easily bending to grasp the man beneath the shoulders and drag him out the door.

They were forced to wait until the unconscious Mr. Foster was over the threshold before they could begin tugging Edward to safety. Biddles could hear Bianca's rasping breath, but there was no hint of fear or even panic upon her countenance.

Nothing but grim determination.

At last able to drag Edward backward, they had barely stepped out of the door when a sudden mob appeared and Biddles found a dozen hands reaching to grasp hold of Edward and rush him from the hungry flames.

Momentarily knocked aside, Biddles and Bianca sucked in deep breaths of the crisp air. They had only been within the cottage for a few moments, but it was enough to fill their lungs with thick ash.

At least he knew that Edward was alive and seemingly unharmed except for a nasty gash on his temple, Biddles acknowledged with sharp relief. Even as he had been jostled aside, he had witnessed the Earl's eyes begin to flutter open.

Digging out his handkerchief, Biddles mopped the sweat and soot from his countenance. Then, with a wheezing cough, he turned his attention to the lady at his side.

At first he did not notice more than the fact that her hair had come loose to tumble about her shoulders and her dress appeared to be singed by the flames.

It was only when she slowly fell to her knees that he noticed the fierce blisters that marred her beautiful hands.

"Oh lord," he muttered as he bent beside her and took her hands in his own. "Edward is going to castrate me."

CHAPTER TWENTY

It was the relentless throbbing in his temple that at last wrenched Edward from the dark oblivion that held him.

For long moments he floated in an odd sort of limbo, not quite awake but aware enough to sense that he had somehow been carried to his private chambers and that the light was slowly fading to dusk.

For long moments he attempted to recall what had occurred after he had entered the cottage. He remembered carrying Mr. Foster toward the door, and the searing heat that had surrounded him. There had been something blocking his way, and then there was nothing more than darkness.

Except for . . . an odd unease niggled at the edge of his mind.

As if there were something of the gravest importance that he should recall.

Painful moments passed as he struggled to think past the thickness fogging his mind. Blast it all, what had it been?

A sound. Yes, that was it. A sound that had managed to reach him even as he lay unconscious.

The sound of Bianca's voice.

His eyes abruptly wrenched open as he gave a low groan of dismay.

Dear God, had he truly heard her voice, or had it only been a figment of his imagination?

He had to know. This moment.

Gritting his teeth, Edward began to lift his head from the pillow. He was prepared for the pain that flared through his brain like a strike of lightning. What he was not prepared for was the wave of dizziness that nearly tumbled him back into the waiting darkness.

With a low groan, his head returned to the pillow and he clenched his hands into frustrated fists.

"Ah, the mighty savior at last awakens," a voice drawled before the thin countenance of Biddles appeared directly above him. "And about bloody time."

"Good God, have I gone to hell?" he groaned.

Biddles gave a low laugh. "Not as yet, old friend."

"Bianca . . ." He was startled by the raw huskiness of his voice.

"Rest easy, Edward. Your Bianca is in rather better shape than you."

"I thought . . . I heard her voice when I was in the cottage."

A grimace touched Biddles's face, and a shaft of pure fear lanced through Edward.

"Yes. I fear that I failed you. She managed to slip away, and I was too late in arriving at the cottage."

She had been in that flaming hell?

"Oh God. Is she harmed?"

"Her hands are blistered. A burning chair had fallen atop you, and she pushed it off before it could harm you."

"I need to see her."

Once again he attempted to lift himself from the bed, only to have his companion press him firmly back onto the mattress. Much to his chagrin, it took the small man very little effort.

"Absolutely not. You are to remain in this bed until the doctor returns in the morning."

A warning frown gathered on Edward's brow. "Biddles . . ."

The pale eyes narrowed with their own warning. One that held considerably more weight since Biddles was hovering over him like a ruthless vulture.

"You attempt to move, and I shall call for your servants and have you tied to this bed," he threatened in blunt tones. "Which is what I should have done to your foolhardy fiancée."

Well, Edward certainly agreed with that.

What the devil had the woman been thinking? It was bad enough to have followed him to the cottage. But to actually enter . . . ?

Hell's teeth, he felt as if he had lost at least a dozen years off his life.

"Where is she?"

Biddles smiled wryly. "After a battle I do not relish enduring again, I managed to convince her you were not at death's door, and she went to have the doctor care for her burns."

His heart twisted. It was unbearable to think of her in pain. "I want to be with her. If she is hurt . . ."

"Do not even think of it." With a deliberate motion, Biddles sat on the side of the mattress, his expression warning that he would do whatever necessary to keep Edward flat on his back. Damn his soul. "If you were to appear, she would begin fussing over you and never have her wounds properly attended. Leave her be for the moment."

Firmly trapped, Edward heaved a disgusted sigh. "I should never have gone into the cottage."

"There are any number of us who can make that claim," Biddles drawled.

Edward stilled, his eyes widening as the truth struck him. "You saved me, did you not?"

"Along with your soon-to-be wife and another tenant I did not bother to ask his name of."

"What of Mr. Foster?"

Biddles shrugged. "He has a few burns, and his lungs are still troubling him, but the doctor is certain he will make a full recovery."

Edward heaved a sigh. It seemed all had turned out well despite his bumbling.

"I do not know how I can ever thank you."

A sly smile touched the thin lips. "Oh, I shall no doubt discover some means."

Edward resisted the urge to chuckle. He feared the least movement might make his head explode.

"No doubt."

There was a moment of silence before Biddles regarded him with a somber expression.

"Edward."

"Yes?"

"Do not ever doubt Lady Bianca's love for you," he astonished Edward by insisting. "Never have I seen a woman more frantic to reach a man's side. I truly believe she was willing to die rather than lose you. A rare devotion you would be a fool not to appreciate."

Edward found himself unable to speak as a flood of peaceful acceptance filled his heart.

Biddles was right. He had been absurd to doubt Bianca even for a moment. Even before she had accepted her love for him, he had sensed it deep within her. It shimmered between them with a force that was nearly tangible.

It was only his doubts of himself that had blinded him to her steadfast affection.

Of course, he was quite willing to believe in her love without any further heroics, he acknowledged with a sharp pang of horror. His poor heart could not endure the thought of her in danger.

"I fully intend to appreciate her devotion," he assured his friend, a faint smile curling his lips. "After I throttle her for daring to take such a risk. The mere thought of her being in that cottage will give me nightmares for years."

"Ah, the pleasure of a wife," Biddles drawled. "Trust me, you will never again have peace in your life."

Edward arched a brow. "Thank you, that is quite reassuring."

"On the other hand, nothing will bring you greater happiness or joy."

Edward briefly considered the warmth filling his heart to near overflowing. In truth, he had never thought it possible to be so happy.

"On that we agree, my friend. So, may I assume that you now approve of my choice in brides?"

"Without hesitation. Indeed, I would say you are a greater idiot than I ever imagined if you allow her to slip away."

"She will not slip away," he swore softly. "That I can promise you."

Slowly rising to his feet, Biddles regarded him with a searching gaze. "Is there anything I can get for you? You appear a bit pale."

Edward grimaced. "My head feels as if it has been used as a battering ram, but otherwise I am well enough."

"Then I believe I shall return to London."

Edward glanced toward the window, where he could study the gathering darkness.

"Would it not be best to wait until morning?"

Biddles offered a dismissive wave of his hand. "I prefer to travel during the night. That is when one is inclined to meet the more interesting folk."

"Interesting folk such as cutthroats, thieves, and smugglers?"

"Ah, my very favorite sort."

Edward rolled his eyes. "Why am I not surprised?"

Biddles gave a soft chuckle. "They possess their own charm."

"And beyond the creatures of the night, you are anxious

to return home." Edward easily sensed his friend's restless impatience.

The nobleman gave a helpless lift of his hands. "I do not like to leave Anna when she is still battling her sickness in the mornings. Unless I am there to badger her, she will not eat as she should."

"Then you should go." With an effort, Edward reached up to lightly touch his companion's arm. "And thank you. Bianca is not the only one who has proven a rare devotion this day."

A twinkle entered the pale eyes. "Good gads, do not believe I did anything out of affection for you, old friend. Had it been my choice, I would have left you to rot in that cottage. Unfortunately my poor vanity could not possibly accept being bested by a mere female. How could I show my face at the clubs again?"

Edward smiled wryly. He did not doubt for a moment this man would dare the pits of Hades to rescue a friend in need.

"Be on your way," he murmured. "And take care. I shall never forgive you if you allow your throat to be slit before you can stand beside me at my wedding."

"Do not fear. I shall take the greatest care. I would not wish to miss appearing at your side in all my glory."

With a laugh at Edward's horrified expression, the slender gentleman gave a flamboyant bow and slipped out of the door. Alone once again, Edward heaved a faint sigh.

Damn, he wanted to be with Bianca.

No matter how many times he was reassured that she was well, he would not truly believe it until he was able to see her for himself.

Unfortunately, the pounding in his head had taken on a malicious vigor that made even blinking a painful business.

For the moment, he was trapped in this bloody bed.

As soon as he could move, however, Bianca would not escape him again.

She would be at his side, precisely where she belonged.

* * *

Bianca was more than a bit unnerved as she entered Edward's darkened chamber and set the candle beside the bed. It had been bad enough to have the doctor fussing over her blistered hands as if she were at death's door. But before she could escape to be with Edward, the cook had firmly bustled her into the kitchen and insisted on treating the burns with her own private salve that she swore was far superior.

Even worse, the entire staff had gathered in the kitchen, tears streaming down their faces as they babbled over and over about her miraculous rescue of their master and how she must have been sent by God.

It had all been horridly embarrassing, and, barely waiting for the cook to finish bandaging her hands, she had muttered a need to retire and fled with all haste.

Taking care, she leaned over the bed to study the man asleep upon the pillows. In the blink of an eye, her lingering unease faded and a swell of tenderness raced through her heart.

Dear God, she loved this man, she acknowledged as her gaze clung to his pale countenance. In the flickering candlelight, his features appeared oddly softened, even boyish. Oh, there was no mistaking the raw masculinity or sheer power that was so much a part of him. Or even the hint of stubbornness in his strong jaw. But with his hair tousled onto his forehead and his temple sporting a painful wound, he had never seemed so vulnerable.

Her hand instinctively reached out to smooth back his curls, only to pull back sharply. The doctor had warned that Edward was bound to suffer from an aching head when he awoke. It was surely best that he be allowed to sleep through the worst of his pain.

With a grudging sigh, she turned to head back toward the door. She was desperate for a hot bath and a tray of food. But not quite desperate enough to face the tearful gratitude of the servants.

It seemed there was nothing left to do but return to her own chambers and wait for Edward to waken.

She had taken only a few steps when a husky male voice shattered the silence.

"Surely you are not leaving so soon?"

Spinning about, Bianca met the glittering hazel gaze with a jolt of surprise.

"I thought you to be asleep."

With an obvious effort, Edward shifted higher upon the pillows, the linen sheet lowering enough to reveal the broad width of his chest.

A renegade shiver of awareness inched down her spine.

Oh . . . my. She did not believe she would ever grow tired of such a sight.

Seemingly unaware of her fascinated gaze, he allowed a smile to touch his lips.

"I have been awaiting your arrival."

She was forced to clear her throat. "Where is Lord Bidwell?"

"He is returning to London."

Bianca blinked in surprise. "At this hour?"

"You need not concern yourself with Biddles. He is never quite so happy as when he is sneaking through the darkness. He will come to no harm."

Bianca smiled with dry amusement. She did not fear for the nobleman's life. There was no doubt that Lord Bidwell could best the worst sort of scoundrel with nothing more than his sharp tongue.

Still, it seemed an odd hour to begin such a long journey.

"Yes, but is the neighborhood safe?" she demanded.

"Now, that I cannot promise." He gave a low chuckle that ended in a rasping moan.

Instantly concerned, Bianca moved to perch upon the edge of the bed. Whatever the doctor's assurances that Edward would have a full recovery, she would not be satisfied until he was up and out of the bed.

"Are you in pain?" she demanded. "Is there anything you need?"

His expression became brooding as he studied her delicate features.

"Yes, to both of your questions," he at last retorted. "I am in desperate pain."

Her stomach clenched in fear. "Dear God, I will call for the doctor—"

Before she could lift herself from the bed, his hand shot out to grasp her arm.

"Bianca, all I need is you by my side and your assurance you will never do anything thing so utterly stupid again."

The fear receded to be replaced by a shaft of pure annoyance. Did he think that she wished to be consumed with the terror he was about to die? Or to plunge into a burning cottage because she could not bear to be without him? Or to feel utterly helpless when she realized she did not possess the strength to pull him clear of the flames?

By God. She would take a horsewhip to him should he ever put her through such an ordeal again.

Leaning forward, she stabbed him with a narrow-eyed glare. "I would not have done anything so stupid if you had not done so first."

"But I have always been a thick-skulled ox who is expected to blunder into disaster," he countered. "You, muirnin, are a dazzling butterfly who must take the greatest care of herself. I could not bear to live if anything happened to you."

She gave a lift of her brows. "And why should I feel any differently?"

"Bianca." His fingers trailed down her arm until he encountered the bandages upon her hand. She sensed him suddenly stiffen, a flare of regret tightening his features. "God, your poor hands."

Her heart once again melted. Damn him. He was far too skilled in turning aside her ready temper.

"They will heal," she assured him in soft tones.

"We must send to London for a doctor. There must be one who is proficient in treating such burns."

She could not halt her smile at his fierce tone. There were times when he could be terribly protective.

Something that she did not seem to mind nearly so much as she once had.

Not as long as it was Edward.

"I have already been treated by the local doctor, and in truth it was Mrs. Chester's salve that has proven to be the best cure."

With gentle care he raised her hand to his lips. "Remind me to give her a rise in salary."

A delicious heat spread through her. A heat that had nothing at all to do with the burns on her hands.

"Actually, I shall be the one to give her a rise," she murmured, deliberately settling closer to his hard thigh.

His eyes darkened as the air began to shimmer with a familiar tension.

"Indeed?"

"Oh yes, I shall demand complete authority over the household accounts."

His lips continued to stroke lightly over her fingers, taking great care not to press upon her bandages.

"Complete authority?"

"Complete."

"And what other demands might I expect from my lovely shrew?"

She found it increasingly more difficult to concentrate upon his words as his tongue touched the tip of her finger. Blast it all. This man was supposed to be recuperating, not stirring her passions to a fever pitch.

With an effort, she attempted to keep her mind upon the matters at hand.

Not an easy task when she need only bend forward to place her lips against that gloriously bare chest.

"A generous allowance, of course," she managed to rasp.

His lips twitched as if he were perfectly aware of her unruly desire.

"Of course."

She sternly steadied herself. The dratted man would not always be able to distract her with his potent appeal.

"And a townhouse where I may entertain those gentlemen in position to lend support to your reforms. I shall dazzle them with my charm and wit."

"And perhaps bully them into supporting me?"

She shrugged. Being the daughter of a duke did have a few benefits.

"If necessary."

He regarded her with something that might have been tender pride even as his smile widened.

"Anything else?"

"Not at the moment. However, I do not doubt several more requirements will occur to me once we are wed."

"No doubt." His lips closed over the tip of her finger as he gave it a gentle nip. "Now may we discuss a few of my own requirements, muirnin?"

She did not need to be a clairvoyant to know precisely what requirements he intended to discuss.

Perhaps more than discuss, she acknowledged as his features softened with a desire that made her heart pound.

"Edward, I am quite certain the doctor would not approve. He was very adamant that you should rest," she forced herself to protest.

They had an eternity to indulge their passions. For now all that mattered was that he recovered from his very nasty blow to the head.

"Actually I find that I am feeling considerably improved. In fact—"

Before he could complete his wicked suggestion there was the lightest rap upon the door and Bianca was hurriedly jumping to her feet. She heard Edward mutter a string of frustrated curses as he tugged the blankets to his chin and sent her a smoldering glare.

"We are traveling to a remote cottage in the Highlands for our honeymoon. It seems the only place where we will not be interrupted."

Bianca merely shrugged. Regaining his composure with an effort, he called for the intruder to enter.

With obvious unease, a young tenant stepped into the room and offered an awkward bow toward the bed. Thankfully, he did not seem overly offended by the sight of Bianca in the bedchamber. In fact, he sent her a smile that added an unexpected charm to his round countenance.

"Pardon the interruption, my lord, but there are a few of us wanting to pay our respects."

Edward blinked in bewilderment. "Whatever are you about, Joseph?"

The tenant clenched his hat in his battered hands. "We all seen how you rushed into the cottage to save old man Foster and how your young lady risked herself to pull you out."

A surprising flush touched Edward's cheeks. He clearly was uncomfortable in the role of hero. Bianca, however, felt nothing but a surge of pride.

There were few noblemen who could claim to have the love and respect that Edward inspired among all those he encountered.

He was a rare gentleman indeed.

"Good God, I did nothing that any other man would not do," he gruffly protested. "Although I will admit that my fiancée proved to be a courageous savior."

It was Bianca's turn to blush, but before she could deny the absurd claim, the young man was turning to regard her with a happy grin.

"Congratulations, my lady. You have chosen a fine man."

"Yes, I know," she agreed softly.

His grin widened. "And Lord Harrington has proven he is not quite so stupid as we had feared. He has done well."

She was taken aback by the familiar manner in which Joseph spoke of his master, but Edward merely laughed. The two were clearly friends.

"Enough, you forward pup."

"May I tell the others they may offer their gratitude?" Joseph demanded.

"It is not at all necessary."

The smile upon the round face slowly faded. "It is to them, my lord. They have waited all afternoon to see you."

There was a long moment before Edward heaved a sigh of resignation. No doubt he worried the tenants might wait in the foyer the entire night for the opportunity to see for themselves that he was alive and well.

"Very well."

With a pleased nod, the man turned to leave the room and Bianca prepared to return to her own room. It was bad enough that the entire neighborhood must now know she was staying beneath Edward's roof. She would not add insult to injury by being seen in his bedchamber.

Unfortunately, she had not taken into consideration Edward's stubborn nature. Before she could move, his hand had reached out to grasp her wrist in a firm grip.

"Do not leave," he commanded softly.

She frowned although she did not pull free. She could not risk jarring him unduly.

"Edward, I cannot be seen here. Your tenants will never accept me as your wife if they think me your mistress."

He slowly smiled, his male beauty breathtaking in the flickering shadows.

"Trust me, muirnin. My tenants are not like those of society. They do not judge others upon silly gossip or the cut of their gown. They judge a person by the contents of their heart. You have already earned their respect."

It was a lovely notion, but Bianca was not so easily convinced. She had lived far too long among others who took positive delight in ripping reputations to shreds.

"Edward, I really think it best if I return to my chambers."

His grip refused to loosen.

"Trust me," he whispered.

She heaved out a frustrated sigh. Truly he was the most stubborn of men.

Wishing herself far away, Bianca was forced to remain standing beside the bed as the first of the visitors shuffled into the room. Somehow she even conjured a stiff smile.

It was a smile that became quite genuine as one by one a seemingly endless flood of guests came to pay their respects.

And not only to Edward.

With a somber sense of tradition, they came toward the bed and offered what gifts they could afford. Flowers, pots of honey, freshly made jam, fine linen, lace, and delicately carved pieces of wood. Soon the gifts threatened to overwhelm the entire room.

And each in turn spoke words of thanks, first to Edward and then to Bianca.

Not one regarded her with disapproval or even curiosity.

In their minds she had rescued their beloved lord.

That was enough for them.

At the end of the long line came Mrs. Foster, her round face damp with tears as she pressed her lips to Edward's hand and gently touched Bianca's cheek before leaving the room.

More than a bit stunned by the overwhelming display, Bianca slowly sank upon the edge of the bed.

She felt . . . welcomed.

As if she had been accepted into a far-flung family that had just invited her into their lives.

Sensing Edward's steady regard, she slowly lifted her lashes to meet his searching gaze. A smile of wonder touched her lips.

"What is it, muirnin?" he demanded.

"I feel as if I have just come home."

The tender expression that would always melt her heart touched his features. Then, with great care, he tugged her to lie closely nestled at his side.

"You are home, Lady Bianca," he assured her, his lips touching the top of her curls.

"Our home," she murmured against his chest.

His arms tightened about her. "Yes . . . our home."

Please turn the page for an exciting sneak peek of
Deborah Raleigh's
next historical romance,
coming soon from Zebra Books!

CHAPTER ONE

The townhouse tucked in Lombard Street was a perfectly respectable brick structure, with a perfectly respectable garden, in a perfectly respectable neighborhood.

It was remarkable only for the fact that it managed to meld so easily into its surroundings as to be nearly invisible.

The owner, Mr. Dunnington, was equally successful in blending into his surroundings.

Even his most intimate acquaintances would admit they knew little of the gentleman. Nothing beyond the fact that he had once been a tutor who had come into a small inheritance and after buying the townhouse had converted it into an exclusive school for boys of superior, if not precisely legal birth.

Bastards, some would call them, but with enough money from their fathers to ensure that they received a proper education and the ability to establish decent careers.

Beyond his obvious skill at teaching, Mr. Dunnington, however, remained an intriguing mystery.

Of course, there was no one who could have suspected just how mysterious he would prove to be. Certainly not the three gentlemen currently seated in the library of the townhouse.

At a glance the gentlemen held little in common. Well,

nothing beyond the fact that all three were the sort to cause a riot among the most fastidious of women.

Raoul Charlebois leaned negligently against the mahogany desk and was perhaps the most captivating of the three.

It was more than his pale, golden beauty or the perfection of his lean body. There was simply something in the grace of his movements and the compelling emotions that played over his classic features with a mesmerizing ease. There was no surprise that he was currently London's most celebrated actor.

Ian Breckford in contrast was a dark, smoldering gentleman who managed to succeed in everything he attempted. He was the best swordsman, he held the fastest record of traveling from Dover to London on horseback, he had made a fortune at the gambling tables, and women throughout London referred to him as Casanova.

He was a genuine hedonist who was admired and envied by every gentleman in London.

Fredrick Smith was neither as fair as Raoul, nor as dark as Ian. His hair was a pale honey with an annoying tendency to curl over his ears and at the nape of his neck. His features were delicately carved and had been the bane of his existence when he had been a lad. What boy wanted to look like a cherubic angel? Thankfully, age had managed to add a layer of unmistakable masculinity to the wide brow, the angular cheekbones, and the thin line of nose. Nothing, however, could alter the eyes that were an odd grey that could shift from silver to the deepest charcoal depending upon his mood.

His body was also thinner, although he spent enough time in his workshops to develop the sort of hard muscles that were nicely displayed by the current fashion of skintight breeches and tailored jackets.

Not that he entirely approved of all the latest styles, he wryly acknowledged. There was nothing pleasant about the black slippers that he had hastily purchased for the funeral. They not only pinched his toes, but he feared the laces were beginning to cut off the bloodstream to his feet. Had he known that this appointment was going to take the better part of the day he would have worn his comfortable boots.

It had been nearly an hour since the small, annoyingly fussy solicitor had excused himself from the room, but the shocked silence remained as thick as the moment the will had been read.

Seated near the crackling fire that battled the late January chill, Fredrick sipped on the fine brandy that he had possessed the foresight to bring.

He had expected the day to be difficult. Mr. Dunnington had been more than a teacher to him and his two companions. He had been a father, a mentor, and the cornerstone of their lives. Even after they had left this townhouse to seek their fortunes in the world, they had never lost contact with the man who had given them something none of them had ever expected to discover.

A family.

A rare and precious commodity for a bastard.

To know that he had gone from this world forever left a gaping wound in Fredrick's heart that would not soon heal.

There was a loud pop from the fireplace as one of the logs shifted. It was enough to jerk the three gentlemen from their broodings and with a muffled oath, Raoul rose to his feet and paced toward the bow window.

"I'll be damned," he muttered.

"That seems to sum it up nicely," Fredrick said dryly.

Ian made a sound deep in his throat. "The old man was always a bit batty and we all thought he must harbor some mystery in his past, but this . . ." He gave a shake of his head, the handsome features for once devoid of its wicked smile. "Bloody hell."

Raoul leaned against the frame of the window and folded his arms over his chest. His movements were not the smooth, almost profound movements he usually employed. Raoul

Charlebois was an actor who considered the whole world his stage. It was only when he was with Fredrick and Ian that he allowed himself to lower his guard.

"It does all seem highly unlikely."

"Unlikely? It is a great deal more than that." Ian surged to his feet, a restless energy crackling around his lean body. "It is one thing to possess a hidden lover or even an addiction to the gaming hells. Good God, even an occasional trip to the opium dens would have been less shocking. Who the devil could have suspected he was a brilliant extortionist?"

Fredrick remained seated, his mind methodically working through the stunning revelations that had shaken all of them. When they had been requested to attend the meeting with Dunnington's solicitor, they had all presumed that the old man had left them some small memento, a reminder of the past they had shared. Certainly none of them expected to be told that they were each to receive a legacy of twenty thousand pounds. Or that the money they were each to receive had been bilked from their respective fathers over the course of near twenty years.

Absently, he reached beneath his jacket and pulled out a small notebook and nub of pencil he always kept handy. He was a man who understood that any problem could be solved once it was sorted into manageable details. No doubt it was the result of his career as an engineer.

Or perhaps he became an engineer because he possessed an obsession with details. Fate was a strange thing.

And getting stranger by the moment, he ruefully acknowledged as he began to jot down notes.

Across the room, Ian paced to pour himself a glass of Fredrick's brandy. "What I want to know is how? It is one thing to manage to learn of a scandal. Hell, I do not doubt that I could be blackmailed under the right circumstances. But to have extorted each of our fathers out of twenty thousand pounds . . . Christ, it is nothing short of remarkable."

Raoul narrowed his gaze as he brooded on his friend's words. "True enough. Not that our dear, beloved fathers led blameless lives. We three are proof of that. Still, what sort of dark sin would they be willing to pay such a sum to keep hidden?"

"They must be sins worthy of the devil." Ian gave a short, bitter laugh. "Hell, it almost makes me hopeful. I assumed that my father must have been forced at gunpoint to actually impregnate my mother, the cold bastard. Now I discover he has another sin or two up his sleeve. Perhaps he is mortal after all."

"I think you have something there," Fredrick murmured, scratching on his pad. "Whatever secrets our fathers are hiding must be of great importance. At least to them."

"What the blazes are you doing Fredrick?" Without warning Ian was across the room and standing next to Fredrick's chair. "Making one of your damnable lists?"

Fredrick shrugged. "It always helps me to sort things out to see them written in logical order."

"Let me see." Ian plucked the notebook from his hands.

Raoul stepped forward, his handsome features hardening with a flare of annoyance. "Ian . . ."

"Let it be, Raoul," Fredrick said softly. He understood Ian. Behind his sardonic wit and restless need to forever be proving himself, he was a gentleman who felt deeply. The death of Dunnington, followed by this disturbing legacy, had left him unsettled and battling the desire to strike out.

"Item one." Ian read from Fredrick's notebook. "Dunnington leaves a legacy of twenty thousand pounds to three of his students. Why only three?"

"*Mon Dieu.*" Raoul sucked in a sharp breath, his eyes narrowing as he studied Fredrick. "As usual you have managed to hit on the pertinent point, Fredrick. Dunnington must have had twenty or more boys here over the years. Why would he choose us three?"

Fredrick reached for his brandy and took a sip. "We were the first three he brought in. Maybe it was no random coincidence," he said slowly. "Perhaps Dunnington already had the information on our fathers before opening the school and when it came time to acquire his first pupils, where better to search than three powerful gentlemen who were clearly willing to go to any length to keep their secrets?"

Ian gave a lift of his brows. "So you suggest that Dunnington had managed to stumble across some intriguing information and he used that to fund his school for bastards?"

"Yes," Fredrick agreed.

Ian mulled the notion for a moment. "Do you know . . . I think that it more likely that he started the school *because* of us. He was a sentimental old fool. It would be just like him to have caught sight of us or even just heard about us when he was a tutor at the various households. If he became determined to help us in some way he could have set about discovering information about our fathers. After he had us settled it would have been a natural thing to continue his efforts to assist other boys in need."

There was a short silence before Raoul at last gave a low chuckle. "Egad, Ian. Did you actually make use of the organ located in your skull rather than your breeches?"

Ian smiled with dry humor. "Not nearly as rewarding, I fear."

Fredrick smiled at the affable teasing. The three men were closer than brothers could ever be. They had more than the ties of blood, after all. They had the shared shame and burden of knowing they were unwanted. Not only by their families, but by society who considered them as outcasts.

Their lives would be a constant struggle to make a place for themselves in the world. Thank God they had each other.

"I think it is a reasonable hypothesis." Fredrick reached to reclaim his notebook. "Let us say that Dunnington decided he wished to help us and managed to uncover the sort of infor-mation a gentleman would not wish bandied about."

Raoul nodded. "Not a difficult task for a tutor. They are in an odd position within the household. Not precisely servants, and yet, not a member of the family. They seem to disappear between the upper and lower stairs. It would be a simple matter for them to overhear any number of conversations, or to catch sight of clandestine meetings."

Ian returned to his quick, impatient pacing. "Well, what-ever information he managed to uncover it had to be more se-rious than possessing a bastard. None of us were actually denied by our fathers."

"Just unwanted," Fredrick muttered.

"Here, here," Ian muttered, lifting his glass in a mocking toast.

"Unwanted by our fathers, perhaps, but Dunnington ap-pears to have wanted us. Quite desperately," Raoul mur-mured, his perfect features softening as he recalled the man who had altered all of their lives. "After all, he could have walked away with sixty thousand pounds and lived a life of considerable luxury if he wanted."

Fredrick smiled as he recalled the image of the thin, somber gentleman who was always tidily attired with his hair carefully combed to hide the encroaching baldness. At a glance, he appeared the sort of staid fusspot that young boys detested. Beneath his stoic demeanor, however, he possessed an extraordinary intelligence and a rare ability to inspire the most reluctant student. Even a young Fredrick who had been a shy lad with the tendency to retreat from others.

It had been Dunnington who had recognized Fredrick's gift for anything mechanical. Indeed, he spent a small fortune on providing Fredrick with a variety of materials so that he could build and tinker to his heart's content. The long-suffering man had even occasionally attempted to make use of the strange (and by and large useless) inventions, including a water clock that had leaked so often that it had ruined the floorboards.

"I am not certain that Dunnington could ever have been satisfied unless he was educating some reluctant lad. He devoted his life to teaching," Fredrick said. "However, I do not doubt he was happier to be in charge of his own school as opposed to being at the whim of an employer."

Ian halted at the fireplace and stared down at the flames with a brooding expression. "More the fool him. He should have taken the money and devoted his days to debauching his way through society."

"Not all of us consider debauching a rewarding career," Fredrick pointed out.

"Certainly not you." Ian turned to regard Fredrick with a narrowed gaze. "How you can bear to spend your days in that cramped workroom with all those bits and pieces of machinery . . . it is enough to give a gentleman hives."

Fredrick smiled. His workroom was no longer cramped. Indeed, he now owned several large buildings throughout London and employed near fifty people. Not bad for a gentleman who had started with nothing more than dreams.

"Those bits and pieces have made me a tidy fortune."

"Bah." Ian turned his attention toward the silent Raoul. "At least Charlebois understands the pleasures to be found in debauchery. Eh, old friend?"

Raoul shrugged, as usual far more reserved about discussing the women who warmed his bed. Odd considering most actors conducted their affairs with the same flamboyance as they lived their lives.

"It does offer its share of amusement," Raoul murmured. "Although I must confess that anything can become tedious over time."

Ian gave a lift of his brows. "Ah. Then the rumors must be true that you have ended your torrid affair with the beautiful Mirabelle."

"All affairs must end."

"Of course they must," Ian readily agreed. "Variety, as they say, is the spice of life."

Fredrick gave a shake of his head. He was not a prude, but he had never understood his friends' incessant need to be forever seducing women. He had enjoyed discreet affairs, of course. And he had always chosen women who possessed intelligence and charm and could offer more than just a quick tumble. But on the whole, he had preferred to concentrate on building his business. Deep within, he had always known that *she* was out there. That one special woman who would alter his life forever.

Romantic drivel Ian would call it. Fredrick, however, had never doubted her existence.

"Variety may be the spice of life, but it is also the source of any number of nasty maladies," he muttered.

Ian gave a short laugh. "Good God, I despair of you, Fredrick, I truly do."

Fredrick smiled, not at all offended. Ian was forever chiding him for his dull dreams and lack of stylish dash. But his teasing was always born of affection. Dear God, how different it would have been for Fredrick had he gone to a traditional school. His shy nature and odd fascinations would certainly have been the source of malicious mocking, if not downright brutality. Dunnington had truly saved his life when he had brought him to this small townhouse.

"Because I do not keep a harem of women at my disposal?" he demanded softly.

"Because you were born to be shackled to some harridan who will run roughshod over you until you are badgered into the grave," Ian retorted.

"No, Ian." Raoul regarded Fredrick with a shrewd, piercing gaze. Fredrick found himself resisting the urge to squirm beneath that steady regard. Raoul possessed an uncanny knack of seeing far beneath the surface of a person. Almost as if he could read their very soul. It was no doubt what made him such a good actor. "Our Fredrick is destined for quite another fate."

"And what is that?" Ian demanded.

"Fredrick happens to be one of those rare and fortunate gentlemen who are destined for true love."

"Bah. It still includes a wife and pack of squawking brats, poor blighter," Ian groused.

Fredrick rose to his feet, not nearly so flippant about discussing the future as his friends. He was superstitious enough to leave fate (or whatever one wanted to call it) well enough alone.

"As fascinating as I find your profound predictions, I believe we would be better served to devote our attention to our more pressing matter," he said firmly.

Raoul reached out to give Fredrick's shoulder a brief squeeze, as if sympathizing with Fredrick's reluctance to discuss his very private dreams.

"No doubt you are right, old friend, but at the moment all we are doing is speculating with no real means of knowing the actual truth. Dunnington might or might not have extorted our respective fathers to rescue us and begin this school. There is simply no way of knowing for certain."

Ian grimaced. "Dunnington managed to take his secrets to the grave."

Fredrick paused as he was struck by a sudden thought. "Yes, odd that."

"What?" Ian demanded.

It was Fredrick's turn to do a bit of pacing. "Why did he not reveal the truth when we reached our majority?" he demanded. "God knows we could each have used such a fortune at that time."

They exchanged knowing glances as they recalled the lean years when each of them had been forced to struggle to carve a place in a world determined to offer them nothing.

"Holy hell," Ian rasped. "When I think of the years I spent dodging the collectors and living in flea ridden rooms . . ."

"Oh come, you know Dunnington," Raoul drawled. "He would have told you that a man's character is formed by his suffering, not by his successes. He wanted us to learn to survive by our wits. It is what he preached on a daily basis."

Ian's expression revealed precisely what he thought of such a philosophy, but Fredrick was more concerned with what must have been going through Dunnington's mind.

"That is no doubt part of the reason," he agreed. "Dunnington did possess a strange obsession with teaching a man to stand on his own two feet. Still, I think . . ."

Silence descended in the room as Fredrick struggled to put his thoughts into words.

"Well, do not leave us in suspense, Fredrick," Ian at last prompted.

Fredrick gave a lift of his hands. "Just consider the fact that if Dunnington had given us our legacies, he would have been forced to explain how he came by them."

"You are off the mark if you believe that Dunnington would have been too ashamed to confess the truth of his . . . unique methods of gaining the necessary capital to begin this school," Raoul swiftly countered. "For all his fanciful notions of teaching, he was at heart a practical man who would take full responsibility for his choices."

"Yes, I agree with you," Fredrick said. "I was thinking more along the lines of protecting us."

Ian frowned. "Protect us? From what?"

Fredrick moved to stare out the window. There was nothing much to see on the quiet street. A maid shivering against the frigid breeze as she polished the doorknob across the way, a coal wagon clattering over the rough cobblestone, a young boy and his nanny taking a walk through the garden. It was all quite commonplace, something to be seen out the window of a hundred homes in London.

But this view would always be special, Fredrick acknowledged as a fresh wave of pain rolled through him. It was special because this was home.

"If Dunnington were still alive we would not rest until we had forced him to tell us the truth of what secrets he learned of our fathers."

"Bloody right." Ian refilled his glass with brandy. "We have the right to know what nasty sins our fathers have been committing."

"Perhaps we have the right, but maybe not the will," Raoul said softly. "Is that what you are implying, Fredrick?"

"Yes."

Ian gave a loud snort. "In English, please."

Raoul absently reached to pluck the brandy from Ian's hand. The actor had just celebrated his thirtieth birthday which made him a year older than Ian and three years older than Fredrick. He took his role of the elder brother quite seriously.

"Dunnington would realize that we would have instinctively demanded him to tell us the sordid secrets that he kept. Curiosity is human nature, after all. But, he might have felt that the past was better left undisturbed."

"If he felt that way, then why reveal where the money came from to begin with?" Fredrick muttered. "There was no need to reveal that our fathers were ever involved."

Raoul heaved a deep sigh. "Because it gave us the option of deciding whether we desired the truth badly enough to go in search of it."

"Yes." Fredrick shoved his fingers through his hair. Gads, but he was tired. He had been in Portsmouth when he had received word of Dunnington's death and he had traveled without halt to arrive in time for the funeral. Since then he had been overwhelmed with one endless task after another. When this was all said and done he intended to reacquaint himself with his very large, very comfortable bed. "It is one thing to simply be told of the past, and quite another to have to go to the effort of returning to our families and seeking it."

"Dunnington has ensured that the truth comes with a price," Raoul whispered softly.

Ian firmly took back his glass of brandy and downed it in one swallow. "What you are saying is that he has left us holding Pandora's Box."

Pandora's Box. Yes, that was a perfect description, Fredrick acknowledged.

The sensible choice, of course, would be to keep the lid firmly closed. After all, none of them had any true relationship with their fathers. And certainly whatever secrets their fathers might be harboring could have nothing to do with them.

More importantly, they had each forged lives that gave them satisfaction in their own way. Only a fool would risk such fragile peace to stir up the past.

A silence descended that was broken only by the crackle of the burning logs as the three gentlemen became lost in their own thoughts. At last Raoul gave a sharp shake of his head.

"It would appear that if we had any sense at all, we would take our money, invest it wisely, and forget where it came from."

Ian gave a short laugh. "And when have we ever been wise?"

Fredrick had to admit his friend did have a point. Raoul devoted his life to playing roles upon the stage. Ian lived by the fickle fate of Lady Luck. And even Fredrick took enormous risks with each new patent he invested in.

"I do not suppose it is possible for any of us to know that there is some secret out there and not try to get to the bottom of it," Fredrick admitted with a resigned sigh. "It is like having a splinter stuck in your finger that you try to ignore. Eventually you have to pluck it out or it becomes infected."

"An unpleasant, if apt description." Raoul gave a short, bitter laugh. "*Mon Dieu,* we are idiots."

"And it would seem that Dunnington has at last had his final revenge for all those frogs we hid in his bed," Fredrick said wryly.

Ian held up his empty glass. "To Dunnington, damn his soul."

Fredrick and Raoul exchanged a wry glance. "To Dunnington," they agreed in unison.

And for a taste of something different
please turn the page for a sneak peek of
Alexandra Ivy's
WHEN DARKNESS COMES
now on sale at bookstores everywhere!

PROLOGUE

England, 1655

The scream ripped through the night air. Pulsing with a savage agony it filled the vast chamber and tumbled down the vaulted corridors. Servants cowering in the lower halls of the castle clamped hands over their ears in an effort to block out the piercing shrieks. Even hardened soldiers in the barracks made the sign of the moon, the protector of the night.

In the southern turret, the Duke of Granville paced across his private library, his shadowed features lined with distaste. Unlike his servants, he did not cross his forehead in an effort to ward off the evil eye. And why should he?

Evil had already struck. It had invaded his home and dared to taint him with its filth.

The only thing left was to purge the infestation with a ruthless strike.

Tugging at the hood to his robe to ensure his marred countenance was fully hidden, he grimly squared his shoulders. Patience, he told himself over and over. Soon enough the moon would move into the proper equinox. And then the ritual would at last be at an end. The child he had sacrificed to the witches would become their precious Chalice and his suffering would be at an end.

Turning abruptly on his heel, he marched back toward the slotted window that offered a fine view of the rich countryside. In the distance he could witness the faint glow of fires. He shuddered. London. Filthy, peasant infected London that was being punished for its foul sins.

A punishment that had spewed out of the ramshackle whorehouses and swept its way to his sanctuary.

His hands clenched at his sides. it was untenable. He was a just man. A godly man who had always been richly rewarded for his purity. To have that . . . vile disease enter his body was a perversion of all that was due to him.

That of course, was the only reason he had allowed the heathens to enter his estate. And to bring with them that creature of evil that was currently shackled in his dungeon.

They promised him a cure.

An end to the plague that was consuming his life.

And all it would cost him was a daughter.

CHAPTER ONE

Chicago 2006

"Oh God, Abby. Don't panic. Just . . . don't . . . panic."

Sucking in a deep breath, Abby Barlow pressed her hands to her heaving stomach and studied the shards of pottery that lay splintered across the floor.

Okay, so she broke a vase. Well, perhaps more than broke it. It was more like she shattered, decimated, and annihilated the vase, she grudgingly conceded. Big deal. It was not the end of the world.

A vase was a vase. Wasn't it?

She abruptly grimaced. No, a vase was not just a vase. Not when it was a very rare vase. A priceless vase. One that should no doubt have been in a museum. One that was the dream of any collector and . . .

Freaking hell.

Panic once again reared its ugly head.

She had destroyed a priceless Ming vase.

What if she lost her job? Granted it wasn't much of a job. Hell, she felt as if she were stepping into the Twilight Zone each time she entered the elegant mansion on the outskirts of Chicago. But her position as companion to Selena LaSalle was hardly demanding. And the pay was considerably better than slinging hash in some sleazy dive.

The last thing she needed was to be back in the long lines at the Unemployment Office.

Or worse . . . dear God, what if she were expected to pay for the blasted vase?

Even if there were such a thing as a half price sale at the local Ming outlet shop, she would have to work ten lifetimes to make such a sum. Always supposing that it was not one of a kind.

Panic was no longer merely rearing. It was thundering through her at full throttle.

There was only one thing to be done, she realized. The mature, responsible, adult thing to do.

Hide the evidence.

Covertly glancing about the vast foyer, Abby ensured that she was alone before lowering herself to her knees and gathering the numerous shards that littered the smooth marble.

It was not as if anyone would notice the vase was missing, she tried to reassure herself. Selena had always been a recluse, but in the past two weeks she had all but disappeared. If it weren't for her occasional cameo appearances to demand that Abby prepare that disgusting herb concoction she guzzled with seeming pleasure, Abby might have thought that the woman had done a flit.

Certainly Selena didn't roam the house taking inventory of her various knick-knacks.

All Abby needed to do was ensure that she didn't leave any trace of her crime and surely all would be well.

No one would ever know.

No one.

"My, my, I never thought to see you on your hands and knees, lover. A most intriguing position that leads to all sorts of delicious possibilities," a mocking voice drawled from the entrance to the drawing room.

Abby closed her eyes and heaved in a deep breath. She was cursed. That had to be it. What else could possibly explain her unending run of bad luck?

For a moment she kept her back turned, futilely hoping Selena's houseguest, the utterly annoying Dante, would disappear. It could happen. There was always spontaneous combustion, or black holes, or earthquakes.

Unfortunately, the ground didn't open up to swallow him, nor did the smoke detectors set off a warning. Even worse she could actually feel his dark, amused gaze leisurely meandering over her stiff form.

Gathering her battered pride, Abby forced herself to slowly turn and regard the current bane of her existence.

He didn't look like a bane. God's truth he looked like a delicious, dangerously wicked pirate.

Still kneeling upon the floor, Abby allowed her gaze to travel over the black biker boots and long, powerful legs encased in faded denims. Ever higher, she skimmed over the black silk shirt that hung loosely upon his torso. Loose, but not loose enough, she acknowledged with a renegade shiver. Much to her embarrassment, she had caught herself sneaking peeks at the play of rippling muscles beneath those silky shirts during the past three months.

All right, maybe she had indulged in more than mere peeks.

Maybe she had been staring. Gawking. Ogling. Occasionally drooling.

What woman wouldn't?

Gritting her teeth, she forced her gaze up to the alabaster face with its perfectly chiseled features. A wide brow, a narrow aristocratic nose, sharply defined cheekbones and lushly carved lips. They all came together with a fierce elegance.

It was the face of a noble warrior. A chieftain.

Until one noticed those pale silver eyes.

There was nothing noble in those disturbing eyes. They were piercing, wicked, and shimmering with a mocking amusement toward the world. They were eyes that branded him a 'bad ass' as easily as the long raven hair that carelessly tumbled well past his shoulders and the golden hoops he wore in his ears.

He was sex on legs. A predator. The sort that chewed up and spat out women like her with pathetic ease.

That was, when they bothered to notice women like her in the first place. Which was not very damn often.

"Dante. Do you have to skulk about like that?" she demanded, desperately aware of the priceless clutter just behind her.

He made a show of considering her question before offering a faint shrug.

"No, I don't suppose I *have* to skulk about," he murmured in his husky midnight voice. "I simply enjoy doing so."

"Well, it's a very vulgar habit."

His lips twitched with amusement as he prowled ever closer. "Oh, I possess far more vulgar habits, sweet Abby. Several that I don't doubt you would enjoy fully if only you would allow me to demonstrate."

God, she just bet he did. Those slender, devilish hands would no doubt make a woman scream in pleasure. And those lips . . .

Abruptly she was squashing the renegade fantasy and stirring up the annoyance she most certainly should be feeling.

"Ack. You're revolting."

"Vulgar and revolting?" His smile widened to reveal startling white teeth. "My sweet, you are in a very precarious position to be tossing about such insults."

Precarious? She battled the urge to glance down and discover if any shards of her crime were visible.

"I don' t know what you mean."

With a flowing elegance, Dante was on his knees before

her, those disturbing fingers lifting to lightly stroke her cheek. His touch was cool, almost cold, but it sent a startling flare of heat searing through her.

"Oh, I think you do. I seem to recall a rather precious Ming vase that used to sit upon that table. Tell me, lover, did you hock it or break it?"

Damn. He knew. She desperately attempted to think of some feasible lie to explain the missing vase. Or for that matter, any lie, feasible or not. Unfortunately, she had never been particularly skilled at prevarication.

And it didn't much help that his lingering touch was turning her brain to mush.

"Don't call me that," she at last lamely muttered.

"What?" His brows lifted.

"Lover."

"Why?"

"For the obvious fact that I'm not your lover."

"Not yet."

"Not ever."

"Tsk, tsk." Dante clicked his tongue as his fingers moved to boldly outline her lips. "Has no one ever warned you that it is dangerous to dare fate? It has a tendency to come back and bite you." His gaze drifted over her pale countenance and the soft curve of her neck. "Sometimes quite literally."

"Not in a million years."

"I can wait," he husked.

She gritted her teeth as those skillful fingers traveled down the arch of her throat and along the neckline of her plain cotton shirt. He was merely toying with her. Hell, the man would flirt with any woman who possessed a pulse. And maybe a few who didn't.

"That finger moves any lower and your stay in the world is going to be considerably shorter."

He gave a soft chuckle as he reluctantly allowed his hand to

drop. "Do you know, Abby, someday you're going to forget to sa
no. And on that day I intend to make you scream with pleasure

"My God, how do you possibly carry that ego around?"

His smile was pure wicked. "Do you think I don't notice
All those covert glances when you think I'm not looking? Th
way you shiver when I brush past you? The dreams that haur
your nights?"

Conceited, puffed up toad.

She should laugh. Or pooh, pooh. Or even slap his arrogar
face. Instead, she stiffened as if he had hit a nerve that sh
didn't even know she possessed.

"Don't you have somewhere you need to be?" she grittec
"The kitchen? The sewers? The fires of hell?"

Surprisingly, the pirate features hardened as his lips twistec
into a sardonic smile.

"Nice try, my sweet, but I don't need you to condemn m
to the fires of hell. That was accomplished a long time agc
Why else would I be here?"

Abby gave a lift of her brows, intrigued in spite of hersel
by his hint of bitterness. For God's sake, what more could h
want? He possessed the sort of cushy life that most oversexec
playboys could only dream of. A glamorous home. Expensiv
clothes. A silver Porsche. And a sugar mommy, who was no
only young, but beautiful enough to make any male hot anc
bothered. His life was hardly in the gutter.

Unlike her own.

"Oh yes, you must really suffer," she retorted, her gaz
flicking over the silk shirt that cost more than her entir
wardrobe. "My heart simply breaks for you."

The silver eyes flashed with a startling heat as the fierc
power that always smoldered about him prickled through th
air.

"Do not presume to speak of things you know nothing
about, lover," he warned.

Just let it be, Abby, she sternly warned herself. Whatever

his easy charm, the man was dangerous. A genuine Bad Boy. Only fools deliberately toyed with fire.

Of course, when it came to men, she might as well have the word IDIOT tattooed on her forehead.

"If you dislike being here, then why don't you leave?"

He regarded her in unnerving silence before his eyes slowly narrowed. "Why don't you?"

"What?"

"I'm not the only one suffering here, am I? Every day you seem to fade a bit more. As if your frustration and sadness has taken another piece of your soul."

Abby nearly tumbled backward at his sharp perception. She had never dreamed that anyone could possibly have noted her desperation at her tedious existence, nor the budding fear that she would soon be too old and tired to care that she was going nowhere.

Certainly not this man.

"You don't know anything."

"I know a prison when I see one," he murmured. "Why do you remain behind the bars when you could so easily slip away?"

She gave a short, humorless laugh. Easily? Obviously he was not nearly so perceptive as she had given him credit for.

"Because I need this job. Unlike you, I don't have a generous lover to pay my bills and keep me in style. Some of us have to earn our pay with actual work."

If she thought to insult him, she was far off the mark. In fact, her sharp words merely returned that mocking humor she found so damn annoying.

"You believe me to be Selena's whore?"

"Aren't you?"

He lifted a broad shoulder. "Our . . . relationship is a bit more complex than that."

"Oh yes, no doubt being a boy-toy to a rich, glamorous woman is astonishingly complex."

"Is that why you try to keep me at a distance? Because you believe I share Selena's bed?"

"I keep you at a distance because I don't like you."

He leaned forward, until his lips were nearly touching her own. "You may not like me, sweetness, but that doesn't keep you from wanting me."

Her heart forgot to beat as she struggled not to close that shallow distance and put herself out of her misery. A kiss. Just one kiss. The tingling need was nearly unbearable.

No, no, no. Did she really want to be a poor joke to relieve his boredom? Hadn't she played that humiliating game before?

"Do you know, Dante, I've met my share of jackasses in my time, but you . . ."

The rather tidy insult was brought to a stunning halt. In the air there was a sudden, crackling heat. As electrifying as a strike of lightning.

Unnerved by the prickling sensation, she turned her head toward the stairs just as a thundering concussion ripped through the house. Caught off guard, she tumbled backward, her breath knocked from her body.

Just for a moment, she lay perfectly still. She half expected the ceiling to come crumbling down upon her. Or the ground to open up and swallow her.

What the blazes had happened? An earthquake? A gas explosion?

The end of the world?

Whatever it was, it had been enough to tumble the pictures from the walls and knock over tables. Suddenly, the Ming vase she had broken matched every other priceless object.

Giving a shake of her head to clear the ringing in her ears, Abby sucked in a deep breath. Well, at least she seemed to be alive, she told herself. And while she was certain to be sporting a few bruises, she didn't think anything vital was actually missing or punctured.

Lying flat on her back, she barely heard the low feral growl, but it still managed to make the hair upon her nape stand upright. Dear lord, now what?

Struggling to push herself upright, she glanced about the littered foyer. Astonishingly it was empty. No wild animal. No approaching madman.

And no Dante.

With a frown, Abby ignored her wobbly knees and forced herself toward the nearby stairs. Where had Dante gone? Had he been hit by the explosion? Or thrown from the foyer?

Had he simply disappeared in a puff of smoke?

No, no of course not. She pressed a hand to her aching head. She was thinking crazy. She must have been knocked unconscious for a moment. That would explain it. No doubt he had gone to check on the damage. Or to call for assistance.

Her job was surely to ensure that Selena was not injured.

Concentrating upon placing one foot in front of the other, a startling difficult task, she managed to climb the sweeping marble stairs and awkwardly made her way down the hallway. At the end of the long east wing, the door to Selena's chambers was already open and Abby stepped over the threshold.

She got no further.

A gasp was wrenched from her throat as her wide gaze swept over the demolished room. Like downstairs the pictures and various objects had been tumbled to the ground, most of them smashed beyond recognition. But here the general mayhem had left the walls blackened and in places crumbled to dust. Even the windows had been blasted from their frames.

Her gaze flew to the large bed that was tumbled onto its side and at last to the center of the room where Dante was kneeling beside a limp, battered form.

"Oh my God." Holding her hands to her mouth, Abby stumbled forward, her heart firmly lodged in her throat. "Selena."

Noticing her presence for the first time, Dante jerked his head up to regard her with a frown. Almost absently, Abby noted the even sharper pallor of his skin and the oddly hectic glitter in his silver eyes.

Obviously he was as shaken as she was.

"Get out of here," he growled.

She ignored his warning as she fell to her knees beside the burned body. Whatever her secret dislike for the beautiful, coldhearted woman it was forgotten as tears streamed down her cheeks.

"Is she . . . dead?" she croaked.

"Abby, I said to leave. Now. Get out of this room. Out of this house . . ."

The dark, furious words continued, but Abby was no longer listening. Instead, she watched in fascinated horror as one of the charred hands twitched upon the carpet. Holy freaking hell. Could the poor woman still be alive? Or was it some horrible trick of her imagination?

Frozen in shock, Abby stared at the fingers that continued to jerk and spasm ever closer. It was like something out of a nightmare. A sensation that only deepened when the hand snapped upward and grasped her wrist in a painful grasp.

Opening her mouth to scream, Abby discovered her breath wrenched from her body. A coldness was spreading from the fingers that dug into her flesh. A coldness that crawled through her blood with a searing, ruthless agony. With a groan, she desperately attempted to tug herself free of the brutal grip.

She was going to die, she realized in stunned disbelief. The pain was clawing at her heart, slowing its beat until it was doomed to halt. She was going to die and she hadn't even bothered to start living yet.

What an idiot she was.

Raising her head, she met Dante's shimmering metallic gaze. His beautiful, wicked features appeared grim in the dim light. Grim and edged with something that might have been fury, or regret, or . . . desperation.

She tried to speak, but a bright flare of light burst through her mind and with a strangled scream, she plunged head first into the welcoming darkness.

CHAPTER TWO

Surrounded by a silver fog of pain, Abby floated in a world that was not quite real.

Was she dead?

Surely not. She would be at peace, wouldn't she? Not feeling as if her bones were being slowly crushed and her head about to explode.

If she were dead then this whole after-life thing was a big, fat rip off.

No. She had to be dreaming, she at last reassured herself. That would certainly explain why the silver fog was beginning to part.

Curious, despite the vague taste of fear in the air, she peered through the shimmering light. Moments later she could see a dark, stone chamber that was only dimly lit by a flickering torch. In the center of the stone floor lay a young woman in white robes. Abby frowned. The woman's pale face was remarkably familiar although it was difficult to determine the exact features as the woman twisted and screamed in obvious agony.

About her prostrate form sat a circle of women in gray cloaks, holding hands and chanting in low voices. Abby could not make out the words, but it appeared as if they were *performing some sort of ritual. Perhaps an exorcism. Or an enchantment.*

Slowly a gray-haired woman stood and held her hands toward the shadowed ceiling.

"Arise Phoenix and bring forth your power," she called in booming tones. "The sacrifice is offered, the covenant sealed. Bless our noble Chalice. Bless her with your glory. Offer to her the might of your sword to fight the evil that threatens. We call. Come forth."

Crimson flames swept through the chamber as the women continued to chant, hovering in the thick air before surrounding the screaming woman upon the floor. Then, just as abruptly as they had appeared, the flames melted into the woman's flesh.

Abruptly, the gray-haired woman turned her head toward a darkened corner.

"The prophecy is fulfilled. Bring forth the beast."

Expecting some horrid, five headed monster that would fit right into the bizarre nightmare, Abby caught her breath as a man attired in a ruffled white shirt and satin knee breeches was brought forward, a heavy metal collar and chain hung about his neck. His head was bowed, allowing his long raven hair to cover his face, but that didn't halt a shiver of premonition from inching down Abby's spine.

"Creature of evil, you have been chosen above all others," the woman intoned. "Wicked is your heart and yet blessed are you. We pledge you to the Chalice. In fire and blood we bind you. In the shadow of death we bind you. Through eternity and beyond we bind you."

The torch suddenly flared and with a terrifying growl the man lifted his head.

No. It was not possible. Not even in the strange and ridiculous world of dreams. Especially not ones that felt so horrifyingly real.

Still, there was no mistaking his terrifying beauty. Or the smoldering silver eyes.

Dante.

She shuddered in horror. This was madness. Why would these women have him chained? Why would they call him a monster? A creature of evil?

Madness, indeed. A dream. Nothing more, she attempted to convince herself.

Then, without warning, the unease tracing her spine turned to consuming terror. In pure fury, Dante tilted back his head, the perfect alabaster features bathed in flickering light. The same flickering light that revealed his long, deadly fangs.

When Abby at last woke again the silver fog, and the sharpest edges of her pain, had disappeared.

Still, with uncommon caution, she forced herself to remain perfectly motionless. After the day she had already endured, now didn't seem to be the best time to be charging and blundering about in her usual style. Instead, she attempted to take stock of her surroundings.

She was lying upon a bed, she at last decided. Not her own bed, however. This one was hard and lumpy and possessed a funky scent she didn't even want to consider. In the distance she could hear the sounds of passing traffic and closer, the muffled sound of voices, or perhaps a television.

Well, she wasn't in Selena's charred house. She was no longer in a damp dungeon with screaming women and demons. And she wasn't dead.

That was surely progress?

Screwing up her courage, Abby slowly lifted her head from the pillow and glanced about the shadowed room. There wasn't much to see. The bed she was lying upon consumed most of the cramped space. About her were bare walls and the ugliest flowered curtains ever created. At the end of the bed was a broken dresser that held an ancient television and in the corner was a shabby chair.

A chair that was currently occupied by a large, raven-haired man.

Or was he a man?

Her heart squeezed with a building dread as her gaze swept over the slumbering Dante. God. She would have to be demented to think what she was thinking.

Vampires? Living and breathing . . . or whatever it was that vampires did . . . in Chicago? Nuts. Full out, engines roaring, madness.

But the dream. It had been so vivid. So real. Even now she could smell the foul, damp air and the acrid burning of the torch. She could hear the screams and chanting. She could hear the rattling of heavy chains. She could see Dante being pulled forward, and the fangs that marked him as a beast.

Real or not, it had unnerved her enough to desire a bit of space between her and Dante. And perhaps several crosses, a few wooden stakes, and a bottle of holy water.

Barely daring to breathe, Abby sat upright and swung her legs over the edge of the mattress. Her head threatened to revolt but she gritted her teeth and pushed herself upward. She wanted out of here.

She wanted to be in her familiar home, surrounded by her familiar things.

She wanted out of this nightmare.

Taking one unsteady step followed by another and another, Abby moved across the room. She was just upon the point of reaching for the doorknob when there was the faintest whisper of sound behind her. The hair on the nape of her neck tingled before a pair of steely arms wrapped about her.

"Not so fast, lover," a dark voice murmured directly in her ear.

For a moment her mind went blank and she was paralyzed with fear. Then sheer panic took control.

Arching her back, she frantically attempted to kick at his legs. "Let me go. Let go."

"Go?" His arms merely tightened at her struggles. "Tell me, sweet, where do you plan to go?"

"That's none of your business."

Surprisingly, he gave a short, humorless laugh. "My God, you don't know how I wish that were true. We were both released, do you realize that? We were free. The chains were broken."

Abby stilled at his rough, accusing words. "What do you mean?"

He brushed his face over the top of her head in an oddly intimate manner before he was firmly turning her to meet his shimmering gaze.

"I mean that if you had kept that beautiful nose out of matters that are none of your business, we both could have gone upon our merry way. Now, because of your Florence Nightingale act, where you go, what you do, what you bloody well think, is now very much my business."

What the hell was he talking about? Unconsciously, her wide gaze skimmed over the perfect alabaster features. The last thing she needed was more troubles.

"You're insane. Let me go or . . ."

"Or what?" he demanded in silky tones.

Good question. A pity she didn't have a brilliant answer.

"I . . . I'll scream."

The dark brows lifted in sardonic amusement. "And do you truly want to discover just what sort of hero is going to rush to your rescue in this place? Who do you think it will be? The local crackheads? The whores working the lobby? You know, I'd place my money on the drunk next door. There was a definite hint of rape in the air when I carried you past him in the hall."

Suddenly, Abby understood the cramped room, the vile

smells, and echoes of despair. Dante had taken her to one of the endless seedy hotels that catered to the poor and desperate.

She might have shivered in disgust if it hadn't been the least of her worries.

"They couldn't be any worse than you."

He stiffened at her accusation, his expression guarded. "Rather harsh words for the man who might very well have saved your life."

"Man? Is that what you are?"

"What did you say?"

His fingers dug into her shoulders and belatedly Abby realized that confronting Dante directly, might not have been the wisest decision.

Still she had to know. Ignorance might be bliss, but it was also freaking dangerous.

"You . . . I saw you. In the dream." She shivered as the memories burned through her mind. "You were chained and they were chanting and your . . . your fangs . . ."

"Abby." He gazed deep into her eyes. "Sit down and I'll explain."

"No." She gave a frantic shake of her head. "What are you going to do to me?"

His lips twisted at her shrill tone. "Although several enticing ideas have passed through my mind upon various occasions, for the moment I plan nothing more than talking with you. Will you calm down long enough to listen?"

The very fact that he hadn't laughed and told her that she had lost her mind, only deepened Abby's terror. He knew of the dream. He recognized it.

Allowing instinct to take over, Abby forced herself to pretend a resignation she was far from feeling.

"Do I have a choice?"

He shrugged. "Not really."

"Very well."

Weakly following his lead toward the bed, Abby waited

until Dante was convinced of his victory before reaching out to push him sharply away. Caught off guard he stumbled, and in the blink of an eye she was bolting toward the door.

She was fast. Growing up with five older brothers ensured she was well practiced in running from a potential massacre. But shockingly, she had taken only a few steps when Dante's arms were wrapping about her and lifting her off her feet.

With a muffled scream, she reached her arms over her head and grasped two handfuls of his silky hair. He gave a low grunt as she gave a violent tug. Still keeping grasp of his hair with one hand, she shifted the other to dig her nails into the side of his face.

"Dammit, Abby," he muttered, his grip loosening as he sought to ward off her attack.

Not pausing for a moment, Abby wriggled free and turning, she aimed a kick that over the years had proven to bring even the largest of men to a screeching halt. Dante gasped as he doubled over in pain, and not pausing to admire her handiwork, Abby lunged for the door.

On this occasion, she managed to actually touch the knob before she was roughly hauled up and over a broad shoulder and carried back to the bed. She screamed again as Dante easily tossed her onto the foul mattress, and then shockingly followed her downward to cover her struggling form with one much larger, and much harder.

More frightened than she had ever been in her life, Abby gazed into the pale face with its unearthly beauty. She was sharply, disturbingly aware of his lean muscles pressing against her. And the knowledge that he held her completely at his mercy.

Uncertain what was about to happen, she was startled when a slow smile curved his lips.

"You possess powerful weapons for such a tiny thing, lover," he murmured. "Have you practiced those rather nasty tricks often?"

Somehow his teasing managed to ease a portion of her rabid terror. Surely, if he were going to suck her dry he wouldn't be indulging in conversation?

Unless of course vampires preferred a bit of pre-dinner chat?

"I have five older brothers," she gritted.

"Ah, that would explain it. Survival of the fittest, or in this case, survival of the one with the dirtiest arsenal."

"Get off me."

He gave a lift of his brows. "And risk becoming a eunuch? No thanks. We'll finish our discussion without anymore scratching, hair pulling, or low blows."

She glared into his mocking expression. "We have nothing to discuss."

"Oh no," he drawled, "nothing beyond the fact your employer was just barbequed to a crisp, the fact that I'm a vampire, and the fact that thanks to your stupidity you now have every demon in the vicinity after your head. Nothing at all to discuss."

Barbequed employers, vampires, and now demons? It was too much. Way, way too much.

Abby closed her eyes as her heart squeezed with horror.

"This is a nightmare. Dear God, please let Freddy Krueger walk through the door."

"This is no nightmare, Abby."

"It's not possible." She reluctantly lifted her lids to meet the glittering silver gaze. "You're a vampire?"

He grimaced. "My heritage is the least of your concern at the moment."

Heritage? She swallowed a hysterical urge to laugh.

"Did Selena know?"

"That I was a vampire? Oh yes, she knew." His tone was dry. "In fact, you could say that it was a prerequisite to my employment."

Abby frowned. "Then she was a vampire too?"

"No." Dante paused as if carefully considering his words. Ridiculous, since he could have informed her that Selena was Beelzebub and she couldn't have twitched a muscle as long as he held her in his relentless grip. "She was . . . a Chalice."

"Chalice?" Her blood ran cold. The woman screaming in agony. The crimson flames. "The Phoenix," she breathed.

His brows drew together in shock. "How did you know that?"

"The dream. I was in a dungeon and there was a woman lying on the floor. I think the other women were performing some ritual upon her."

"Selena," he muttered. "She must have passed a portion of her memories onto you. That's the only explanation."

"Passed on memories? But that's . . ." Her words trailed away as a mocking smile curved his lips.

"Impossible? Don't you think we're beyond that by now?"

They were, of course. She had tumbled into some bizarre world where anything was possible. Like Alice in the Looking Glass.

Only instead of disappearing cats and white rabbits there were vampires and mysterious Chalices and who knew what else?

"What did they do to her?"

"They made her a Chalice. A human vessel for a powerful entity."

"So those women were witches?"

"For lack of a better term."

Great. Just great. "And they put a spell upon Selena?"

The silver eyes shimmered in the shadowed light. "It was rather more than a spell. They called forth the spirit of the Phoenix to live within her body."

Abby could almost feel the crimson flames that had seared into the woman's flesh. She shivered in horror. "No wonder she was screaming. What does this Phoenix do?"

"It is a . . . barrier."

She eyed him warily. "A barrier against what?"

"Against the darkness."

Well, that made everything as clear as mud. Impatiently, Abby wriggled beneath the man pinning her to the bed.

A bad, very bad move.

As if a lightning bolt had suddenly struck her, she was vibrantly aware of his hard body branding her own. A body that had haunted her dreams more than a few nights.

Dante's jaw tightened at her unwittingly provocative movements, his hips instinctively shifting in response.

"Do you think you could possibly be a little more vague?" she managed to choke out.

"What would you have me say?" he demanded in rasping tones.

She struggled to keep her thoughts focused. Good God. Now was no time to be thinking of . . . of . . . that.

"Something a bit more clarifying than *the darkness*."

There was a moment of silence, as if he were waging his own battle. Then at last he met her gaze squarely.

"Very well. The demon-world refers to the darkness as the Prince, but in truth it isn't a real being. It is more a . . . spirit, just as the Phoenix is a spirit. An essence of power that demons call upon to enhance their dark skills."

"And the Phoenix does something to this Prince?"

"Her presence among mortals has banished the Prince from this world. They are two opposites. Neither can be in the same plane at the same moment. Not without both being destroyed."

Well, that seemed like a good thing. The first ray of hope in a very bleak day.

"So, no more demons?"

He gave a lift of his shoulder. "They remain but without the tangible presence of the Prince, they are weakened and chaotic. No longer do they band together to attack in strength and rarely do they hunt humans. They have been forced into the shadows."

"That's good, I suppose," she said slowly. "And Selena was this barrier?"

"Yes."

"Why?"

He blinked at the abrupt question. "Why?"

"Why was she chosen?" Abby clarified, not quite certain why she even cared. She only knew that at the moment it seemed important. "Was she a witch?"

Oddly Dante paused, almost as if he were considering not answering her question. Ridiculous after all he had already revealed. What could be worse than the fact she was being held captive by a vampire? Or that the one person who kept away all the scary, bad things in the night was now dead?

"She was not so much chosen as offered as a sacrifice by her father," he at last grudgingly confessed.

"She was sacrificed by her father?" Abby gave a startled blink. Hell, she had always thought her father was a shoo-in for scumbag of the year. He had been a brutal jerk whose only redeeming act had been tossing aside his family for a bottle of whiskey. Still, he hadn't offered her up as fodder to a band of crazed witches. "How could he do such a thing?"

The elegant features hardened with ancient anger. "Quite easily. He was powerful, rich, and accustomed to having his way in all things. Or he was, until he was struck down with the plague. In exchange for a cure, he gave the witches his only daughter."

"Holy crap. That's horrible."

"I suppose he thought it a fair trade off. He was cured and his daughter made immortal."

"Immortal?" Abby caught her breath with sudden hope. "Then Selena is still alive?"

The beautiful features sharpened even further. "No, she is very much dead."

"But . . . how?"

"I don't know." His tone was rough with coiled emotions. "At least not yet."

Abby bit her bottom lip, attempting to wrap her aching brain around the consequences of such a death.

"Then the Phoenix is gone?"

"No, it is not gone. It is . . ." Without warning, Dante flowed to his feet, his head turning toward the closed door. A tense silence filled the room before he at last returned his gaze to her startled face. "Abby, we must go. Now."

Put a Little Romance in Your Life With
Georgina Gentry

Cheyenne Song
0-8217-5844-6   **$5.99**US/**$7.99**CAN

Apache Tears
0-8217-6435-7   **$5.99**US/**$7.99**CAN

Warrior's Heart
0-8217-7076-4   **$5.99**US/**$7.99**CAN

To Tame a Savage
0-8217-7077-2   **$5.99**US/**$7.99**CAN

To Tame a Texan
0-8217-7402-6   **$5.99**US/**$7.99**CAN

To Tame a Rebel
0-8217-7403-4   **$5.99**US/**$7.99**CAN

To Tempt a Texan
0-8217-7705-X   **$5.99**US/**$7.99**CAN

Available Wherever Books Are Sold!

Visit our website at **www.kensingtonbooks.com**.

More Historical Romance From
Jo Ann Ferguson